THE HERO REBELLION 2
RIVEN

BELINDA CRAWFORD

HENDRIX & FAUST
PUBLISHERS

SECOND EDITION
Published by Hendrix & Faust, Publishers in 2026
Text copyright © Belinda Crawford 2016

ISBN: 978-0-6488745-4-6 (ebook)
ISBN: 978-0-6488745-5-3 (paperback)

PRINTED AND BOUND BY INGRAMSPARK.
Australia: Ingram Content Group AU Pty Ltd, Melbourne, Victoria. US: Lightning Source LLC, La Vergne, Tennessee / Allentown, Pennsylvania / Jackson, Tennessee, United States. UK: Lightning Source UK Ltd, Milton Keynes, United Kingdom. Europe: Lightning Source UK Ltd, with facilities in Germany, France, and Spain.

The authorized representative in the European Economic Area is Lightning Source France, 1 Av. Johannes Gutenberg, 78310 Maurepas, France.
compliance@lightningsource.fr

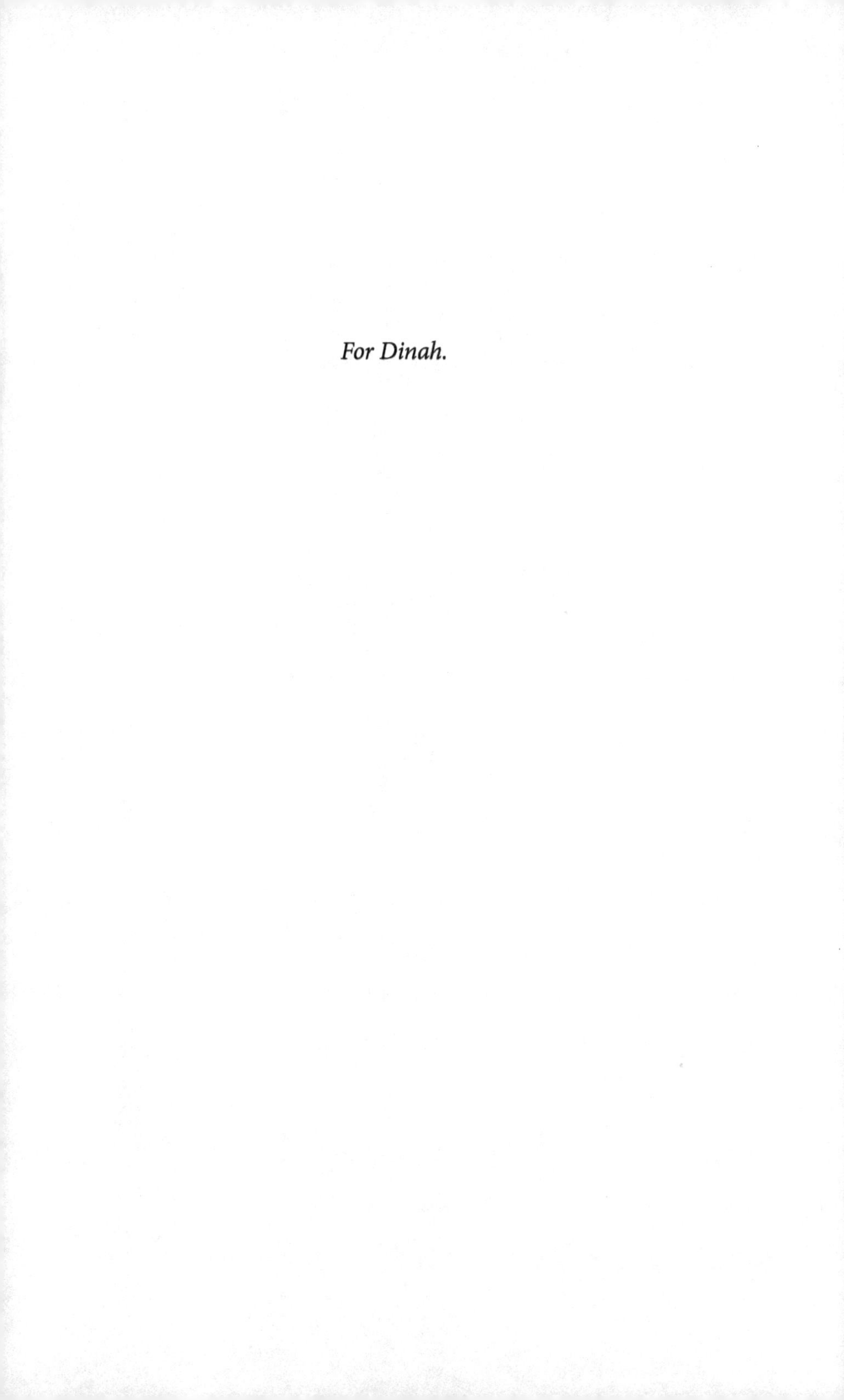

For Dinah.

Books by Belinda Crawford

The Hero Rebellion
(Hunter)
Hero
(Race)
Riven
Regan

The Echo
Cold Between Stars
Dark Between Oceans
Echo Between Worlds
(Brother)

Gamer

I Am Maggie Volume 1

Demons & Battleskirts
Volume 1
Volume 2
(coming late 2026)

Gods of Sundered Heaven
Through Soul to Flesh
(coming June 2026)

Short Bits
Short Bits Collected Edition 1
(collecting volumes 1–4)
Volume 5
Volume 6

www.belindacrawford.com

IN THE BEGINNING

Humans colonised Jørn; they travelled across the galaxy intent on a better way of life, away from the influence of Earth. But the drones they sent ahead, the ones that told them that Jørn was their new paradise, missed something; a native spore toxic to all Terran life.

Genetic engineering, blending DNA from Earth and Jørn species, saved their crops and livestock, but the colonists refused to use the same technology on themselves. Instead, they took to the skies, turning their five great colony ships into cities that floated above the spore's reach.

But one colonist, Dr Augusta Woolsey, had a different vision of humanity's future, one where humans could walk Jørn's surface without the protection of suits or re-breathers. A vision of a humanity genetically altered to live in harmony with the planet they called home. She put into motion a plan that would take centuries to come to fruition and set two artificial intelligences to oversee it, Ayumon and the Librarian.

For three hundred years Ayumon and the Librarian carried out Dr Woolsey's instructions, carefully engineering a new subspecies of human.

After generations, they were ready to enact the ultimate step.

And then Hero blew it to smithereens.

Literally.

CHAPTER 1

The yellow floor numbers hovering before the lift's door ticked over with the same speed her mother had approved her transfer to a regular school. Slowly, so very slowly.

It was still faster than she'd approved Hero's request to join her school's barrier racing team. Which was to say, not at all.

One hundred sixteen.

Hero shifted in her saddle, Fink's ribs expanding and contracting between her knees, and frowned at the girl reflected in the door. The girl frowned back, all round cheeks and big eyes, skin a little sallow under her usual tan and the dark barely there fuzz of her hair swallowed by the blue-white halo of her helmet.

Timon Dane had called her a pixie, right there at the start line surrounded by all the other race teams. He hadn't said it out loud, but she'd caught the thought as it flittered across his mind, dark orange-brown and pink at the same time – like a tingly, fuzzy rash. It had come with an image of her sitting astride Fink, a short, stocky girl atop an enormous tawny beast, her navy jacket done all the way up to her chin, the thick black saddle harness almost swallowing her thighs and pouches hanging from her belt.

It hadn't been the word – she wasn't sure what a pixie was, some Old Terran frog she guessed – but something about the *way* he thought it had a thousand tiny needles prick-pricking their way through her brain and all the way down to her stomach.

One hundred seventeen.

She shifted in the saddle, twisting her nose and frowning at her reflection in the lift doors. *Pixie my ars—*

Fink snapped his jaws and shook his head, pinning her with a big black eye. He didn't think it at her, but she caught the message.

Hero snorted. Like 'arse' was even a swear word.

One hundred eighteen.

After that, Dane's scruffy little scout with his dumpy oad-hawk had called Fink a menace. Said it right out loud, as if she and Fink weren't standing right there, glaring at him. The runt didn't even flinch, like Dane's snooty toa-mare – all sleek purple skin and snappy, sinuous tail – could protect him from Fink's six-hundred-and-seventy-eight kilos of teeth and claws. Let alone her.

Maybe if the long abandoned arcade hadn't been jammed with people and the holocams hadn't been swarming thicker than flies, she'd have shown him what a real menace was. But illegal or not, even the street races had rules, and she was pretty sure hacking the biocomputer wrapped around the scout's wrist, so that it zapped him every time he looked in her direction, was against them.

Hero crossed her arms and the girl in the door did the same. Together their fingers tapped the bracer wrapped around their forearm, igniting sparks of colour that danced and caught in the veins of energy coursing through the biogel.

She narrowed her eyes and bared her teeth. The girl in the door snarled back.

It didn't matter, she'd show them. She and Fink, they'd leave Dane, his scout and his snooty toa-mare in the itch-dust. Then they'd see just who was calling whom a pixie.

Beneath her, Fink grumbled and twitched, his whiskers doing an agitated dance in time with his ears. His long, hairless tail thumped against the lift's sides in sharp little half jerks. Even if his skin hadn't rippled with tension, bunching and twitching against her calves, she would have known he was unhappy from the way his thoughts crouched in the back of her mind, a dark, huddled mass of grumpiness.

One hundred nineteen.

Almost there, she thought at Fink.

The grumpiness unwound, just a little, and his whiskers paused in their dance. In their reflection, his dark eyes narrowed and she felt anticipation ripple through his skin.

All they had to do was win this race and they'd be another step closer to freedom.

One hundred twenty.

Tension crawled up her spine. Just one more level.

Prepare to eat dust, Timo—

The lift jerked, a violent shudder that almost threw them to the floor. Fink's claws screeched over the plasteel, all six legs braced. Adrenalin shot straight to Hero's heart, the heady fuzz of anticipation turning sour when the lights flickered, the doors stayed closed and the yellow numbers hovering in front of them stuttered and died.

For a second the only illumination came from the glow of her holohelmet, washing the lift in blue-white and picking out the hairs in Fink's ruff in icy highlights and shadows. She had time to think that it was a fine time for another blue-out before the lift shuddered again, the lights flicked back on and it was over. There was a faint hum and the numbers on the door changed.

One hundred twenty-one.

The doors cracked open.

Fink burst out of the lift, neck stretched, paws pounding the floor of the narrow arcade. Jammed side-by-side, thin shopfronts and thinner autovenders blurred in Hero's peripheral vision, the light from their holos strobing red and green and violet, flashing in her face, making the shadows darker, longer.

Behind them, barely heard over the pounding of Fink's paws and her own heart, came the old-fashioned ding of another lift. She chanced a glance over her shoulder to see Phara thunder out, the toa-mare's hooves striking sparks from the steelcrete, Timon Dane crouched over her sleek neck.

She turned back, just as a streak of green and purple screeched through the air in front of her, tail feathers grazing her nose, talons batting a round object out of the air. The bomb that had been about to impact her visor exploded in a puff of purple knockout gas somewhere above her head.

'A little warning next time?' she said to the voice in her ear.

'A little gratitude perhaps?' the voice retorted, and Hero's visor flickered. Norah appeared on the inside of her helmet. Her best friend scowled at her, eyes dark and brows in a single black line. 'Harish just saved your arse, you know. Again.'

The green and purple streak – Harish, with his glossy wings and sleek, scaled underbelly – whizzed past her ear with another ear-splitting screech.

'Sorry,' she said, more to Harish than Norah.

A sphere shattered on the ground, releasing a violet miasma ahead of them. Fink swerved, almost running into a shop window and narrowly avoiding the puff of sleeping gas. He leapt violently to the other side as another purple sphere dropped from overhead.

The cloud brushed her shoulder, the tingly fuzz of the sedative clogging her nose for a second before they whipped past.

Hero sneezed. 'What's with all the Violet Nights?'

'Look up.'

Hero looked up. Hiding amongst the holographic clouds was a swarm of drones, their shiny white bellies heavy with multi-coloured spheres. The inside of her helmet changed, yellow outlines appearing around the two dozen triangular shapes hovering above her head, tactical readouts flying from each one until her visor was a cluster of graphs and numbers she had to shake to the sides of her vision.

'A gauntlet,' Hero said.

Norah's frown turned thoughtful. 'Yeah, but they're waiting for a trigger before they drop the rest of their payload. I think we can use it, to get Dane off your tail. I just have to hack…'

'Use that new program I installed on your bracer.'

'I know.'

'Well, last time you used the—'

'I said.' Norah bit the words out. 'I. Know.'

Fink leapt and twisted again. The saddle harness pulled at Hero's legs, and only the urgent red pulse of her visor had her ducking in time to miss Timon's oad-hawk as it dive-bombed her head.

Hero scowled but ignored the urge to glare over her shoulder. She could see Timon well enough in the small screen on the edge of her visor, him and his snooty 'mare eating up the ground between them, her helmet helpfully providing the distance. Eighty-nine metres. Eighty-seven.

'Timon's catching up,' she said.

'I've almost got it.'

Seventy-six.

Hero reached for the pouch strapped to her thigh. 'My drones—'

'No! Not after last time. We need to delay him, not blow him up. Just hang on, I'm almost done.'

Seventy-one.

The oad-hawk – squat but graceful, with its blunt, wide-lipped head and a wingspan wider than she was tall – flew at her again, a round shiny object clutched in its giant webbed feet.

Hero ducked and swore, just as Norah yelled, 'Got it!'

She had a moment of anticipation at seeing just what Norah had done before her visor screamed a warning and she looked up. The outlines around the drone swarm flashed from orange to a bright, screaming red and a multi-coloured hailstorm dropped from the sky.

The first fist-sized glob exploded in a puff of orange, and she hunkered low over Fink's neck, digging her fingers into his ruff as he slid and skidded, his claws leaving scratches in the steelcrete as he scrambled around the itch gas.

'I thought this was just supposed to get Timon!'

'It was booby-trapped.'

'Didn't you run the Rabbit first?'

Norah looked straight at her, big black eyes wide and her skin a shade whiter than its usual golden glow. She hadn't. 'Sorry.'

'Whatever.' Out of the corner of her eye, she could see the toa-mare – closer now, the boy on its back focused, his eyes narrowed on Hero, lips moving as he talked to his scout. His oad-hawk swooped and dipped in front of the pair, knocking bombs out of their way.

Harish dived in front Fink, swatting a bomb with his tail, sending it crashing into a shopfront, the sphere leaving a sickly green light behind. More and more bombs dropped from above, the drones keeping pace with the riders below, staining the old arcade a multitude of shimmering, wafting colours.

Fink leapt and twisted, his neck stretched, his hearts beating hard, his lungs sucking air. She held on with knees and hands; half-standing in the stirrups, her legs springs that moved with every bound, the wind rushing around her visor and her eyes focused on the ground ahead. Still, the drones continued to drop their bombs and Timon and his toa-mare closed the distance.

Fifty-one metres.

Ahead, the arcade dead-ended in nothingness. No more arcade, no skybridge, just the yawning darkness of a skylane punctured by the zip and flash of hovers and the dim glow of an old holoboard, more fizz now than sparkle.

Fink sat back on his haunches, claws screeching over plascrete. Hero's visor flashed red and she looked up. A sickly green bomb arrowed for her face-plate. There was barely time to widen her eyes—

Harish smacked it into the skylane. Hero's visor tracked it, following the green ball into the emptiness and then down, down, down until it smashed into one of the small floating ledges spiralling towards the dark ally below.

'That's where we're going?'

'Yes,' Norah said, even as Harish dived past Hero's ear, tucking his wings against his chest and plummeting downwards. 'Harish is mapping the ledges.'

The visuals on Hero's visor became a dizzying rush of darkness, the hover ledges picked out in red, windows and even a startled face flashing by in her periphery.

Hero shook the vision away and looked back over her shoulder. Phara closed the distance.

Her thoughts went to the pouch strapped to her leg, and the little egg-shaped drones inside. 'How much further?' The drones were safe – she was sure they were safe.

'Down the hover ledges and then five hundred metres straight to the finish line. Don't do anything stupid. You'll make it.' Nothing stupid. She didn't need to read Norah's mind to know what she meant. Nothing stupid was code for 'not the drones'.

They wouldn't make it, not unless she evened the field. On the flat, Phara was too fast.

Hero reached for the pouch on her leg. No way she was going to lose, not now, not when they were so close.

'Don't!' Norah's eyes were wide. 'You promised!'

The pouch opened with a small pop. She didn't have to say anything, just wrapped her fingers around the first small egg-shaped drone and threw it towards the boy. The rest followed, a dozen black eggs streaming after the first, sprouting stubby black wings as they went, a split second before Fink leapt over the edge.

She didn't look back, but then she didn't need to. Timon's yelp was loud and high.

By the time they'd skidded down the last plank, the drones were back in their pouch and Fink was galloping towards the finish line.

Harish winged ahead of them. The lights came closer and closer, until she could see herself on the huge holoscreen hovering over an even bigger crowd, and could feel all those minds, pressing against the wall around her brain.

Three hundred metres, two, one. The distance ticked down, the red numbers growing large on the inside of her helmet and the sound of the crowd loud in her ears. Fifty, forty, ten—

Fink's chest passed through the holotape.

The screen exploded in a shower of stars.

She looked up at the screen and grinned at herself, her face, beneath the transparent plasteel of her visor, red and streaked with sweat.

Elation filled her chest and a sharp punch of triumph added an extra kick to her smile. They'd done it, made it another step closer to the finals and the talent scouts that would be there. But most of all, she was another step closer to feeling the planet's surface under her feet, the chill air against her face and the dusty scent of freedom on the wind.

It didn't even matter if they won the finals, all *she* had to do was not get caught.

Harish landed on Hero's shoulder, jerking her out of reverie. The screen had changed, showing Norah's scowling face beside her own. She turned to look for Norah among the lines of scouts still guiding their riders to the finish line. The other girl stood with her arms crossed and her mouth set in a thin line. Hero felt the lavender-scented brush of Norah's mind, too faint to be directed at her, before Harish lifted off her shoulder and glided to Norah.

A guy shoved a holocam in Norah's face. She didn't even glare at him before she turned her back and disappeared into the crowd.

Hero slapped open the vacuum seals keeping her in the saddle, but she didn't have time to swing her leg over Fink's back before Rom, the referee, tall and thin, with a voice too deep for his skinny chest, was at her side.

He was dragging her arm into the air before her foot touched the ground. 'Everyone, let's hear it for Team Hero as they advance to the finals!'

The crowd roared and screamed and then there was the white sphere of a holocam in Hero's face and people pressing her against Fink's side, and her chance to follow Norah was gone.

Rom yanked her arm higher, stretching her out until she was on her tippy toes, and the crowd roared again.

The crowd's approval – a warm, effervescent glow – settled over her and tingled against her brain. She basked in it, letting it fill her chest, even as the roar pressed on her ears, until it all burst out of her free arm, her fist shooting into the air.

Around them, the crowd surged forward. A hovercam was shoved in her face, blinding her with a flash brilliant enough to bleach her eyeballs, pressing her deeper into Fink's shoulder, his hearts beating hard against her back.

A snarl ripped the air.

The noise and lights stuttered, a few heartbeats of silence during which Hero managed to blink the stars from her eyes.

Fink's ears were flat against his head and his foreshoulders hunched. He growled, the white of his fangs flashing in the bright lights, and the wall of people slowing backing away quickened its pace, leaving them in a bubble of tension and silence.

Woolsey. She heard the name whispered among the crowd, passed from one mouth to another, carrying with it the hint of fear that surrounded all the species the first-gen colonist had engineered out of Terran and Jøran DNA. It didn't matter that out of all the animals and plants the first generation colonists had created when their Earth-born ones had started dying, Woolsey's had adapted to the Pollen, the toxic spore that saturated the planet's atmosphere, the best. It only mattered that the scientist had plucked the Jøran portion of her creations from some of the biggest, scariest predators on the planet.

Hero ignored the whispers and reached for Fink's shoulder. 'Fink?'

Head low, he scooted out of reach, ears still lost amidst his ruff. He huffed once and stalked in the direction Norah had disappeared. The crowd parted around him in a wave of wide eyes and whispers. A few people were forced to jump out the way as his tail lashed from side to side, the end thwacking against the legs of those too slow, or too stupid to move.

Slowly the crowd filled back in behind him.

'Right. Well.' Rom cleared his throat, his voice booming above the crowd. 'Let's let the 'pard have his room then, while the rest of us get set to PARTY!'

The crowd roared and the Fink-sized bubble that held it back popped. People rushed into the space left behind, hands and thoughts reaching out to buffet Hero from all sides. The elation of the win wore off quickly, eroding with every flash of a holocam and slap on the back. The tingle of the crowd's approval was a cloud and then a hover and then a skytower weighing on her mind – the colours and flavours of their thoughts twisting and mixing in her head until she felt like she might explode.

She felt it coming, recognised the force pressing against the inside of her skull and clamped down even as she charged after Fink. She shoved and ducked and weaved, and with every new body she touched, the force in her head grew, straining against bone, skin and hair. She had to get out of there, had to find Fink, an abandoned store, a break in the crowd, anything.

Hero burst through the mess of people a split second before the psionic blast ripped through her skull. She squeezed her mind tight, felt the shockwave hit her mental shields, felt them stretch and shudder, the rich brown bubble around her thoughts thinning until it was barely there at all.

She had to hold it. She had to. Just a little longer…

Strength rose from her bones, a blue rush that ate the psionic blast and turned her shields to glittering stone. She breathed, power heavy in her veins, the scent of roses heavy in her nose, and for one thrilling heartbeat the crowd's minds were open to her and she felt everything and everyone.

They sparkled and shone, thoughts fizzing and popping in her brain, feeling like they were going to come out of her nose and ears.

Exhaustion hit, a giant ball slamming into her ribs, pushing the air out of her lungs and making her head spin. She had time to think, *no, not now,* before her legs buckled.

Hands grabbed Hero before she hit the ground. 'Hey, dude, are you all right?'

Dread curled in her gut. Sweet Terra, someone saw. No one could see, because then her mother might find out and then there'd go her dreams of exploring the planet's surface, freedom in her nose, solid ground beneath her feet.

She dragged air into her lungs, forcing her ribs outwards with a wheezy shudder. One breath and her head stopped spinning. Two breaths and she could shove some of the stuffing back into her knees, stiffening them enough to stand straight and scowl at her rescuer.

It was okay, she was at a street race, no one here was telling her mum anything.

Timon Dane, ebony skin and darker hair, looked down at her.

She wrenched herself from his grip. 'I'm all right,' she said and locked her knees tight against another wobble.

'Hey.' Timon raised his hands palm out. 'I'm just trying to help.'

'I don't need your help,' Hero said, even as she spied Fink and Norah over the boy's shoulder. She pushed past him, her knees still wobbly but firm enough that she could walk without falling on her face. 'I won, remember?'

CHAPTER 2

The taxi was silent. Tension held the air still.

Across from Hero, Norah sat with her chin pointed towards the window and Harish draped over her shoulders, his tail feathers cascading over her crossed arms. Through the window – fuzzed and cracked with age – the holoboards and lights of the city painted her profile green and orange and red. Her fringe, long and black, had fallen across her forehead and all Hero could see was the dark line of her lips, but it was enough to imagine the matching frown.

At least Norah wasn't giving her *that* look, like her friend was looking for something behind her eyes. Like she was scary. That was an expression Hero'd seen more and more over the past year, ever since she and Norah had been kidnapped by a group who'd wanted to use them to wipe out the Pollen. Ever since she'd—

Hero pushed the thought from her mind, crossing her arms and slumping further into the seat. The seat was older than she was, so old the nanofibres barely had enough oomph left to clean themselves. She was surprised the taxi's mag-levs even managed to get them above the Grip, where the magnetic field generated in the city's bowels was weaker. Not as weak as in the Horizon, where she lived, or the Upper, where only the latest hover engines could fly.

Way back when the first-gen colonists had decided to take to the skies as their only way to survive the Pollen, the floating cities they'd built had been smaller, and old clunkers like the taxi had been all they needed. Now Cumulus City, and the four others like it, had towers so tall they kissed the vacuum of space. It was no wonder they kept having blue-outs if the power generators hadn't been upgraded in the three hundred years since the cities were built, like the newscasts said. Personally, Hero didn't believe it – only an idiot made something bigger without giving it more power, and the city AIs wouldn't have let them if they'd tried. Not that anyone would listen to what she thought, not unless she hacked into the city AI and plastered "you are stupid" over all of Cumulus City's holoboards.

Hero sighed and kicked the pack at her feet, boot thunking against the saddle and helmet inside. At least Norah cared what she thought. Hero fingered the drones still nestled in their pouch against her leg. At least Norah did most of the time.

Fink shifted his head on the bag, and a mawberry-flavoured memory played in her brain. In it she was Fink, lying on the floor of the same cab just a few hours earlier, eyes on the shiny black drone hovering over Hero's hand.

'No,' Norah said. '*You can't, not after last time.*'

Hero rolled her eyes. '*Relax, I fixed the power flux, it won't overload.*'

'*That's what you said last week, two hours before you fried the kitchen terminal. My dad still hasn't figured out how to get the scorch mark out of the marble-wood, but it probably doesn't matter because the technician said they'd have to replace the whole unit anyway.*' Norah leaned across the tiny square of carpet, made smaller by Fink sprawled between them. '*Promise me, you won't use the drones.*'

Hero frowned harder. *So?* she thought back.

Fink nipped her knee, hard enough that she could feel the sharp points of his teeth.

'Ow.'

She promised, was all he thought back to her.

She rubbed her knee and glared at him. 'We won, didn't we?'

Hero sensed the lavender pressure of Norah's mind before she met the other girl's glare.

'You said you wouldn't use the drones,' Norah said. Harish lifted an eyelid to add his stare to Norah's. 'We agreed.'

'Timon was going to win!'

'You could have killed him!'

She sat back in her seat with a thump. 'I *fixed* the drones and even if I hadn't, they wouldn't have killed him.'

Norah leaned forward. 'You sure?'

She matched Norah's hard, accusing gaze with a glare. 'Yes. I swapped out the power units with weaker ones. They don't last as long, but they won't explode.' She paused a heartbeat, before something in Norah's gaze made her add in a smaller voice, 'Not unless they overloaded all at once.'

Norah's eyes narrowed until they were black slits and Hero felt lavender, hard and sharp, pushing against her mind.

She let Norah in, just a little. Lavender filled her nose and crept down the back of her throat as the other girl shifted through her brain, a pale purple wind skimming her thoughts. She knew when Norah found the memories of the night before, let Norah not just see her at her workbench but feel what she had felt. The concentration, the certainty the moment she'd found the corrupt genes, and the elation when the drone hovered above the bench and the stun field turned her fingers numb, the power levels holding steady.

She didn't think about the other moment, the one where she stared at the innards of a half-finished stun-stick-that-wasn't-a-stun-stick and wondered not just how she'd made it, but how she'd even known where to start. Hero left *that* moment in the back of her mind, hidden in a dark little corner not even Fink could see.

Norah's mouth unclenched and her presence in Hero's mind withdrew, leaving the hint of lavender and the sour taste of scepticism in its wake.

Norah looked back out the window. 'You still shouldn't have done it,' she said.

'It was our last chance at the finals.'

Norah spared her a glare. 'We're a team, and we agreed. No. Drones.'

'I knew what I was doing.'

'Right, just like you knew what you were doing when you…' Norah's face screwed up, and her eyes went darker than dark before she turned back to the window. 'When you did *that*,' she said softly.

That. Norah didn't have to say what it was. The word was almost visible in the air, shivering with the memory of a man falling to the ground, his eyes glazed, blood trickling from his nose.

That. Not even Fink knew about *that.* Or the other time, the one before, the one she kept locked away in a corner deeper and darker than the stun-stick, the one she hid even from herself.

A touch of mawberry wound through her thoughts and Hero shoved the memories back into their corners.

Fink's ears perked and his whiskers pricked forwards. *What did she do?*

Hero didn't answer, just sat back in the barely clean seat and turned her face to the window.

Fink propped his head on her knee, the weight of his massive skull pressing her into the cushions, and fixed her with a steady black eye.

She ignored him, or tried to, focusing on the vehicles that zoomed around and over them, endless streams of plasteel and light weaving in and out of the dark corridors made by skytowers. Holoboards illuminated the spaces in between buildings, multi-coloured beams of light projecting into the traffic, assaulting drivers with shouted slogans and the temptations of glowing drive-thrus.

The skybridges, slung between the towers, cast sparkling strings of light: some tall and thick enough to house an entire city cube, others as thin as a spideruck's web. Below, the city descended into a never-ending abyss of hazy lights vanishing into a deep, dark squirmy black.

The taxi wove through the traffic, shifting first left and then right, merging with one stream of hovers after another, climbing higher and higher through the city. They rose through the bright lights and busy skylanes of the Grip, their taxi just one amidst the eclectic stream of hovers, battered and new, small and large, some crammed with people, others with their windows tinted an inscrutable midnight. But not as inscrutable as the wave rushing towards them from the end of another endless skylane.

Hero pressed her hand to the plasglas and peered at the glob of darkness. It grew, swallowing skytowers, bridges and hovers. She had enough time to wonder what it was before the wave took them.

One moment they were a speck in a sea of lights and people, and then they weren't. Outside was nothingness, inside was cast in the dim orange of the taxi's single dome light. Hero's wide eyes met Norah's and her hand clenched in Fink's ruff before the taxi plummeted.

They were weightless, and then they weren't. Her stomach met her heart, squished right up against it, a split second before her back was plastered against the roof. The old plasteel ground into her spine even as Fink crushed her chest, her face buried in his coat, the hairs getting in her nose, her mouth, stopping her lungs.

Panic, hers and Norah's and Fink's, even Harish's, flooded her mind. A jumble of colours and flavours that made her sick, made her gasp for air only to choke on Fink's coat. Her lungs burned, her vision danced, and then it was over.

She hit the floor, half-sprawled over Fink, the coat that had been choking her now cushioning her fall.

Fink whined, his ears flat against his head before turning to nuzzle her side, his worry sharpened by adrenalin and the last vestiges of panic.

Hero buried her face in his ruff, breathing in the familiar sweet and dusty scent, before pushing herself up to look out the window. Outside, holoboards flickered and spat where they had any life at all, while the towers and bridges remained dark. Only the traffic cast any real light, the flight lights of countless hovers illuminating a scene that was eerily still.

'Is it over?' Norah righted herself against the other seat, Harish clutched to her chest. The linch-adder's feathers were puffed out, his wings half-mantled and his long sinuous tail wrapped tight around Norah's forearm.

Hero shook her head. 'I don't know.'

A holoscreen came to life in the middle of the cab, flickering where it bisected Fink, still sprawled on the floor, each of his six legs braced, claws deployed.

The taxi driver, brow creased as much with age as concern, looked out at them. 'Everyone okay?'

Hero nodded.

The driver nodded back and the taxi swerved, the engines whining before it dropped again.

Norah's eyes went wide and Hero's heart clenched, but it wasn't the same stomach-hollowing plunge as before, and a few seconds later they came to a stop.

The door opened.

Outside the vehicle it was dark. Hero could only tell they rested on a hover pad because of the orange-red glow cast by the taxi's flight lights.

On the holoscreen, the driver thrust his chin towards the open door. 'You two can stay here or get another taxi.' The driver shook his head. 'My girl ain't going nowhere till this blue-out is sorted. Her engine won't take another fall like that.'

Norah rubbed her arms, Harish peeking out from beneath the fall of her waist-length hair. 'Why did we fall?'

The driver shrugged, but the furrows in his brow had deepened to canyons. 'I don't know. You staying or going?'

'Going,' Hero said. She grabbed her backpack with one hand, Norah's arm with the other, and pulled them both out the door.

'Hey.' Norah tried to yank her arm back, but Hero ignored her until they were on the pad. Fink lumbered out last and the door slid closed.

Norah jerked her arm from Hero's grip. 'What are you doing? We didn't even pay him, and we still have to get home.'

'I know.' Hero unzipped the sleeve of her jacket, revealing the blue-white glow of her bracer. 'But I don't have time to wait. If Mum or Tybalt find out I snuck out again…' She didn't finish the sentence, but next to her Fink shuddered.

'You think it's any better for me? If one of my dads calls your mum and they find out I'm not sleeping over at your place, they'll send me to the New Gobi academy like they did my sister.' It was Norah's turn to shudder.

Hero ran her fingers over her bracer, holding her breath as a holoscreen popped to life above it, the words "breaking news" leaping out. She felt the knot in her shoulders unwind. The blue-out hadn't affected the prime-net. 'Which is why I'm getting us another taxi.' She activated the holo that interacted with the city's transportation AI.

Nothing happened.

She touched it again. Nothing.

She frowned.

Norah shifted closer to Hero until their shoulders touched. 'Why isn't it working? The prime-net is still up, right?'

'Yeah.' Hero looked up at the still-dark skytowers and flickering holoboards. Hovers had begun to zip through the darkness, the lights and soft buzz of their engines making them seem like so many angry stars. Except… She took a step, and then another, until she was at the edge of the hover-pad, staring out at the fast-moving traffic.

Some of those angry stars weren't moving.

Fink poked his head over her shoulder, his whiskers tickling her cheek.

She swung her backpack around to her front and had it open in one smooth move. A second later, her holohelmet was on, screens popping into life around her head, visor zooming in on the hovers that sat like stones in the torrent of traffic.

They were all the same. Squat and orange, with stubby triangular wings that tilted back and forth, holding the hovers stationary against the currents of passing vehicles, and an unmistakable 'T' projected above and below them.

'Taxis,' she said.

'What?' Norah peered out at the traffic with her.

'The automated taxis aren't moving.'

Norah frowned. 'But why?'

Hero shrugged. 'The blue-out must have scrambled the transport AI.'

Norah didn't say anything, just turned on her heel and headed back towards the taxi they'd just abandoned.

Hero stared after her. 'What are you doing?'

'Getting back in.'

'What if the blue-out lasts for hours? What about your dads?'

Norah paused and bit her lip before shrugging. 'I'll think of something.'

Fink rumbled, his ears twitching backwards, forwards and sideways, his tail making agitated little jerks. He nudged Hero's shoulder. *She should get back in the hover too. He could hear things skittering in the dark, and he didn't think they were the blue and white hover things.* A mental image of a police security drone popped into her head.

'That's it,' she whispered, before raising her voice. 'Wait, I have an idea.'

Norah turned back. 'Yeah?'

Hero nodded and activated the police holo on her bracer. 'Yeah.'

The hover that settled next to the old taxi was big and boxy, its windows as black as its sides.

Beside Hero, Norah shifted her feet and hugged her arms while Harish peered from behind the curtain of her hair. 'Are you sure about this?'

A door on the side of the hover slid open, revealing a dark interior.

Fink rumbled, his nose lifted to the breeze, and took one slow step forwards.

Nerves were exploding in Hero's stomach, but she frowned and lifted her chin anyway. 'It's the only way,' she said, eyes glued on the open hover.

'But her?' Norah said, as a tall, curvy woman, her white, curly hair cut close to her head, stepped out of the hover.

The woman stood, feet planted, hands on hips, and frowned at them, green eyes hard and her mouth turned down. Dressed head to foot in light-sucking black, Imogen had never looked less like one of the Old Terra lambs Hero had once nicknamed her for.

Hero had only seen Imogen once since the day she'd blown up a chunk of the city. Imogen had been at a café, pretending to read a newssheet while peering at her partner – a short thin man with blue eyes – as he talked to a woman with hair as dark as her skin. Imogen hadn't changed.

'What is it, Hero?' Imogen sounded as fierce as she looked.

Hero lifted her chin a fraction higher, took a breath, and dragging Norah along behind her, marched towards the open hover. 'We need a lift.'

'A…' Imogen's green eyes grew wide as strapples, and her mouth fell open.

Hero sensed, more than saw, the apologetic smile Norah gave Imogen, and figured that was the reason they managed to get two steps past the planetary agent before her mouth snapped closed.

'A lift?' From the way Imogen enunciated each word, Hero figured she was gritting her teeth.

'Mm-hmm.' Hero cast a glance over her shoulder and then wished she hadn't. Imogen's face was blank, not even a wrinkle creasing her brow, but her eyes were something else. They boiled, an angry green that made Hero's skin shrink.

Even Fink, walking in their wake, ducked his head and skittered away from that gaze.

Imogen didn't say anything, but the sharp, hard sparkle was

warning enough. 'I'm not your minder anymore, Hero.'

Hero swallowed but kept her chin high. 'It's an emergency.'

Imogen's eyes narrowed to slits, then flicked to the backpack slung over Hero's shoulder, and the one dangling from Norah's hand. Imogen's brow creased, just a fraction, and Hero could feel the thoughts clicking together in her mind.

Something very like a smile made Imogen's eyes gleam. 'You were at the race,' she said.

'What race?' Norah said, her voice barely even squeaking at the end.

Imogen's smile widened, but she didn't say anything. She just walked past them and into the hover before looking back expectantly. 'Do you want a lift or not?'

Hero didn't wait for a second invitation, climbing in the back of the hover and settling in a rear-facing seat. Fink curled at her feet, paws and tail tucked tightly against his body and tension riding the fur standing up along his spine. Norah sat beside her, with Harish's tail brushing Hero's cheek.

The door closed.

Imogen took the seat facing them, still smiling.

There was something in that smile, like a well-fed skunk-wolf waiting outside a mouse-rahm's den, that had nerves creeping up Hero's back. She shifted on the seat. 'Where's your partner?'

'You mean Dorich? He's on another assignment.' The words were light, but even from across the cab, Hero felt the tight, sour pinch of a lie on the edge of Imogen's mind. The woman slung an arm over the back of her seat. 'Did you win?'

Norah squirmed.

'Win what?' Hero said.

Imogen shifted her gaze to Norah and her smirk widened, just enough to show a hint of teeth, stark white against red lips.

'Of course you won, you're Team Hero after all.' She leaned back, swinging one leg over the other. 'I guess it's off to the finals for you. Congratulations.'

Norah spoke. 'You can't prove anything.'

The hint of Imogen's teeth became a blinding flash. 'Are you sure?'

Norah's thigh pressed into Hero's. *Do you think she's lying? If my dads find out I'm racing…*

I don't know, she thought back. But she wasn't going to take chances.

Hero crossed her arms and scowled at Imogen. 'What do you want?'

'From you, Hero? Nothing except, perhaps, for you to stay out of my way. From you, though, Ms Joshi…' Imogen leaned forward, the lights from passing hovers painting her face in shades of red and green. 'I believe we can help each other out.'

There was a bump as the hover landed, and the side door slid open as silently as it had closed.

Hero frowned. The hover pad outside wasn't the half-circle of steelcrete with its shield of plasteel to separate them from the endless traffic and dark canyons outside of Norah's house. Instead, the view outside the open door was of a nondescript grey wall that Hero knew, from long acquaintance, rose two storeys above the hover.

'You're home.' Imogen indicated the door with an inclination of her head.

Hero looked at Imogen, then Norah. Imogen smiled her secret smile but Norah looked at her with wide brown eyes.

Hero turned her gaze back to Imogen. 'What do you want Norah for?'

Imogen's smile deepened – the shunk-wolf smiling at the mouse-rahm. She gestured once more to the open door. 'Your mother's going to be home soon.'

Narrowing her gaze, Hero reached out to touch Imogen's thoughts. If Imogen wouldn't tell her then, she'd just—

Manners, Fink growled and pushed her out of the hover.

'Hey!' Hero stumbled when she hit the hover pad, barely righting herself in time to swing around as Fink alighted, saddle bag held between his teeth.

Norah was half out of her seat, clutching her own bag, but then Imogen was there, hand around the girl's arm, holding her back.

Hero pushed past Fink. 'I want to know what's going on.'

Imogen smiled at her, eyes amused chips of green. 'I know,' she said.

The door snapped closed, leaving Hero facing her own puzzled frown reflected in the hover's shiny sides.

The mag-levs hummed and Fink, his teeth in her shirt collar, tugged her backwards a split-second before the vehicle lifted off, buffeting them in a backwash of displaced air. Hero didn't move, eyes glued to the hover as it rose another three metres before angling sideways and plunging into the tangle of traffic below, heading for the skylines that would take it back into the Grip and Norah's home.

Fink purred and bumped her shoulder with his.

The hover disappeared amongst the traffic, but she continued to stare after it, pretending she could see it in the darkness. 'Why doesn't Imogen want me?'

Did it matter? Norah would tell her anyway.

Hero crossed her arms. 'I guess,' she said. But it did matter, she just didn't want to tell Fink about the hollow, ugly feeling swirling in her chest. She spun on her heel and headed for the solid grey chunk of wall that was the service door. 'Come on, before someone finds out we're gone.'

CHAPTER 3

Chaos spilled out of the double doors and onto the pristine marble-wood floor beyond. A trail of microcircuits and empty boxes that, no matter how often the cleaners swept, tidied and discarded, always reappeared in the morning. Each time the mess crept a little further down the hallway, with its sharp white walls and bright windows.

The cleaners had long since given up on the room behind the double doors.

An old holoboard was shoved up against the wall, covered in gelpaks – some plump and green, sparkling in the afternoon light, others dull grey, squished and twisted, biogel oozing out of cracked skins and filling the room with the stench of old fish. Old drone casings, some bigger than Fink's head, others smaller than a thumb, turned the floor into a minefield of plasform. A trio of crates with the Bayard logo – a 'B' in a sharp black square – emblazoned on their sides took up one wall.

Only the workbench – a spotless white rectangle – belied the mess. It sat in a bubble of serenity, the marble-wood floor – golden brown with veins of sparkling red – clear of the creeping mess that had swallowed the rest of the makeshift lab.

A matt silver cylinder the length of Hero's hand lay cradled on a transparent plinth atop the bench. A thick white sheet of biogel, grooved with the indentations of fingers, wrapped its middle, and its two ends were hollow, waiting for something to slip through.

Around the object – the stun-stick she couldn't remember constructing – holoscreens showed everything from the power running through the stick's stun circuits to the neural output of her bracer, glowing blue-white on the other side of the bench.

Hero sat cross-legged on the stool, her elbows on her knees, and stared hard at the swirling shards of DNA on the screens. Whatever the stick-that-wasn't was, it did the same thing as a stun-stick, it just did something else as well; connected with something. Something like her bracer, but not.

Maybe if she… Hero bit her lip and rearranged the molecules in the stun-stick-that-wasn't's programming.

Above the bench, a pale blue aura appeared, engulfing the device. On another screen, the slider that measured the strength of its stun field hovered in the sweet spot, a tiny stretch of green that was just strong enough to fell a snippy toa-mare but not enough to harm. Slowly but surely, the stick's aura turned pale violet, and the slider nudged upwards until it flirted with the slice of yellow that would make the toa-mare's rider numb for a week.

She leaned closer, the stool obediently gliding forward with the shift in weight. She pulled back before she came nose-to-holo with the rotating lines of code, her eyes glued to the chromosomes controlling the stick's energy output.

Peripherally she was aware of the stick's aura morphing from violet to purple, and the slider easing out of the yellow and into the orange, but her eyes never left the code. Not even the scent of her mother's fur-roses, sweet and just a bit spicy, could distract her.

The smell crawled up her nose, and as it hit her brain she saw the problem – the molecules lighting up in her mind's eye – the way they controlled the flow of power to the stun field, and the lone molecule that disrupted it. She reached out and replaced the offending molecule with another, shinier one.

The alarm almost knocked Hero off the stool. She slapped her hands over her ears. Above the bench, the stun-stick's aura turned bright, screaming red and the output slider joined it. She stumbled off the stool, almost falling to her knees before she slammed the emergency panel.

The bench went dark, the stick-that-wasn't's aura gone. Only her bracer continued to glow, its white-blue light a little dimmer but still enough to illuminate the wreckage.

Fink poked his head through the open balcony doors, his ears pricked forward, and coughed.

'I'm okay,' she said and pushed the stool back down so she could sit on it, her eyes on the stick. She'd had it, the key to stabilising the stun field, she knew it, so what had gone wrong this time?

She wrinkled her nose at the scent of her mother's roses wafting back in through the open doors. The gardener must have been experimenting with another of her fertilisers. The buds had been closed up tight this morning, but now they smelled like they'd been open for days.

Footsteps in the corridor, the hard clack-clack of shiny black shoes, gave her a second's warning before Tybalt burst through the doors. He filled the space, lean and dark, the thick line of his brows lowered over black eyes, his jacket open and his vest askew. The puckered, shiny scar creeping over his chin was the only hint of the explosion that had left him up to his neck in nanomeds for almost a week the year before.

He let out a breath, his shoulders falling back towards their usual position. 'You're okay,' he said.

She frowned and gestured to the workbench. 'It's just a stun-stick.'

'Mm-hmm.' Tybalt stepped out of the doorway, winding his way through the clutter with the ease of practice, and took the only other functioning stool, flicking the ends of his jacket out as he sat. 'I still remember the hole that bot you "borrowed" from your mum made in your bedroom wall.'

She crossed her arms. 'I was eight.'

'Yes, I know.' Tybalt folded his hands in his lap. 'It was a big hole.'

She poked her tongue out at him.

He smiled.

Hero turned back to the bench, reaching under it to switch the power back on. 'Don't you have people to organise or something?'

'No,' Tybalt said, and she didn't need to look at him to know he was settling in. His mental presence was as solid as he was, an inscrutable black that tasted like liquorice and felt like patience.

A few keystrokes and a red square came to life on the workbench. Carefully, Hero prodded the stun-stick towards the containment field.

Tybalt's stool hummed and his shadow loomed over Hero's shoulder. 'Do I want to know what you're doing?'

'I'm turning it back on.'

'Will it blow up?'

She shrugged and clicked the screen to send power back into the stick. 'Maybe,' she said.

Tybalt's hand shot out and gripped her wrist. 'Maybe?' he said.

Hero scowled and tugged at her wrist, but Tybalt's long bony fingers were bands of steelcrete. 'It's in a containment field.'

His brows rose. 'Set to contain a power surge or just projectiles?'

'Both.' Hero tugged some more and this time Tybalt's grip loosened enough for her to slip free. She rubbed her wrist and scowled. 'I'm not stupid, you know.'

He sighed. 'Then why do you keep blowing things up?'

'*I* don't blow them up,' Hero said, turning back to the stick-that-wasn't. 'They do that all on their own.'

Night had set outside and her mum's fur-roses cast pale-blue light through the open balcony doors, but Hero didn't notice.

The workbench was the only real light in the room, and her eyes were fixed on the silver tube still sitting in its red square. The stick's aura fizzled and spat, brilliant purple sparks of energy crackling in the hollow ends.

The solution was right in front of her, it had to be, but her mind felt full, too full, her thoughts running over each other. No matter how hard she stared or fiddled, the solution just wouldn't come. The fur-roses weren't helping, their sweet, cloying scent crawling up her nose and getting tangled in her thoughts, making them thick and slow.

Hero stood, jumping off the stool with enough force to send it rocketing backwards, and marched towards the open balcony. She had her hand on one sliding plasglas door, muscles tensed to slam it closed, when she caught a glimpse of the rose bushes. She froze.

Fink, a dark shadow curled up on the balcony, nudged her arm and rumbled, the question clear in his mind.

'They're closed,' she said.

He cocked his head. *What were closed?*

'The roses. The flowers haven't opened yet.'

Fink looked at the roses, then back at her. *Was that bad?*

She shook her head. 'No. I mean, I don't think so.' But she'd smelled them – how could she do that if the flowers weren't open? She took a step onto the balcony.

From inside came a sharp crunch and the thunk of something heavy hitting the floor.

'Ow. Dammit, Hero, why can't you keep this room tidy?'

A tight, angry coil slithered up Hero's spine before she ducked back inside to watch the thin shadow that was her mum pick herself up from the floor. 'Because it annoys you,' she said. And because, no matter how hard Hero nagged and wheedled, her mum wouldn't let her anywhere near the exploration arm of Bayard. As the company's CEO it wasn't like she didn't have the clout.

'Of course, why'd I even ask?' Patricia Regan rose, her silhouette slim and straight, and Hero knew, even in the dark, that not a single hair would be out of place. 'Lights,' her mother snapped.

The darkness faded and there her mum stood, blonde and perfect, except for the dark circles under her eyes and the smear of old biogel slowly sinking into her trousers. Her mum tried to brush it off only to scowl at the goo that stuck to her hands. 'Really, Hero, this is just…' Frustration bottled up inside her mum's shoulders and for a second Hero thought her head would pop right off, before she sighed.

All the tension in Patricia's shoulders eased with that breath and she picked her way across the room to slump on a stool, or as close to a slump as Hero had ever seen her.

'What are you working on now?' Patricia gestured to the stick-that-wasn't.

The angry coil still knotting her nape, Hero slunk towards the workbench. 'A thing,' she said.

'"A thing".' Her mother nodded and reached out to flick through the screens above the bench. 'You're usually better with your descriptions.' Patricia paused in her flicking, leaning in to examine one screen in particular.

Hero rubbed her nose, trying to dislodge the scent of roses, but the twisting spheres of DNA her mum was studying sent ice up her spine. She didn't know why, didn't know what it was about that collection of chromosomes, but she didn't want her mum looking at it.

Ten strides and she was close enough to slap the screen back into the workbench. 'What do you want?'

Her mum jerked back, neat blonde brows snapping together, putting lines in her perfect forehead. 'I was just coming to spend some time with my daughter, but now I want to take a closer look at that code.' She reached for the bench.

Hero slapped her hand away.

The sharp crack echoed in the silence.

Her mum stared at her, a strange expression on her face. Hero stared back, heart beating hard and the sweet, sticky scent of roses clawing at her brain.

'What are you hiding, Hero?'

'Nothing.'

'I don't believe you.' Quicker than Hero could catch, her mum grabbed her chin, turning it left and right. 'When was your last appointment with Doctor Zass?'

She ripped out of her mother's grip. 'You should know, she works for you.'

Patricia stood, peering at Hero like she wished she had a microscope, before grabbing her shoulders. 'Hero, this is important. Have you had any headaches, experienced any memories that...' Her mother's face screwed up like she didn't know how to say the next bit. 'Memories that aren't yours.'

'No.' Hero tried to shake her mum's hands loose, but they wouldn't budge. The scent of roses was so strong she could see it, a subtle blue haze between her and the world, between her and her mum. With it came something else, an acidic churning in her chest that made her sick and giddy at the same time. She breathed and felt that the air should have been fire.

'Let go of me,' Hero said from between gritted teeth.

Her mother's fingers tightened and the sense of her flooded Hero's mind, the cool taste of cinnamon curdling in her brain. 'Are you sure? I know it might be difficult but—'

'I said.' Hero put both hands on her mum's chest and shoved. Hard. 'Let. Me. Go.'

Peripherally, she was aware of Fink out on the balcony. Ears alert. Eyes focused on her. His ruff half fluffed out.

Her mum stumbled back, hands falling to her sides. Surprise disturbed the lines on her face before concern wiped them away and she stepped forward again. 'Hero, I think you should come with me.' Patricia reached for Hero's arm.

The acid in Hero's chest boiled over, the scent of roses exploded in her nostrils and something very much like glee curled her hand into a fist.

Fink yowled.

Her mum turned at the sound.

Hero's fist sailed past her chin.

Patricia stumbled backwards.

Blue soaked Hero's vision. Roses were tangled in her mouth and in her brain. She felt the smile pulling at her lips, drawing them back over her teeth. There was something else too, a crack, somewhere way, way back in her brain.

She advanced.

Fink yowled again.

Her mum raised her hands, palm out. 'Hero, stop.'

Her fist tightened. She could already see it, bigger, browner, rocketing towards her mum's nose.

Someone grabbed her from behind.

The scream that came out of her mouth was a great blue torrent of hate. She tried to twist, to turn, but the arms – Tybalt's arms – held her tight while her mum backed away.

There were words, Tybalt's chest rumbled with them, but she didn't hear what they were. All she could hear, all she could think, was blue. She breathed it. In and out. It scorched her nose, her throat, her lungs, suffused her chest, her bones, her fingers.

Her mum's mouth moved, but her words too were lost in the rush. Her eyes were wide, white around the edges. She took a tentative step forward.

Glee rooted Hero to the spot.

Her mum came closer.

Hero tensed.

Tybalt yelled something.

Her mum was gone.

Frustration ripped another shriek from her throat.

The blue burned in her chest and in her brain. Burned and burned and burned. She kept screaming, pouring it out of her throat and her nose until it faded and she could see other colours, breathe other scents. There was the warm spicy tang that was Tybalt, the white glow of the workbench, the brown-gold of the floor with its veins of red beneath her knees, and Fink's big black eyes.

The blue was gone. Her chest felt empty, her throat raw. There was steelcrete in her bones, dragging her limbs to the floor, making her sag in Tybalt's arms.

Fink whuffed, his whiskers tickling her nose, and she was pretty sure Tybalt said something, but all she could summon was a sigh before she closed her eyes.

CHAPTER 4

The first thing she saw was the afternoon sky, bright blue and cloudless, framed by green and purple leaves. It shimmered and the scene on her bedroom ceiling changed.

The next thing was Fink's big red and black flecked head, half-resting on her stomach, his gaze and ears focused somewhere beyond them.

The third was Tybalt, slumped in the chair beside her bed, bushy black brows almost touching, lines embedded deep on his forehead, his skin a shade or two paler than its usual dusky brown.

Fink flicked an ear her way and whuffed. His thoughts touched hers. He showed her going to sleep in Tybalt's arms and Tybalt calling someone while he carried Hero to her room. *That wasn't all. Look*, he thought to her, *listen*.

She turned her head on the pillow and did.

The door between her room and private lounge was open. Through it she could see her mother, blouse pulled out of her trousers, bits of hair straggling around her ears. Her mother's lips moved, talking to a woman in a white coat. Tall enough, but round, with small shoulders and big hips and a long wave of pale brown hair trailing down her back.

Why was Doctor Zass here?

'You said it was stabilising,' her mother said.

Doctor Zass pursed her lips. 'It was, but there have been other changes and those are producing issues of their own.'

'Changes that are only affecting *my* daughter.'

'I've already explained—'

'Yes, I know. Fundamental differences in the Jørgen gene, suggesting the existence of separate races within the subspecies.' Her mum's hand went to her hips and the sound that came out of her mouth made Hero jerk in surprise. She'd never heard her mum growl before, and couldn't tell if it was anger or frustration that twisted her expression. 'That only explains why Norah isn't experiencing the same issues. Dammit, Doctor, I don't care about the why, I just want the how. How are you going to stop what happened to my brother from happening to my daughter?'

Zass was silent for several long heartbeats. 'I don't know,' she said.

The bedroom door snicked closed. Hero looked up.

Tybalt didn't smile at her, but he didn't frown either, he just looked tired, shirt-sleeves rolled back to the elbow and his vest undone. 'You're awake,' he said.

She pushed herself up, Fink's head moving from her chest to her lap. 'I want to hear what they're saying.' She nodded towards the door.

Tybalt sat back in the chair, one leg over the other, his elbows on the armrests, hands folded in his lap. 'No,' he said.

Hero scowled but didn't argue. Instead, she reached out to touch her mum's mind. And ran smack-bang into a mawberry-flavoured wall. She glared at Fink.

He twitched an ear. *Manners*, he thought to her.

She pushed his head out of her lap, but she didn't even get to throw the blankets off her legs before a large, weathered hand was pushing her back into the pillows.

'Not yet,' Tybalt said.

'But—'

'No.'

Before Hero could retort, the door swung open and Doctor Zass strode towards the bed. 'Good morning, Hero, how are you feeling?'

Hero turned her glare to the doctor. 'What were you and Mum

talking about?'

Doctor Julia Zass didn't blink. 'There are some tests I need to run,' she said.

'I don't want any tests, I want to know what you were saying about my life.'

The doctor perched on the mattress beside Hero's hip. 'You're one of the only two known people in an emergent subspecies of human, and less than seven hours ago, you had a what appears to be a psychotic break before collapsing.' The doctor stared at Hero, hard, but without anger or fear. 'I am running these tests and you will sit still for them.'

Hero wanted to say 'or what?', but something in Doctor Zass's gaze and the brush of her mind, a hard golden-brown, like crystal, stopped the words in her throat. She didn't even glare that hard, just slumped against the headboard while the doctor slipped a half-circle of biogel-filled plasglas around her forehead.

With his head still in her lap and the rest of his body half on and half off the bed, Fink sighed. Mawberry-scented approval flooded her mind. *That was good. He'd been worried.*

About what?

On her head, the half-circle beeped.

'No telepathy please.' Doctor Zass didn't look up from the readout on her palm-unit.

One of Fink's memories played in her mind. In it, she was advancing on her mum, teeth bared, and there was something wrong with her face. It was squarer, broader and her hair was green.

Hero shuddered. She remembered that hair, but on another woman, one whose expression had been slack and empty, a thin line of blood trailing from her nose. A woman whose thoughts had smelled like roses.

Dread shivered down Hero's spine. 'That was what I looked like?'

Fink's ears flattened. *To him,* he thought at her. *He didn't think that was what her mum saw.*

Tybalt leaned forward, elbows on his knees. 'What's Fink saying?'

She stared at Fink, her eyes wide and felt her heart pound in her chest. 'Nothing.'

Doctor Zass reached out and adjusted the band on Hero's head. 'That's not what your vitals say.'

'Hero.' Tybalt's voice was soft. 'Look at me.'

Slowly, she did.

The deep lines had disappeared from his forehead, and there was concern in his eyes. 'We can help you better if you tell us what's wrong.'

She shook her head.

He sighed and rubbed his hands over his face, and when he stopped the lines were back and he was looking at Fink. 'Fink, can you show me?'

Fink went still, freezing in her lap, neither tail nor whiskers so much as twitching. He rolled one big, black eye to look up at Hero.

She frowned at him and crossed her arms.

He whined, just a little.

She frowned harder.

With a grumble, Fink turned his gaze back to Tybalt and shook his head.

Tybalt sighed and rested his forehead against his palms. 'Dammit, Hero.'

'No matter.' Doctor Zass plucked the band off of Hero's head. 'The neural scans will tell us more than the animal's recollection.'

'He's not an animal.'

'Mm-hmm.' The mattress bounced as the doctor rose. 'I'll be scheduling more tests for you at Bayard. Until then, get some sleep.'

CHAPTER 5

An oad-hawk squatted at Hero's elbow, casting a long, fat shadow over her slice of the group's workbench. It had perched there for the last half of the xenobiology period, without a single rustle of its dark cinnamon-coloured wings or a twitch of its scaly, webbed feet. Hero wasn't even sure it breathed. She only knew it was alive because she could feel it, a muddy green lump on the edge of her mind.

She tried not to look at it, but every time she summoned a new screen it popped up right where the companion stood; like now. She caught the screen with the tips of her fingers, scooting it across the bench, and caught the 'hawk's eyes.

It blinked, the long slow slide of its twin set of eyelids so hypnotic she almost didn't notice it cranking open its stubby, wide-lipped beak and—

'Crrroaaak.'

The sound reverberated throughout the classroom before sinking into the pale grey shimmer of the holowalls.

From the other end of the workbench, a giggle grated its way up Hero's spine, then a titter and a snort, until the entire classroom was lost in laughter.

Hero hunched her shoulders and glared at the flyer. She didn't know what was so funny about it: the oad-hawk had breath like a bag full of sweaty socks, and she'd just caught the brunt of it.

The tutor clapped her hands. 'All right, all right. More xenobiology, less frivolity.'

The laughter was stuffed back into mouths and hidden behind hands but passed around in nudges and giggle-filled glances. Hero let it wash over her and stole a glance at Norah at the workbench opposite. The other girl grinned and nudged right along with everyone else, and Hero tried to ignore the resentment building in her gut. It wasn't like she couldn't make new friends, it was just... no one wanted to know her. Even now, she sat in her own little bubble; the other three members of her work group huddled at the opposite end of the bench, as far away from her as they could get.

The low tone that signalled the end of class bonged through the room.

Holoscreens vanished, chairs slid back and the oad-hawk took flight, buffeting her with its wings.

The classroom was empty in less than thirty seconds.

Hero hopped down from her stool.

Norah hadn't even waited for her.

The dining hall was loud, the hubbub of students' voices circulating in the air, their thoughts a gentle pressure against Hero's skull.

The golden-red bundle of teeth and claws that was Fink play-wrestled with a mauve and tan dobber-shepherd in front of gigantic floor-to-ceiling windows. Hovers flashed through the darkness outside while a small cluster of students watched the two companions stalk each other with yips and mock growls, the 'shepherd's long, lean body dancing around Fink's heavier one.

Hero ignored them, focusing instead on Norah, who was sitting by herself with a micropage in one hand and a sandwich in the other, Harish curled on the sofa beside her.

Movement caught Hero's eye, and she took her gaze from Norah long enough to glare at the blonde girl making a beeline for the space beside Norah. The girl didn't notice Hero at first, but a touch of her mind to the blonde's was all it took for the girl to scurry away.

She sat next to Norah with a plop, making the cushions bounce and sending Harish tumbling off the sofa. The 'adder squeaked when he hit the ground, but was quickly back on his feet and, with a flap and a hop, in Norah's lap. He puffed out his purple chest and hissed at Hero.

She ignored him and did her best to look relaxed, leaning back against the cushions. Her fingers tapped on the armrest. She took a deep breath and made them stop. Her foot started jiggling instead and while she was trying to stop that, her hands forced themselves into fists and crossed over her chest.

The sound that came from behind the micropage was less of a sigh and more an explosion of breath. The 'page came down with a slap and Norah glared at her. 'What?'

Hero's foot jiggled, and she frowned at it. 'Did you get home okay?'

'Yes. My dads didn't even blink when Imogen dropped me off. They assumed the van was one of your mum's.'

'That's good.' Hero's knee jiggled. 'So,' she said.

'So?'

Hero shifted on the sofa.

Norah continued to frown at her.

She unwrapped her arms, drummed her fingers. It would be so much easier if she could just read Norah's thoughts. Hero cast the other girl a considering glance but didn't need to send a thought her way to know Norah's brain was impenetrable as ever.

Hero sighed, stopped studying her feet and lifted her head, mouth open to ask.

'No,' Norah said.

Hero blinked. 'What?'

'I'm not telling you what Imogen said.'

Hero blinked again. 'But—'

'No.'

She frowned. 'Why not?'

'Because.'

'That's not an answer.'

It was Norah's turn to cross her arms, and she did so with a determined look in her eye that Hero knew well. But there was something else there too, behind the hard set of her jaw and in the way Norah hugged her chest and clenched her hands. Too tight, too hard, nervous. Sick almost.

Suspicion snuck into Hero's thoughts and a tiny, cold knot formed in her belly. Did Imogen know about *that*? She'd been there, had probably seen it or read about it or heard about it. Had Imogen asked Norah about what had happened that night? A chill worked its way down Hero's spine and she felt some of the blood leave her face. 'Was it about me?'

Norah sighed. 'Not everything is about you, you know.'

The knot in her stomach grew colder and tightened. 'It was about me.'

Norah rolled her eyes, her arms unclenching from her middle. 'No. It wasn't.'

Something about the look on Norah's face, in the way she'd rolled her eyes, and the sharp, lavender scent of her thoughts, made the knot in Hero's belly unclench. She took a deep breath. Relief poured through her, making her head light and her muscles slack. She slumped against the cushions.

Norah kicked her in the shin. Her scowl was ferocious.

'Ow.'

'You thought I'd tell.'

Hero didn't need to ask her about what. *That* hung between them, just like it always did. She shrugged. 'It scares you.'

'It doesn't scare you?'

She thought back to the day before, to her mum and the blue-coloured hate that had taken her. The chill came back, knotting her stomach. She swallowed but didn't say anything.

Neither did Norah.

The silence stretched. The knot in Hero's stomach thawed. Her foot jiggled. 'If you didn't talk to Imogen about me, why can't you tell me what you did talk about?'

'Because, I promised I wouldn't.'

'Why would Imogen tell you something and not me? She was my minder.'

Norah scoffed. 'For like three months, and only because she was spying on your mum. And maybe she didn't want to tell you because the last time you blew up a chunk of the city *and* an AI.'

'You helped.'

'Maybe, but at least it wasn't my idea to start with.'

'It wasn't mine either.'

'Whatever. I'm still not telling you, and don't even think of reading my mind.' Norah spared her one last glare, before raising her book. 'I'll give you a migraine if you try.'

Harish mantled his wings and hissed at Hero again, while across the lounge, Fink followed it up with his own mental warning.

'Fine,' she said to all of them. She'd find out, it was just a matter of figuring out how. In the meantime… She squinted at the cover of Norah's book. A beautiful, plump woman with sharp blue eyes and thick strands of silver through her dark hair stared at Hero, the title *Unconventional: The geneticist who saved the world* stamped over the top. 'Why are you reading Woolsey's biography?'

'I'm not.'

'Well, that's not what the cover says.'

'What?' Norah flipped the micro-page over. She glared at Hero and flipped the 'page back. 'Stop messing with me. I'm not telling you anything.'

'I'm not…' Hero let the denial hang and squinted at the cover. She snatched it out of Norah's grip.

'Hey.'

The cover was different, the title even. Woolsey no longer stared back at her; instead, a girl with fire in her hair clutched a boy above an Old Terran city. Hero held her thumb to the shiny surface. A screen popped up, and she scowled at it. There was only one book in the 'page's memory, and it wasn't the one she'd seen.

The 'page was ripped from her hands, the edge cutting into her palm, blazing a line of fire in its wake. 'Ow.'

Norah's frown was half annoyance and half puzzlement. 'Get your own book.'

'But I saw—'

'Whatever.' Norah thumped against the back of the sofa and lifted the 'page in front of her face.

Hero's mouth opened, closed, and then she did her own thumping against the sofa back.

She glared at the flame-haired girl on the back of Norah's micropage. 'I saw it.'

Norah's knuckles whitened, but she didn't move, Harish curling up in her lap.

Hero stood. 'Fine.' She glared at Norah for a heartbeat, before stalking to an abandoned stretch of holowall, not bothering to grab a chair before plonking herself in front of it. She'd find that damn book, if for no other reason than she could.

The Library responded to the touch of her fingers, the tiny white avatar of its AI popping out of the wall. 'Hero Regan, how may I help you?'

Hero stared at the little white figure, no bigger than her hand. 'You're talking to me now?' The Librarian hadn't spoken to her since she'd destroyed Ayumon. Not even to ask her how it could help.

'Of course, Hero Regan.'

'I'm looking for a book—'

'I know, Hero Regan.'

A book spun up on the wall.

Hero frowned. 'The cover was white, as devoid of features as the Librarian itself. 'That's not it,' she said.

The avatar remained silent.

The book twirled in front of her, spinning slowly, back to spine to front. It paused a second, the light catching the ridges of a figure embossed on the cover. Hero looked closer. Whatever it was rustled its wings.

She jerked back. Could it be? Hero looked over her shoulder, lip caught between her teeth, but no one looked her way. The zip-seal on her sleeve gave way with a sigh when her thumb found the pressure pad, the material parting over her forearm. Beneath, blue-white veins of energy shone under her bracer's skin, and a second later the book was safely stored in its memory.

She glanced over her shoulder. Students, companions, and the smattering of tutors were intent on their plates or books or each other. No one was looking at her. Nonetheless, she made the screen above her bracer a small one.

The book, now barely bigger than her two fists, hovered above her wrist. The bird embossed on the front cover didn't ruffle its feathers, but the shape of a robin was unmistakable. Hero held her breath and touched it.

The book slid open until it was no longer a book but a landscape of words and holos that curved around her head. In the middle of it the holo of a man, with smooth golden hair and the hint of trouble in his blue eyes, smiled back at her.

'Uncle Paris,' she whispered.

Hastily, she squashed the screen, until it was back to being no bigger than her two fists, before detaching it from above her wrist and sticking it on the wall. She spent a second staring at her mum's twin. Had he been as uptight as her mum, as strict? Something about his eyes, in the way they seemed to gleam, and the tilt at the corner of his mouth, told her no.

Could he have told Hero about her telepathy? Could he have stopped her parents from making her take the meds? Could he have told her what was happening now?

She bit her lip. Maybe, but it didn't matter, couldn't matter. Paris was dead, and the Librarian had dumped a mountain of data in her lap. In it, somewhere, might be the answers she needed, but surer than that, there was a catch too, a trail of data leading her all the way to a starring role in the AI's next grand plan.

Hero bit her lip harder, worrying it between her teeth, fingers hovering over the screen. What was the plan this time? Ayumon was gone; the scheme to change human evolution, centuries in the making, destroyed with it. Or was it? Perhaps the Librarian had found another way. What if it had? Did she care?

She glanced over her shoulder to where Norah sat, the girl's face still obscured by the 'page. Her mind went back to the door on the big black hover sliding closed and Norah and Imogen flying away.

She turned back to the screen. An itching, nagging ball of curiosity settled in her gut, squashing the sour feeling of being left out. Her fingers touched the holo.

The data was endless, made up of news clippings and holos. Not just the static shots or short clips taken by journalists and friends, but long rambling vids. Hero hovered over one, debating whether to watch it then and there, but shook her head and kept flicking through.

A vid stilled her fingers. It was taken from above, the angle awkward like it had been shot from a security-holo, but her uncle's bright blond hair was easy to make out. He ran down a hallway, long heavy coat flying out behind him, and barrelled through a door. The vid jumped, cutting to another security-holo, and there was her uncle, sliding to a halt in front of an airlock as the massive door cycled open. Hero didn't know what she expected to see on the other side of the airlock, but it wasn't the tumble of sand-coloured boulders or the blue-grey tangle of leaves and thorny bushes. Her breath caught in her throat and she leaned closer, as if she could squeeze through the holoscreen and down to the planet's surface far, far below.

A huge bird swooped into the airlock and Hero jerked back from the screen. The animal stretched long muscular legs, coming to rest on slender feet covered not in scales but in a short, satiny coat the colour of graphite, its toes tipped with ebony talons. It settled on the airlock's pale grey floor and cocked its long triangular head, as brightly coloured as its double set of wings, its muzzle the same dark, satiny grey as its feet. It stood still as a statue, the points of its tufted ears level with her uncle's sternum, and regarded him with bright blue eyes. Outside, a shadow lumbered across the tumbled boulders.

'It's too soon.' Paris's voice made her jump. 'I need more time.'

The vid ended and the screen changed, flipping through words and holos until all she saw was a blur of colour. She wanted to go back, wanted to know why Paris had needed more time and why he'd been talking to the bird, but the computer ignored her commands and Hero could only hope that whatever the Librarian wanted her to see next held another clue.

The rush of words and images stopped. Doctor Julia Zass, sharp violet eyes and waves of curly brown hair, stared back at her.

The scowl that settled over Hero's face was automatic. 'What does *she* have to do with anything?' She didn't exactly expect an answer, but when the robin holo popped up next to the image and ruffled its feathers, she wasn't surprised.

The bird opened its beak, closed it and fizzed from existence.

'Hey—'

Something huffed against the back of her neck, and only the familiar mawberry touch of Fink's thoughts kept her from jumping out of her skin.

With another huff, Fink slumped to the ground, his head on his paws and his ears flat, the tip of his long hairless tail making a hollow sound as it thumped against the carpet.

'What's up *your* tail?'

He grumbled, but his thoughts were silent.

Hero frowned and pushed against his mind.

He lifted a lip, flashing a hint of fang.

'Did you just …?'

His ears flattened a little more and his whiskers drooped. He whined, and she felt the apology in his mind. There was a hint of something else behind it, a half-caught image of a dober-shepherd before his mind closed down again.

It was enough that Hero raised her eyebrows until they just about touched her hairline. She glanced across the dining hall. Beside the huge plasteel windows the dober-shepherd sat, its furry mauve and tan chest puffed out, ears pricked high while the girl at its side smiled smugly at Hero.

Hero blinked. The other girl's pride made her thoughts so loud, Hero barely needed to touch her mind, and once she did…

Hero turned back to Fink. 'The 'shepherd beat you?'

Another grumble. *He didn't want to talk about it.*

CHAPTER 6

'You're late.' Doctor Tachi – tall, with thin shoulders, a pudgy belly and tired face – didn't look up from the guts of the head-size drone spread across his workbench. Behind him, plastered across the lab's transparent walls, code flowed in a never-ending stream of As, Ts, Gs and Cs.

Hero scrunched her nose and crossed her arms over her chest. 'Doctor Zass dragged me off to her lab.' And she made her stand stiller than a holostatue while she stuck Hero with that stupid headband and a thousand other things. She rubbed the spot on the side of her rib cage where the one of Zass's monitors had pinched her skin. It had been the second longest thirty-six minutes of her life. Not that Hero could tell Doctor Tachi; as far as he was concerned she was interning in Zass's lab, not a human-Jøran hybrid and the subject of a million and one tests.

'Huh. I shall have to have another word with her about hijacking my interns. Of course,' Tachi looked up this time, and the lines on his forehead deepened, his old brown eyes considering, 'you're the only one in whom she's shown interest. Perhaps I should have a word with her instead about the indelicacy of using the boss's daughter to advance her career. Unless, of course, you prefer the biology department?'

Hero snorted. 'No.' The doctor's brows rose, and she hastily tacked on, 'Thanks.'

'Hmm.' He turned back to the drone scattered over his bench.

'We're working on the power issue today.'

Snagging the only other lab coat from the hook beside the door, Hero hurried over to the bench, pushing her arms into the shiny green sleeves as she went. 'The swarm AI held up in field simulations?' Not that she'd ever doubted it – she thought back to the race – she'd been conducting field tests of her own after all.

'Yes.' He looked down his nose, as Hero had learned was his habit when he was thinking, and pushed the drone's thumbnail-sized innards around. 'Your gene-splicing did wonders. Unfortunately, using the swarm mode to enlarge the stun field is still proving problematic.' He picked up a tiny green sphere and placed it in the blue circle glowing in the middle of the workbench.

The surface hummed, and the generator rose until it was hovering a hand span above the surface.

Hero leaned in close. 'The generators are overloading.' Just like hers had before she switched out the power packs, but with a bigger bang.

'Indeed.' Doctor Tachi made a gesture and a holo of the generator's innards, three times larger than the thing itself, appeared above the bench. Another gesture and the twisting lines of the generator's biocode appeared on a new screen. 'Despite suggestions to the contrary, I'm of the opinion that the generator itself is adequate. The problem is in the genes.'

Hero frowned, all her attention glued to the holographic ladder that was the drones' programming. She snagged a hover-stool from beneath the bench, aware of Doctor Tachi moving away, but the code absorbed her attention. Perfectly matched spheres – the drones' chromosomes – danced around each other. She selected first one and then the other, blowing them up and spreading the tight spiral of their component genes across the bench.

'There,' she whispered to herself before pushing in on a segment of DNA.

Hero stared at it, scanning the molecules that made up each gene until her eyes crossed and her brain fizzed. She knew there was something wrong with the code but, like the stun-stick, she couldn't see it. Frustration rose in the back of her throat, the scent of roses coming with it. It rushed through her bones, curling her fingers into fists, knuckles aching with the desire to hurt something, and then she saw it: the gene that told the drones' generators to produce more power and the mismatched collection of molecules that blocked it. No wonder the things blew up, she thought as she set about untangling the code.

A hand appeared between her and the screen. Hero blinked, before turning to look at Doctor Tachi.

The lines on his face were deeper than usual, and there was a hint of confusion in the brush of his mind against hers. 'Hmm.'

'I found the problem,' she said. 'I'm fixing it.'

'So I see.' He leaned one elbow on the bench and rifled through the new code. His frown deepened.

Nerves lit up Hero's chest.

With a final 'hmm', Doctor Tachi straightened before pinning Hero with a strange look.

She swallowed but returned his gaze.

'This is not your code.'

Hero blinked. Anger buzzed in her stomach and pride made her back rigid. 'I didn't steal it.'

'I never said you did,' Tachi said patiently. He shifted the screen, so he was looking at her through it. 'But the fact remains, this is not your code. Or rather, your style.'

She glared at him through the screen, arms crossed tightly.

'Look for yourself,' he said.

Grudgingly, she did, tracing the way one gene connected to another. It was her code – she smelled roses again and rubbed at her nose, masking it with the scent of chocolate – and then it wasn't. She blinked. Her spine went cold.

The genes hadn't – couldn't have – rearranged themselves; it was an impossibility but the logic that had, a moment ago, been so clear, was foreign. Clunky, brutal even. It might have come from her fingers, but that wasn't her code.

She looked up.

Doctor Tachi raised his tired brown brows. 'Well?'

She opened her mouth. Closed it.

The doctor sighed and bent over the bench. 'Might I suggest, the next time you go hunting through the Bayard archives, you focus your attention on objects that are slightly less brutish.' A cylinder, the length and width of her forearm, spun up on the screen. 'Or at least, spend less time studying them, then you shall be less likely to ape the style of less talented individuals.' Tachi laid a hand on her shoulder, flooding her mind with the slate colour of his thoughts and a deep sense of patience before he walked away.

A cold shudder worked its way up to her nape. She knew that cylinder; it sat on her workbench, surrounded by old drone casings and gelpaks. She spun the holo around. 'What is it?' she whispered.

The Bayard AI, pale blue and slender, appeared beside her fingers. 'The jwak: originally designed to subdue large prey by disrupting the central nervous system. The strength and duration of the shock it delivered could be controlled from the user's bracer or palm-unit. However, the device was added to the prohibited weapons registry and development abandoned when field tests produced unexpected results.'

'Such as?'

'The jwak delivers a power surge along the neural pathways that connects the user to their biocomp. In severe cases the surge resulted in a dire state of neural decay that led to loss of motor functions and memory and was accompanied by chronic pain.'

Hero's brain froze, the scent of roses twisting around her thoughts. She was building that; she knew it like she knew Fink hated the way mud squished between his toes. But... why?

The answer was in the original jwak, it had to be. Hero slipped off the stool. 'I'm taking my break now.'

Doctor Tachi gave her a quick, searching glance before turning back to his screen. 'Of course,' he said.

She didn't immediately turn right when the lab closed behind her. Doctor Tachi would see her going the wrong way and ask questions when she came back. Instead Hero waited until she was four labs away before turning towards the archives.

Peare sat in his usual spot, his scalp gleaming in the glow coming from the screens festooning his bulky workstation. He lifted his head at her approach, even though her shoes made no sound on the sparkling white floor.

'Break already?' he said.

Hero shrugged and smiled.

Peare grunted, his shoulders rising and falling with the sound. 'Just don't swipe anything from the active jobs. Accounting's been getting a little touchy about the increase in inventory turnover.'

'Sure,' she said. 'Thanks.'

Peare grunted again, but the corner of his mouth tilted upwards. 'Your mum's the one footing the bill kid, even if she doesn't know it.' He pressed a button on one of the screens, and a section of wall behind his workstation slid to the side, revealing an open lift. 'Happy browsing.'

Hero grinned all the way around the station and into the lift. The door closed, and the lift swept her downwards. A heartbeat later it stopped and opened into a small, well-lit chamber with a massive plasteel wall that looked out into the dimly lit cavern of the Bayard archives.

Everything Bayard had ever invented found its way down here, plus a few things they hadn't.

The plasteel wall glowed when she approached, softly at first and then brighter until it formed a head twice the size of her own. The Bayard AI smiled at her. 'Ms Regan, how may I help you today?'

'I'm looking for this.' A thought and a twitch of her thumb and a holo of the jwak spun above her wrist.

'Of course, one moment.' The AI disappeared. Out in the archives, a drone detached itself from the wall, a glowing blue blob that zipped into the darkness.

It was more than a moment before the drone dashed back, a transparent cylindrical case caught in its antigravs. A hatch opened, and the drone dropped the container.

The wall glowed, and the Bayard AI reappeared. 'Your item, Ms Regan. Will you be taking it to your home lab?'

She shook her head. 'No, I'll just look at it here.'

'As you wish.' The AI disappeared and the floor hummed, a section rising to form a workbench in the centre of the room. In the middle of the bench sat the cylinder.

Hero had the container open and a screen running diagnostics before the workbench finished moving. The jwak's code was brutal and fascinating and all-too-familiar for comfort. It was also incomplete.

Hero's bracer shivered against her skin a split-second before the Librarian's head, glowing white and bald, appeared above her wrist.

'Demona Thy,' it said.

'What?'

'Demona Thy.' A woman's face appeared above the bench. It was a round face with green eyes and greener hair, the lips thin, the expression hard.

The blood left Hero's head. She knew that face.

The Librarian continued. 'A former Bayard employee and the individual responsible for the jwak. Currently in a coma after participating in events leading up to and including your kidnapping.'

'You've been monitoring her?'

'I have, as I have been monitoring you. The incident with your mother was quite illuminating, as is the stun-stick you've been constructing. By now, I assume you're aware of its similarity to the object before you.'

Hero remained silent but an ugly knot of dread curled in her stomach.

'The development is not without precedent. After he rendered an individual comatose, Paris Regan also displayed possession of knowledge and skills he should not have had. I suspect the ability can be linked to your particular Jørgen strain.'

'Jørgen what? And, wait – my uncle put someone in a coma? No,' Hero said, holding a hand up before the AI could respond. 'I don't want to know that. What's any of that got to do with me?'

'Everything, Hero Regan.'

'In what way?'

'I require your assistance. There are still those who seek to implement the plan laid down by Penelope Klaude. The destruction of Ayumon has not changed that – it has only made their task more difficult and the lengths to which they will go more extreme. It is not only for the sake of the human species that I ask this of you, Hero Regan, it is for the survival of Jørn itself.'

Hero cocked her hip and crossed her arms. 'You said that last time too, right before you failed to mention that *Woolsey's* plan would also kill billions.'

'It does not change the facts, Hero Regan. The peril in which the human species finds itself has not abated. Your defiance in destroying Ayumon has merely increased the severity of the situation.'

She scowled. 'What situation?'

'Cumulus City is failing.'

'You mean the blue-outs?'

'The blue-outs are symptoms of the larger issue. The groundside machines that generate the magnetic field on which the city is kept aloft are no longer sufficient to the task. Cumulus City's outer 'burbs will fall first.'

'What do you mean, "fall"?'

'Out of the sky, Hero Regan, much like Ayumon did when you initiated its self-destruct. Except the 'burbs will not explode before they hit the surface and the damage will be considerable.'

'So why doesn't someone fix it?'

'No one knows how.'

'How can no one know how to fix it? Humans built it.'

'Not all of it.'

She blinked at that, waiting for the words to stop ricocheting around her brain. 'Huh? But...' She shook her head, trying to assemble the words in some logical order, but they remained jumbled. 'What?'

The Librarian was silent.

'Answer me.'

'Your questions are not relevant to the current situation. Human survival will only be assured if Doctor Woolsey's plan is completed, and for that I require access to Doctor Zass's research.'

'So, get Tybalt to do it.'

'Tybalt Rom will no longer follow my instructions.'

'So, what makes you think I'll do it?'

'This,' the Librarian said before the screen above the bench disappeared, and a holovid appeared in its place.

At least a part of the vid was a reconstruction, the edges of the room – dark and dingy with the lights and door-panel smashed – were a little too smooth, the lighting not quite right. That didn't stop recognition from exploding in her gut, or her skin turning to ice. She knew that room. Not just how it looked, but how it had felt, how it had smelled, how the door panel's gelpak hadn't just been pulled out but smeared across the floor. And she knew what happened next, even before the figure that was her appeared in the vid, shorter, chubbier, dark shoulder-length hair tangled and mused.

'Stop,' she said, eyes glued to the vid.

The Librarian didn't answer, and the vid continued to play. The door opened, and a woman came in. Demona – green eyes, green hair – grabbed Hero's arm. There were words, she saw the woman's lips move, but no sound accompanied the vid. She remembered them though. *Going to jump me kid? Think you left it a little late.* The rest happened faster than she remembered. The woman staggered before her back hit the wall, her knees buckled and she slid to the ground. Eyes wide, face pale and a bright red trail of blood trickling from her nose.

The vid paused.

Hero stared at it, heart pounding, the scent of roses thick in her nose. The scent of Demona Thy's thoughts. Hero paled, swallowed and tried to speak. Not even a squeak came out.

The Librarian said nothing.

She stepped back and tried again. 'Where did you …?'

'Although uninhabited, many of the sensors in that part of the city remain functional.'

Her heart trembled and her stomach roiled, but she gritted her teeth and pushed her chin into the air. 'It doesn't prove anything, and even if it did, she'd kidnapped me. That.' She pointed at the scene frozen on the vid. 'That was self-defence.'

'I do not disagree. However, your mother may not, particularly in light of your recent actions and the suggestion that your neurological structure has become unstable. I believe it is a fault in your particular hybrid strain; your maternal uncle displayed the same abnormality.'

Unstable. Abnormality. The words struck her chest, robbing her breath and squeezing her heart. 'There's nothing wrong with me,' she said, forcing the words out between constricted heartbeats.

'Yes, Hero Regan, there is.'

She breathed deep. 'So?' she said and was glad when her voice didn't wobble. 'Mum won't care.' She'd just never let her out of the house again.

'Perhaps, but do you want to spend the rest of your life in a med-lab?'

There was a hiss from the workbench, and a data slide popped out of its surface. 'The data slide may be inserted into any workstation in Doctor Zass's laboratory. It will take a few moments to infiltrate the system and install the necessary codes.'

The slide shone, a long sliver of plasglas and biogel the length of her thumb. It stuck out of the workstation, a tiny rectangle sucking the light and air out of the room. Her heart thumped, squeezed, thumped again, each beat louder and more painful than the last. Her eyes flicked back to the vid, to Demona slumped against the wall.

Her fingers closed around the slide, tugged. The workstation held onto it for a second and then it was nestled in her palm, warm and smooth against her skin.

'Hero Regan.'

She looked up.

The AI stared back, blue eyes unblinking, impassive. 'Bayard Explorations possesses the only known copy of Doctor Woolsey's notes regarding her human experiments. They do not reside in the archives, but I am confident you will find them among Doctor Zass's records. Should you wish answers to your earlier questions, you will find them there.' The Librarian winked out.

CHAPTER 7

The faint scent of strapples teased Hero's mind as she swung the flat racing saddle high into the air – shiny black nanoleather gleaming in the light of a holosign – and onto Fink's back. A stray strap smacked his ear, and the 'pard growled.

'Sorry,' she said, reaching up to rub the injured appendage.

He grumbled but ducked his head so she could reach the spot between his ears. *That skinny purple thing was staring at them.*

She looked over her shoulder. Across the square, an octagon lit by portable light drones and crowded with street racers. Some had come just to race but most were finalists seeking to size up the competition in the last practice race before the finals.

'What skinny purple thing?'

A toa-mare – all sleek muscle and long, slim legs – tossed its head and flattened its ears. If the dark violet colour of its hide hadn't given away the 'mare's identity, the boiling resentment crouching in the back of Fink's mind would have clued Hero in. Whether Phara was just snooty by nature or had singled Fink out for special treatment was hard to tell, but in the last two months, he'd stopped trying to make friends and started cultivating his glower.

Fink peeled back his lip and growled at the 'mare.

Slowly, her head high in the air, Phara turned her bum to them, finishing off the insult with a dismissive flick of her long, sinuous tail.

Fink's ruff puffed around his head, and his snarl ripped through the air.

The 'mare bolted, or would have – the big muscles in her arse bunching and her front hooves leaving the ground – were it not for Timon Dane hanging on to her lead, his feet skidding over the ground.

Phara wasn't the only one to panic: a tall red-haired girl was barely holding on to her doe-oc – its enormous raindrop-shaped ears pricked, big black eyes ringed in white – and there was a spideruck halfway up a wall, feathers puffed and black hairy legs quivering.

It was over in a handful of heartbeats, riders soothing their mounts with calm, practiced motions, and then it was silent. Eyes turned to Fink, flicked to Hero, and a second later a wave of whispers rose over the square, louder and louder. Another heartbeat and it was like nothing had happened, except for the bubble of space that emerged around them.

A trill mixed with the babble and Harish's purple and yellow form dived at them from above.

'What's wrong with Fink?' Norah dumped her bag next to Hero's, gear chunking inside. 'I've never seen him do that before.'

'Phara,' Hero said, slapping the saddle's vacuum seals into place.

Harish settled on Fink's head, his tail curling under the 'pard's jaw, immovable even when Fink tried to shake him off.

'*Just* Phara?' Norah's brows were high.

Hero scowled. 'Does he need another reason?'

Norah gestured over Hero's shoulder. 'Maybe,' she said.

Hero turned. There was the Rom, tall and skinny, black biocomp wrapped around his throat, sparkling with golden veins of energy. He walked towards them, his shoulders hunched, halted a 'pard-length away and cleared his throat.

'Look,' he said, his voice surprisingly deep for his skinny chest. 'A few of the other teams have expressed concern about Fink—'

Hero glared at him. 'He's fine.'

'Well, yeah, okay, but I run a clean race here. So, you know, ruc-pards aren't exactly the friendliest and like, if Fink's not feeling too well… Well, I can't let you race if he might, you know, *attack* someone.'

'I said.' Hero stepped closer to Rom until she had to stretch her neck to keep glaring at him. 'He's. Fine.'

Behind her, Fink added a growl and, she was sure, a hint of fang for good measure.

'Ugh, right.' Rom backed away, both hands raised.

She watched him back away into the crowd.

Norah giggled.

Hero frowned at her. 'What?'

She shook her head. 'Nothing.' She giggled again. 'Did you see his face?' Norah stretched her expression, making her eyes wide and her mouth open in a big 'O' as she pretended to back away from Hero. 'I thought he was going to faint.'

Hero grinned back. She looked at Fink, sitting on his haunches, ears sideways and his foreshoulders hunched, the end of his tail flicking back and forth. Harish stretched out on Fink's head and yawned.

The last vacuum seal sucked itself into place. She pulled on the saddle once, making sure it wouldn't slip, and then turned.

Timon's eyes caught hers. He smiled.

She glowered in return. What was he planning? She reached out to touch his thoughts.

Fink nipped her arm.

'Ow.' She swung around and glared at him

Manners, he thought at her, his tone grumpy.

She punched his shoulder and gave another hard jerk on the saddle. 'Look who's talking, grumpy bum.'

He grumbled and swung around to nip at her again.

She slapped his nose.

He flashed a fang.

She bared her teeth—

'Umm, if you two are finished?' Norah stood with her arms crossed and her hip cocked, her visor and bracer already glowing.

Hero harrumphed and snatched her helmet out of the saddlebag, jamming it on her head. 'He started it.'

Norah rolled her eyes. 'Whatever. Just get on, will you? It's almost time to start our run.'

With one last frown at Fink – at which he gave a grumbled response – Hero swung herself into the saddle, snapping the straps into place across her legs. A touch to her bracer and both it and the transparent plasteel dome of her helmet came to life. Both glowed blue-white, with veins of energy running through the bracer's biogel circuits and the helmet projecting a holoscreen around her head.

Fink shifted. She could feel his hearts even through the saddle, his primary heart a steady thump-thump between her knees while his minor heart thrummed its own beat. There was no difference in the beat, but she could never quite forget that it wasn't his heart, just a collection of cells grown in a tank to replace the one shredded by a bullet.

The memory took her, just for a second, of Fink on the ground, his legs twitching as he tried to get up, and the blood, black in the darkness, staining his chest and the floor. She shuddered and pushed the memory aside. They had a race to run.

'How many bombs do you think Zorina's packing this time?'

'We're not racing against Zorina.'

Hero's gaze snapped to Norah. 'But I thought—'

Norah shrugged, her eyes sliding away. She cleared her throat. 'The course we were allocated was too easy. We need something more challenging if we have a hope at the finals and Zorina didn't want to switch.'

'*Riiiight.*' There was something about the way Norah fiddled with her bracer and the twist of her lips that made Hero think there was more to it. 'So, who are we up against then?'

'Who do you think?' Norah gestured.

Hero's spine crawled even before she turned around.

Timon Dane finished clicking the last of his saddle straps over his legs while Phara arched her neck and swished her tail. Next to them,

Henry Dane bent over his palm unit, his black hair all but gleaming in the overhead lights.

Fink growled, ears flat to his head, and lashed his tail, while on Norah's shoulder, Harish ruffled his feathers and hissed.

Hero reached for the pouch strapped to her leg, feeling the small egg-shaped objects hum under her fingers.

A hand gripped Hero's wrist. 'No,' Norah said, brown eyes hard in her dusky face. 'You are not using the drones.'

Hero shook Norah's hand off. 'There's nothing wrong with them.'

Almost too fast for Hero to see, Norah zapped the seal holding the pouch in place and ripped it off Hero's leg.

'Hey,' Hero said.

Norah glared at her. 'No drones.'

'But they're all I packed. I need them.'

'What are we? Chopped wombacow?' Norah gestured to herself and Harish before she backed away, stuffing the pouch of drones in her saddlebag. 'Besides, it's not like you can't hack a holosign or a lift or something. One of the other teams said something about the big bomb drones – hack one of those if you're desperate.'

'In the middle of a race?'

Norah put her hands on her hips. 'It's not like you haven't done it before.'

Hero glared at Norah.

Norah glared back.

Beneath her, Fink grumbled and flicked his ears, and a mawberry-flavoured image of Timon and Phara lining up at the start line appeared in Hero's mind. From the way Norah's nose scrunched up, she saw it too.

'Fine,' Hero said, her arms crossed over her chest. She nudged Fink with her knee. 'Let's go.'

He swung around and headed towards the start line. There were no more grumbles; instead as Fink stalked closer, anticipation bubbled in her veins and thrummed in the air between them. It flowed up Hero's spine and through her limbs until her arms tingled and her legs itched. Fink's stalk became a trot.

Phara threw her head and skittered sideways at their approach, Timon moving on her back like his pants were glued to the saddle.

An oad-hawk circled overhead, and Rom stood on his other side, as far away from Fink as he could get.

Hero ignored them, activating her visor and staring into the darkness of the arcade ahead of them.

'All right, racers.' Rom's voice boomed through her helmet. 'On three. One. Two. Three.'

Fink leapt off the start line.

They streaked over the skybridge, the skylane outside only slightly brighter than the arcades they'd been racing through, before plunging back into darkness. The dull glow of the scattered hover drones barely provided enough light to distinguish the shadows of old benches and dusty fountains, leaving the occasional functioning holosign to throw jagged streaks of colour over the windows of old shops.

Fink leapt onto a hover ledge, springing from it to another and then another, each one crumbling under their weight, the sickly green aura of a slip-field nipping at their toes. The clatter of hooves signalled Phara catching up.

The arcade branched, the left swallowed by darkness while the ledges and the slip field twisted to the right. Fink leapt, angling towards the right—

'Go left,' Norah said.

'What? Are you sure?'

'Just do it.'

Hero frowned but said nothing. The scent of mawberries was in her nose and Fink's senses bright in her mind. She dug her hands into his ruff, felt his muscles bunch and braced herself for the last leap. For a moment they hung in mid-air – Fink twisting sideways – and she could see Timon, the frown on his face smoothing into surprise as Phara thundered up behind them. Then they were off again, Fink's foreshoulders buckling when they hit the ground, even as his mid and hindquarters pushed them forward.

Only the saddle's straps kept Hero in place, the nanoleather cutting into her thighs and calves. The left branch of the arcade was dark; the shops shuttered, wrappers and boxes piled under their windows, without so much as the glow of an old holosign to light their way.

A dozen metres in and Harish peeled away, disappearing behind a mound of old crates.

A chill twisted through Hero's gut and Fink slowed, then stopped.

Norah's face appeared on the helmet's holoscreen. 'What's wrong, why did you stop?'

Hero shook her head. 'This doesn't feel right. Are you sure it's the right way?'

'Yes!' Anger thinned Norah's lips, but there was something else, a shadow behind the hard glitter of her eyes and a tick in her jaw that spoke of nerves. 'Why do you always have to argue?'

There was enough venom in Norah's voice to make Hero's heart clench. 'I—' she began, but Norah cut her off.

'Stop wasting time. Do it,' Norah said and then her face vanished from Hero's screen.

Hero closed her mouth and felt Fink's shock as an echo of her own.

A clatter came from behind, the sound of hooves on plascrete. She didn't need to look back to know it was Timon, but she did anyway, catching a glimpse of Phara's sleek purple hide before the pair became just another shadow.

Fink leapt forwards.

Timon whipped past them, and then his scout, something long and oval-shaped clutched in the oad-hawk's talons. She squinted and the view on her visor changed, zooming in on the object. The warning popped up instantly. Shock bomb.

Ahead, the arcade ended in a narrow corridor, barely broad

enough for one person to squeeze through at a time. Timon and Phara raced through it but Hero only had eyes for the oad-hawk as it attached the bomb to the wall.

'Norah.' The other girl popped up on Hero's screen. 'We need Harish.'

Lip between her teeth, Norah had her gaze on something off-screen. 'He's coming. Hold on.'

'We need him now.'

'Hack something!'

'There's nothing to hack.'

Norah's mouth became pinched. 'Just—'

From somewhere not-too-distant came the sound of an explosion. It echoed off the shopfronts and rolling along behind it came darkness. Hero had enough time to see it rushing towards them before it hit. Her helmet went dead, and they plunged into shadow.

CHAPTER 8

Everything was… still. She could hear her heartbeat, felt Fink's skin shiver and the breath he missed. Felt his sides start and shudder as his lungs made up for it. Her hands clenched in his ruff.

It was so dark. Where her eyes even open? She reached up, the cold touch of her visor making her start. She fumbled with it, lifted it up. Then her hands were on her face and yes, her eyes were open.

Fink rumbled.

Hero opened her mouth. 'I—' The word seemed loud, too loud, like it should echo. She swallowed. *I don't know,* she thought to him. *Can you see?*

He rumbled again, and Hero felt him shake his head.

Okay. She swallowed. *The pulse took out the barrier, so if we move forward slowly…*

Fink whined, and she could imagine his ears flattening. The image that popped into her mind, of Fink's nose touching the barrier, came with the memory of a sharp jolt from a stun drone. *Was she sure?*

She took a deep breath. *Yes.* Mostly.

Fink took one cautious step forward. Nothing. He took another. Tension rode up his body and into Hero's bones, shooting its way to the top of her head and down her arms.

Fink kept sliding forward and with each step the tension grew until Hero's thighs cramped from squeezing the saddle and her knuckles hurt from clenching his ruff. Eventually, her back stiff and a thin trickle of sweat slipping down her spine, she took a deep breath and forced her fingers to unclench. *I think we're past it.*

Fink stopped dead. She could almost feel his paw, half-raised, dangling in mid-air. *Was she sure this time?*

She thought back to before the pulse and the barrier shimmering at the other end of the corridor. The corridor hadn't been that long, and no matter how slowly Fink had crept, they were surely at the end of it now. She nodded. *I'm sure.*

He sighed and relaxed.

Her own tension followed his, flowing down her back and draining out her feet—

Fink growled.

The tension came back. *What?*

He saw something. There was a strange shudder and jerk as Fink pulled Hero's mind into his, and then she saw through his eyes.

It was dark, and if it hadn't been for the warm scent of mawberries all round her, she might have been sitting behind her own eyes. Except her own eyes wouldn't have been able to see the purple smudge coming towards them. She felt Fink crouch as though his muscles were hers – his midquarters shifting over *her* ribs, his claws flexing at the ends of *her* fingers – and together they stalked the smudge.

Whatever it was, it glowed, and it was big. It brightened as they drew closer, bright enough for Fink's eyes to pick out the shadows of walls and shopfronts. He halted, ears twitching.

What?

Listen. He shared his ears with her.

Something clip-clopped towards them, the sound echoing off the shopfronts. *Phara?* Hero projected an image of the toa-mare and her rider.

Fink grunted, and she felt realisation dawn in his mind, but he didn't rise from his crouch; instead he went lower and his tail lashed. *There was something else behind the sound of Phara's hooves, something that skittered.*

A chill ran over Hero's skin. She remembered that sound. Roaches.

Up ahead, the toa-mare screamed.

Fink leapt forward, a snarl already ripping from his throat. Or was it hers? She didn't know, didn't care. Roses were creeping up her nose, her hand reaching for the familiar touch of a hard black grip in a holster strapped tight against her ribs. Except it wasn't there, it had never been, and her thoughts fractured – roses and the bitter taste of chocolate mixing and then splintering in her brain. The mental dissonance made Fink stumble and knocked her out of his mind.

He regained his feet, but then they were skidding around a corner and there was no time to wonder what had just happened, only to hold on and ride the dark mawberry wave at the edge of her mind.

There was Phara, her hide glowing a vibrant purple. Timon clung to her back as she lashed out with hooves and teeth, her long sinuous tail a battering ram doing its best to keep the roaches at bay.

The roaches had the 'mare surrounded. Half the size of Fink with pointy legs, they mashed their mandibles and clicked to each other, shifting and sliding under the flash of the 'mares hooves, always keeping her surrounded.

Fink's snarl ripped the air.

Everyone froze.

The roaches chattered and clicked, their thick oval shells gleaming purple in the light from Phara's hide, their antennae twitching. One made a questing move towards Phara's hocks.

Fink snarled again, the sound rippling out of his chest.

Slowly, the roaches backed away, disappearing into the shadows until only their antennae were visible, and then they too were gone.

Fink grunted and sat.

Hero, the scent of roses still in her nose, stared at the shadows. Adrenalin and something else, something hotter and darker, slowly stopped its swirl in her chest.

'Thanks.'

Hero jumped. She turned and tilted her gaze upwards to meet Timon's. 'What?'

'Thanks,' he said, gesturing to shadows where the roaches had departed. 'For saving us. Not sure what we'd have done if you guys hadn't come along. I think Phara might've been able to fight off one or two, but not that many and not that big.'

'You should see the ones in the Tunnels.' Hero shuddered.

'You've been to the Tunnels?'

'Ugh, yeah.' Hero cast her eyes over Timon, his helmet, his bracer. There wasn't so much as a glimmer of power. 'Your gear's not working either.'

Timon's hand went to his wrist, and he frowned. 'Yeah, no. Not so much as a fizz. My scout's missing too. Hope he's all right – Henry loves that oad-hawk. It's a good thing toa-mares are bioluminescent though, or we'd've stumbled right into those roaches.' The 'mare threw her head and he patted her shoulder. 'I didn't even hear 'em coming.'

Fink grunted and lifted his lip in the 'mare's direction. *If she hadn't been glowy, the roaches wouldn't have found her.*

Silently, Hero agreed, but they could use Phara's glow now. 'We should go. Whatever that surge was, I bet the city AI is scrambling repair bugs.'

Timon nodded. 'And with the bugs will come the security drones and we don't want to be here for those.'

'Do you know the way back?'

'Me?' Timon's eyebrows rose, and he grinned. 'Nah, I was just following you.'

Fink snorted and Hero crossed her arms, eyes narrowing in suspicion. 'Why?'

He shrugged. 'Wanted to see the competition in action. Plus, you know, get you back for those stun drones.' He grinned again. 'How'd you like my little barrier back there? Cool, huh? M' brother made it.'

'Right,' Hero said, rubbing her forehead. Timon's peppiness was starting to give her a headache.

'Aww, don't be blue. It's all in good fun, right? Besides.' He leaned down and his grin turned a little evil. 'You kinda deserved it.'

Beneath her, Fink pruckled and Hero couldn't help the snarl that came to her lips.

Timon chuckled and even Phara's sibilant *huss-hn-hmmm* seemed amused. 'Come on.' Timon pulled the 'mare around. 'We should probably head back.'

'I thought you didn't know the way.'

'I don't, I'm still following you, remember?'

Hero huffed, but Fink rose and turned back the way they'd come. Phara followed.

With Phara's glow to guide them, they made it back to the little corridor where Timon had planted his barrier in no time.

'So,' Timon said as they squeezed through the space. 'You reckon this EMP thing is because of the blue-outs?'

'What?' Up ahead, Hero spied the haphazard stack of boxes Harish had disappeared behind. Was he okay? Why had Norah sent him back there? The memory of her taking off in a hover with Imogen played in the back of her mind.

'You reckon this is another blue-out?'

She spared Timon a look. Idiot, she thought. 'No. A blue-out wouldn't have shorted our gear.'

Fink picked his way forwards, nudging boxes out of the way with his nose before rearing up and shoving with his forepaws when they wouldn't move. Boxes tumbled across the arcade, Phara dancing out of their way, hooves clattering.

A crate, a grey square as tall as Fink's shoulder, defied his efforts and Hero leaned lower over his neck, hands deep in his ruff when he reared to his full height. Hindquarters braced, fore and midpaws clamped on the crate, he pushed. The box screeched across the floor, the sound splitting her ears, revealing the thin corridor behind it.

Would he fit? Hero asked.

Fink grumbled and marched forwards.

'Ugh, that isn't the way we came'.

'Harish came down here. I want to make sure he's not in trouble.' And to ease the niggle in her stomach.

'You mean that pesky little linch-adder?' She practically heard the shudder in Timon's voice. 'Man, that little dude's got some moves. Almost took my head off in that last race and the race before that he actually bit Phara's ear.'

Fink swung his head towards the 'mare and grunted in sympathy.

Phara huss-need back and followed them into the long narrow service corridor. The clip-clop of her hooves drowned the snick-snick of Fink's claws, and her glow threw his shadow ahead of them, stretching it out into the dark.

'You know, I reckon we're right up against a freight elevator,' Timon said.

Hero looked back at Timon, his hand against a wall. 'What makes you say that?'

'The wall's vibrating.' She caught the white flash of his teeth, the rest of his expression lost to the darkness. 'Even behind a metre of steelcrete, the big loads tend to do that.'

'How do you know?'

'I spend a lot of time down here, exploring, checking out the architecture.'

'The architecture?'

'Yeah. Most of the stuff down here was built by the first-gen colonists, you know.'

The service corridor ended, spilling them out into a small square. All the shopfronts were dark and abandoned, their windows coated with a thick layer of dust and dirt. All but one. Sandwiched between two other shops at the end of the cul-de-sac, one store stood with its front window shattered. Shards of plasglas were littered in a wide arc across the arcade's tiled floor, glittering purple in the glow from Phara's hide.

Hero slid off Fink's back and stepped towards the mess, stray shards shattering under her boots.

There was a thump as Timon slid off Phara's back and then more sharp little explosions of plasglas as he came to Hero's side. 'That's some mess,' he said.

'Yeah.' She crunched her way closer to the broken window, only casting a glance over her shoulder when Fink gave a frustrated cough. She frowned at him, all but prancing around the edge of the debris. 'I'm just going to look inside.'

He coughed again, a faint burr to the edge of the sound. *He didn't like it. He should come.*

'You'll cut your paws on the glass.'

He whined.

Hero rolled her eyes. 'It's not like I can't look after myself, you know. Besides, he'll be with me and someone has to watch that.' She waved her hand in Phara's direction.

'Hey,' Timon said, just as Phara threw her head up and snorted in indignation. 'And you were being so nice too.'

Hero and Fink snorted in unison. She turned back to the shattered window, standing on her tiptoes to look through it.

'You know,' Timon said, 'that whole silent talking thing you two do is kinda disturbing.'

There was something in there. Phara's glow was weaker here, barely highlighting the spaces between shadows, but Hero could make out the lumps of scattered furniture and what looked like a holoterminal. She crunched over more glass until she was standing at the edge of the floor-to-ceiling window. Carefully, she stepped over the remaining toothy edges.

'Huh,' Timon said, following her in. 'That's kinda strange.'

She glanced at him. 'What is?'

'Well, the arcades in this part of the Industrial have been abandoned for generations. No people, no shops, no lights, just a few maintenance bots to keep the vital things running. But that.' He pointed to the small curved form of the holoterminal. 'That model came out last year. I know 'cause my daddy grumbled about gettin' one when our old terminal bit it.'

'So?'

'Soooo… what's a new terminal doing where no one works anymore?'

Hero looked around again, eyes catching on the rounded shape of a mug and the mouldy, half-eaten core of a strapple.

'Hey.' Hero jumped when Timon appeared beside her. A black lump, a third the size of his hand and egg-shaped, sat in his palm. 'What'd you think this is?'

Familiarity tickled at the back of Hero's mind. Gingerly, she picked it up. It was light and smooth and beneath the soot it left all over her fingers, it shone. Her thumb followed the distinctive pattern of dots along its spine and the tickle of familiarity became a hard lump of certainty. It was one of her drones.

She remembered Norah taking the pouch of drones from her thigh and felt her lips thin. 'Where'd you find this?'

Timon frowned. 'You know what it is?'

She bit her lip. 'Just… tell me where you found it.'

The boy looked at her, right in the eye. It was disconcerting, and Hero could feel her brow furrowing with the beginnings of a glare, but then Timon nodded somewhere behind him. 'Over there,' he said. 'There are more of those things too.'

Hero rose, clutching the drone, and found the spot at the back of the shop Timon had indicated. It was darker back here, the bodies of her drones harder to see, but she found them all, and the shredded remnants of the pouch she'd last seen them in. Every last one was as dead as her helmet. Because of the EMP, or something else? She rubbed the soot on her fingers. An EMP wouldn't char the plasform.

What had Norah been doing?

'You know,' Timon said, 'I don't think you're here looking for your scout.'

'Do you have a pouch?'

'A what?'

'A pouch, a pocket. I want to collect the drones.'

'Drones? That's what those lumps are?' There was a soft fuzz and then Timon slapped a pouch in her outstretched hand. 'It's got my lunch in it.'

She dug a vac-wrapped oval out of the pouch and handed it to him, before snatching up the drones and stuffing them in.

'Thanks,' Timon said, voice muffled.

Hero frowned at him as she rose. He had the vac-wrap peeled back and was busily stuffing a sandwich in his mouth. She turned back to the corner, eyes scanning the darkness for some clue as to what Norah had been using the drones for. It wasn't like they were good for much, not yet at least – she weighed the pouch in her hand – now, maybe not ever.

'So.' She could practically hear the food sloshing around in Timon's mouth. 'You're not here looking for your scout and those black lumps are drones.' He paused. She hoped he was swallowing. 'Are they *your* drones?'

She glared at him.

He stuffed another bite of sandwich in his mouth. 'I'll take that as a yes.' There was another pause, and when he spoke his voice was clear. 'So, does that mean you blew up the shop?'

Hero snorted, eyes catching on some sort of hole in the wall. 'I don't leave evidence.'

'You… *don't* leave evidence, not you *wouldn't* leave evidence?' The vac-wrap crinkled as Timon took another bite. 'That sounds like you do this sorta thing a lot.'

The hole was jagged, with bits of plascrete sticking up and inwards, some of it crumbling under Hero's arm when she stood on her tiptoes and reached inside. Cheek pressed against the wall, she felt around the hole. One side was smooth and cold, steelglas perhaps – she glanced up and thought she saw the corner of a wall safe – while the back of the hole was warm and gooey. Her fingers closed around something.

'You do, don't you?' Timon whistled. 'I bet you're always grounded too, right? Oh, but wait, you don't leave evidence behind. Man, what do *you* want to be when you grow up, some kinda criminal mastermind or something?'

Hero glared at Timon and drew her hand out of the hole. 'No,' she said. 'I'm going to be Rider.'

'Like a professional barrier racer?'

'No, like the first-gen Riders, who explored the planet.'

Timon stared at her for several seconds. 'You do know there haven't been any of those for like a hundred years?'

She huffed and turned her attention to the thing she'd dragged out of the hole, and the biogel that had come along with it. 'Yes,' she said.

'Oh. Okay then.' The vac-wrap crinkled one last time. 'What'd you find?'

Hero moved closer to the front of the shop so that Phara's glow shone over the piece of plasglas. It was a fragment of a tube, large enough to fit her arm inside, lined with something slimy and the faint tracks of old biocircuits, long-since burned into its surface. 'I *think* it's a subline.'

The last mouthful of Timon's sandwich almost burst out of his mouth. 'A subline? The tubes that supply power to the *whole* sector? Like the one that ruptured last year and almost collapsed an entire skytower?'

She scrunched her nose and wondered if all boys were as disgusting. 'Yeah. Someone tried to use my drones to open the wall safe but put them in the wrong spot. Instead of opening the safe, they blew a hole in the wall, ruptured the subline and probably caused the EMP.'

'Drones can do that?'

Hero shrugged. 'The line was old, and my drones have an... issue.'

'What kind of issue?'

She cleared her throat and walked around him. 'We should get going. The explosion probably triggered some kind of sensor. The police'll turn up soon.'

'Wait, hang on.' Timon grabbed her arm. 'Did those drones have an *issue* when you used them on me?'

Hero jerked her arm out of his grip and kept marching towards the front of the shop. 'They're safe,' she said.

'Ugh, yeah.' Timon danced in front of her, blocking the way. 'One, they have an *issue* and two, they blew a hole in a plascrete wall, ruptured a subline and caused an EMP. I don't call that safe.'

'Well you're fine and they're dead now, okay?' Hero shouldered her way past him and back over the shattered window.

Fink chortled, ears pricked forwards as she crunched her way towards him over the scattered plasglas. Beside him, Phara stood with her hindquarters cocked and her eyes half-closed.

Hero was almost to Fink when she heard Timon's boots crunching behind her.

'Hey,' he called.

She quickened her pace and was swinging onto Fink's back before the boy caught up.

'Hey,' Timon said again and made to grab Fink's harness.

Fink growled, flashing a hint of fang.

Timon jerked back and glared at Fink a second before turning the expression on Hero. There was no humour in his eyes now, just something dark and serious. 'You could have killed me. If Rom knew, you'd be blue-listed.'

'So tell him,' she said, before spinning Fink on his haunches, leaving Timon and his 'mare to light the darkness behind them.

CHAPTER 9

Hero slumped on the bench beside Tybalt, the spot behind her left ear still vibrating from the last sensor Doctor Zass had stuck there.

Tybalt sat with his back against the short half-wall that separated the Bayard stable's training ring from the people and companions that walked, flew and trotted around it. 'How was Doctor Tachi today?' he asked.

'I wouldn't know,' Hero said, her eyes on the two companions stalking each other around the sand, and the woman in the grey Bayard uniform watching over them. 'Zass hustled me off to her lab.' Where she'd been held for the last four hours, standing, sitting and thinking really hard at nothing in particular while the doctor and her flunkies stuck glowing sensors to her head.

Tybalt sat straighter and she could feel his eyes lock on the side of her head. 'Why?'

She shrugged, just as Fink leapt at the other companion, the massive snow-white sternard meeting him halfway. The meaty thunk of Fink's tawny chest colliding with the thick scales of the sternard's belly was audible. 'Doctor Zass didn't say.' But she hadn't had to; the doctor's mind had been easy enough to read.

It hadn't been good.

On the sand, Fink and the sternard were still chest-to-chest, Fink's forelegs wrapped behind the sternard's while his mid-paws struck at the other's belly, claws catching in the joints between its belly scales.

'Hero.' Tybalt leaned forward.

A whistle pierced the air.

Blood ran down the sternard's belly, Fink's claws still caught in its scales, and the grey-clad woman was on the sand, stun-stick pressed into Fink's side. He released the sternard with a snarl, the larger animal stumbling but still managing to place itself between him and the trainer. There were words, gestures, and before Hero was even on her feet, Fink was slinking off to a corner while the grey-clad woman strode towards them.

'Trainer Ella.' Tybalt rose.

'I can't train him here anymore.' The woman spoke before her ponytail finished bouncing. 'The ruc-pard's too dangerous.'

Tybalt frowned a moment before nodding in the sternard's direction. 'Orth looks to be more than a match for Fink.'

'Looks can be deceiving.' Ella sighed and put her hands on her hips. 'Fink's young and human-raised, which means he's never had a chance to play with other 'pards and really learn what he's capable of. Right now, he's operating off what little training we've given him, instinct and hormones. It's a dangerous combination. In a pack, he'd have the older males to teach him and a matriarch to pull him into line if need be, but here?' She shook her head. 'He's still got a solid five, maybe eight years of growing to do and he's already outweighing Orth. He's the biggest sternard to come out of the Farm. Ever.'

Tybalt cocked his head. 'What are you trying to say?'

Ella sighed again. 'We can't train Fink here, not with the sternards. Sooner or later, someone's going to get hurt, or worse.'

'Slale-bears are almost as large as a full-grown 'pard,' Hero said.

'No,' Ella said. 'If the issue were just Fink's size, we could see about adding a slale-bear to the stable, but it's the psionics as well. Nothing fights like a 'pard.' The trainer sighed. 'He needs a pack.'

'I'm his pack,' Hero said.

The woman snorted and looked at Tybalt.

Tybalt raised a brow.

The amusement on Ella's face vanished. She looked from Tybalt to Hero. 'You're serious? Look, even if you are his "pack"' – she hooked her fingers into air quotes – 'you can't teach him what he needs to know, and you certainly can't stop him once he starts tearing things up. That right there.' She pointed to where Fink snicked towards them. 'That is six hundred kilos of brute force, with twenty-six claws, thirty-two very sharp teeth, and jaws that exert over nine hundred pounds of pressure per square inch, which is more than enough to crush your skull. And when we add in the psionics? You think you can handle a telepathic predator?'

Hero crossed her arms tighter. She could take three of them, right after she punched the trainer in the nose.

'Na-ugh. We are not equipped to handle this.' Trainer Ella sighed. 'He needs to go to the Farm.'

'What?' The word burst out of Hero's mouth.

At the same time, Tybalt said, 'No.'

Ella paused a moment. 'Look, I checked Fink's records and not only does the Farm have the closest pack, but it's also the one he was born into. 'Pard's never forget a pack member; he'll slide right back in like he was never gone. He'll have to stay with them for a few years, but the Farm's close enough that you can visit whenever you want.'

The scent of roses tugged at Hero's brain and crept over her taste buds. In the back of her mind she felt Fink, the surprise and first stirrings of alarm pushing aside the grumpy, sour taste of his thoughts. No words passed between them, but in the space between heartbeats, she told him everything.

Out the corner of her eye, she saw Fink's ears go back and his head go down as he stalked towards them, eyes focused on the trainer's back.

'We can't keep training him here and the Farm is the best option,' Ella said.

'He's not going,' Hero ground out. Roses filled in her nose until she thought she should be puffing it out with each breath like some

Old Terra dragon.

'I really don't think you have a choice.' The trainer's hands went to her hips. 'He might have been cute and cuddly when he was a cub, but he's dangerous now and he needs the proper training. Honestly, you've done great with him so far, but a 'pard—'

'It's not him you should be worried about,' she said, even as, behind the trainer, Fink growled.

Ella blinked, turned, but didn't flinch at the sight of Fink's fangs.

'Hero.' Tybalt put a hand on her shoulder. 'Stop it.'

She shrugged Tybalt's hand off her shoulder. 'She's not sending Fink to the Farm.'

'No one ever said she was. Now calm down. You're working Fink up.'

'It's fine,' Ella said, her voice smooth and calm, but her eyes never left Fink. Hero snuck into Ella's mind then and felt the fear swirling in the trainer's belly, but it only made the woman's thoughts sharper, clearer. There was no panic, just purpose and a cold, clear ruthlessness. Hero caught the image of the pistol flashing through Ella's mind before the trainer's hand twitched and dropped towards her belt.

Girl and 'pard growled in unison.

Ella froze. She looked at Hero, her eyes growing wide. 'Did they just…?'

'Yes,' Tybalt said. He took Hero's shoulders, forcing her to tear her gaze from the trainer and look at him. 'Enough. You've made your point. And you.' Tybalt faced Fink. 'You've made yours, but no one's separating you two, so you can stop showing off your fangs.'

Fink snarled one last time, the fur around his neck rippling before he backed away. Even when he lay down, his head on his forepaws, there was still tension in the line of his body and his eyes never left the trainer's face.

Orth appeared at Ella's side, the scales on the sternard's massive chest still bleeding, and growled softly.

Fink growled back.

Ella's hand twitched towards her pistol. *Farm Control can be here in an hour.*

Hero caught the thought as it skittered across Ella's mind. Blue clouded her vision and her fist clenched of its own accord. She stepped forward.

'Hero.' Tybalt shook her shoulders. 'You need to calm down before you do something we'll both regret.'

'She's going to tell Farm Control that Fink's a menace and she thinks he'll hurt someone. They'll come and take him.'

The trainer's hand dropped from her pistol. 'How...?'

'No,' Tybalt said, with a warning glance over his shoulder at the woman. 'She won't, not if she values her career.'

'What? Hey, I'm just doing my job.' Ella pointed to Fink. 'Without the proper control, he *will* hurt someone.'

'Then we'll get him what he needs.' Tybalt turned back to Hero. 'No one is calling Farm Control.'

Hero glared at Ella before turning back to Tybalt. 'If she even tries...'

'I know.' Relief made the liquorice flavour of his thoughts a little sweeter, and the frown on his forehead a little shallower, but his expression didn't change. 'You'll do your best to make her life unliveable.'

The blue haze was clearing from her vision but the scent of roses stayed, tangling in her thoughts until out of them came a new thought – strange and foreign, but somehow still hers – and a surge of violent joy. *She'd do more than make Ella's life unliveable – she'd kill her.* Images rushed in behind the thought: weapons, scenarios... A small explosive attached to the trainer's hover. A short in the mag-levs. The vehicle plummeting out of the sky. A pistol in the dark. A thin blade between the ribs. Poison. Her hands around the woman's neck—

Hero saw the last so vividly – felt it right down to the pulse in Ella's throat, the way her eyes bulged, her lips went blue, and knew seeing that, doing that, would be fun – it sent a jolt straight to her heart. She almost choked, almost heaved up her breakfast spice-berry muffin right there, on Tybalt's shoes. Instead, she clamped a hand over her mouth and watched puzzlement and then worry cross Tybalt's features before she spun on her heel and ran.

She made it to a bathroom before the force behind her hand exploded. She threw up the muffin and then she threw up lunch and then she threw up bile, and she didn't stop until her stomach was twisted and raw and her face was wet with tears and snot.

At some point, while she was still throwing up lunch, she became aware of Fink trying to crowd into the stall behind her. His thoughts, soft and bluey-red, pushed up against hers, heavy with concern.

She pushed them and him away, with her mind as much with her hand. Felt his confusion and his hurt, twin stabs to her heart. She didn't want him to see the thoughts, the images that had gone through her head, but mostly she didn't want him to feel the anticipation or the joy that flooded in with them. She wouldn't be able to bear it if he did.

When Hero's stomach was dry, she sagged against the wall of the stall. It was cold against her shoulder and the floor was hard on her knees, but it was better than throwing up and better than horrible rose-laced images of—

Her throat choked up.

Tybalt squeezed in beside her. 'Here.' There was a towel in his hand.

She took it. Wiped her face. It was thick and nubby and damp and felt good against her skin. She gave it back.

Tybalt took it, held it loosely, so it dangled on the bathroom floor while he crouched in the toilet stall behind her. His suit pants stretched over his knees, his coat undone over his vest.

She didn't look at him, but she felt his gaze. Dark and patient. 'I don't want to talk about it,' she said.

He didn't say anything, and she almost looked up at him, just to see if his eyes were open. 'Are you sure?'

She nodded. 'Yes.'

Silence stretched. She could hear Fink breathing and the snick-snick of his claws on the tiles.

Tybalt sighed, a deep breath out through his nose. 'You haven't told Fink.'

She didn't say anything for a moment and then, 'No.'

'He's worried.'

She shifted, looked at Fink. Looked away. 'I know.' She could feel his worry, pressing against her mind.

'Was this anything like what happened with your mother?'

Hero didn't say anything, and the silence stretched again.

Fink, his shoulders a little hunched and his ears a little flat, nudged Tybalt's arm and coughed once. The affirmation was as clear as if Fink had put it in Tybalt's mind.

Hero glared at Fink.

He rumbled an apology, but the touch of his mind made it clear he wasn't sorry.

Tybalt sighed again. 'I can't keep this a secret, Hero, not after what happened with your mother and not if you won't talk to me.'

Hero turned her glare from Fink to Tybalt. 'Fine,' she said. She stood, sliding with her back up against the stall wall when her knees wobbled. 'Go and tell your girlfriend all about it. Doctor Zass already thinks I'm nuts. For real this time, not some freaky conspiracy cooked up by you and the Librarian to hide my telepathy.'

'She's not my… girlfriend.' Tybalt's mouth twisted, and there was a line between his brows, like the word tasted funny on his tongue. 'And she doesn't think you're unstable.'

'Oh yeah? Then one, you should stop thinking so much about how her eyes look like dansies or sunsets or whatever; and two, ask your not-girlfriend about how my genes are so like Uncle Paris's. You know, the crazy uncle.'

She didn't hang around to see Tybalt's brow turn thunderous. She'd seen it often enough before; instead, knees firm, she stepped over him, brushed past Fink and stalked out of the bathroom.

Fink followed, his claws snick-snicking on the floor behind her, and then he was at her side and then in front of her. He planted his big tawny body in the middle of the tiny corridor, blocking it.

'Out of the way.' She tried to push past him.

He huffed and butted her in the chest, knocking her back a step.

'Hey.' She pushed back but did little more than move his nose. 'You were the one who went and tattle-taled.'

He grumbled. *He was worried. Why wouldn't she tell him what was wrong?*

'Because.' Because she couldn't stand it if he looked at her differently, like she was some kind of monster. But she kept that thought locked tight in her mind.

That wasn't an answer.

'Well, it's all you're getting. Besides, I'm not the only one with problems, Mr Beat Everyone Up. If Trainer Ella gets her way, they'll make you go to the Farm.'

Fink growled. *There wasn't anything wrong with him.*

'Yeah, well now you know how I feel.'

From behind came the soft whoosh of the bathroom door and the flat clack-clack of Tybalt's shoes. Hero didn't need to look to confirm that Tybalt's frown was still thunderous; the feel of it proceeded him down the hall. A roiling cloud of liquorice-scented anger and underneath it all, the faintest hint of embarrassment.

Hero didn't wait for Tybalt to catch up. With both hands against Fink's shoulder, she pushed, hard, adding a mental shove for good measure, forcing him to sidestep just enough for her to shimmy past.

She scurried to the lift at the other end of the hall, and as she stepped in and waited for the doors to close, she didn't turn around to glare at Tybalt or Fink.

Whatever was happening she would deal with it just fine.

CHAPTER 10

Hero squirmed in the plush purple chair, ripping the cushion from behind her back and stuffing it in the other corner.

Another cushion, this one a solid velvety green, smacked her in the face.

'Stop wriggling,' Norah said, her back against a mound of pillows piled high against her bed's headboard. 'I'm trying to study here.'

Hero stuffed the green cushion beside the purple one. 'Like you need to study,' she muttered, not quite under her breath.

She caught the next pillow, a deep mawberry-pink and tucked it behind her back, squirming just a bit to moosh it into place.

Hero brought her micropage back up and tried to concentrate on the equations, but the physics blurred in front of her eyes. The last week had her spine tied in knots.

It was more than just the Librarian or Tybalt's constant presence, unseen but felt, the liquorice flavour of his mind sharp with concern. It was more, even than Fink's sullen mood or his sudden aversion to her company. It was the way the scent of roses hugged the back of her mind whenever she looked at the jwak and the fantasy of Trainer Ella's throat between her hands.

Not even smashing the pouch of scorched, half-forgotten drones from the practice race had helped. It had just made it worse when she found the gel inside hard and cracked, whatever clues they might have held as to why Norah had tried to blow up a safe, lost.

Hero chewed her lip and stared at Norah through the mess of

diagrams and numbers scrolling across her 'page. What was it that Norah had wanted so badly?

The question nagged at her, easier than thinking about Woosley or why the scent of roses kept crawling up her nose. If only she could get Norah to talk or, simpler still, slip into her mind.

Hero chewed her lip. Perhaps she could slip into Norah's mind. She'd have to be subtle about it and touch her mind but not actually *touch* it.

Hero took a deep breath and stretched her mind sideways, like looking at someone from the corner of her eye.

It was hazy at first, a faint wash of purple on the edges of her mind. Concentrating without concentrating was hard, especially when she caught a shadow crossing Norah's thoughts. She started to chase after it, but the stiffening of Norah's shoulders and her glare had Hero skittering away. She tried again. This time, she didn't chase the shadows flicking across the other girl's thoughts, although each time they did, she couldn't help a little twitch.

Norah slapped her micro-page to the bedcovers. 'What?'

Hero jumped and blinked at her. 'What what?'

'You keep twitching. What is it?'

'I'm not twitching.'

'You are. It's annoying.'

Hero frowned and thumped her back against the cushy chair, lifting her own 'page higher and pretending to read. 'Well then, don't look.'

'Ughhh. You're so annoying.'

'You said that already.'

'Ughhh.'

There was silence again, save for the rustling of Harish's wings. Hero bit her lip and tried peeking at Norah's thoughts again, this time attempting to control the urge to twitch as well. It was almost as hard as concentrating without concentrating, and soon enough her heart was beating hard against her ribs and there was a tight, itchy band slowly crushing her head. But there was something else as well;

a lavender-tinged frisson of excitement and power, a half-caught memory of Harish with a bag in his talons, Imogen's face on the comm and a single word. Klaude.

Klaude. The name tickled a memory, but it stuck at the back of her mind, unwilling to come forward. Perhaps, if she knew more…

'What are you doing?'

Hero looked up and jumped. Norah stood in front of her, a frown on her face and her hand already plucking the 'page from Hero's fingers. 'Nothing.' Hero scowled and grabbed the 'page back.

Norah's eyebrows rose. 'Nothing?' She put her hands on her hips. 'You suck at lying, you know. You do this little thing here, with your eyebrow.' She pointed to the corner of one of her own dark brows. 'It kind of kicks up.'

Hero scrunched up her nose. Her mum did that when she was lying and Hero thought she'd conquered the tick.

'But what makes it really easy to tell, are your thoughts,' Norah continued. 'They go hard and just a little green. It's a good thing your mum and Tybalt aren't telepathic too, or you'd never get away with anything.'

She didn't say anything.

Norah sighed and plopped down on the edge of the bed. 'It's not like I don't want to tell you, you know.'

Hero didn't have to ask; the image of Imogen floated between them. There was something else as well, a sour note on the edge of Norah's mind. Her words weren't quite a lie, but they weren't the truth either.

The cloying scent of roses wrapped around Hero's brain and tugged at her mouth, curling it into a sneer. 'Whatever,' she said and hid behind the 'page.

'Hey.' Norah snatched the 'page again. Her brows were drawn tight above her nose, and anger sparked in her gaze. 'I mean it. I want to tell you.'

The sour edge floated across Norah's thoughts, a mere echo of what it was before, but still enough for the roses in Hero's brain to grow thorns.

'No you don't,' she said. 'You're happy you have to keep what Imogen told you secret because it makes you feel better, it makes you feel *special*.' She spat the last word.

That was wrong. Hero had time to think that, to know the words that had just tumbled off her tongue were… bad, not hers. Except they were – they'd been there, in the back of her mind, and she'd spoken them. It was just… Why did she?

Norah looked at her, mouth open and her eyes wide. For a second, Hero thought she'd stopped breathing, and then Norah's brows came down and where before anger had been but a spark in her eyes, now it was an inferno.

A pillow flew at Hero's head. 'That's a lie.' Norah's anger a hot lavender bubble pressing on Hero's mind.

On the bed, Harish mantled his wings and hissed.

The roses tightened their grip on Hero's mind while something dark, hot and gleeful rose in her chest. She smiled, or maybe it was a snarl, she didn't know – all she knew was that Norah tried to step backwards and ended up sprawled on the bed.

'No, you just *wish* it was a lie, then you wouldn't have to admit that if it weren't for me, you'd still just be a *freak*.'

Her friend stared at her, and the hurt in her eyes made Hero's heart leap in her chest, a sick lurch that thrilled even as it repelled, before the look changed, confusion pushing the hurt aside. 'Why does your brain smell like roses?'

The question made Hero blink, and for a moment, the awful glee subsided. 'What?'

'Your brain, it smells like roses.' Norah leaned forward.

Norah's mind pressed against Hero's, tugging at the scent of roses and dislodging a memory. Panic flooded Hero, and she clamped down on it, but not before the image of a green-haired woman slumped against a wall slipped through.

When Norah spoke, her voice was a whisper, her eyes bleak. 'What did you do?'

The glee stuttered, the roses retreating, and with her mind still open the rest of the memory burst to the front of Hero's mind. The way Demona's brain had popped, how she'd staggered, the surprise on her face, the thin trail of blood from her nose, all of it.

Norah recoiled, scrambling all the way across the bed until she was standing on the other side. Shock and a hint of fear trailed after her, and the look on her face…

A hole opened in Hero's chest, a Terra-awful pit right below her heart.

'You did it again.' Norah's voice, no longer a whisper, opened the hole in Hero's chest wider.

Hero didn't say anything, but she didn't need to. The knowledge floated to front of her mind. Not 'again'. Demona had been the first.

'The first? There was a *first*?' Norah's face contorted and Hero felt her heart contort with it. 'How could you?'

There was a lump in her throat, but she choked the words past it anyway. 'I didn't mean to.'

'But you meant it the second time, you *told* me so.' The image of the other man popped up between them. *Your victim,* Norah thought.

'I was going for Meren.' Hero shoved *his* face at Norah, the dead cybernetic eyes, the way his brain had stunk of old meat and tingled with electricity. 'The other man' – she didn't even know his name—'got in the way.'

Norah shoved the image back. 'And that makes it all right?'

Hero stood. 'Meren tried to kill Fink.'

'So?'

So. The word echoed in Hero's mind and slowly, oh-so-slowly, the roses crept back. 'He tried. To kill. Fink.'

Norah shook her head. 'That doesn't make it right. That'll never make it right, and now your thoughts smell like a dead woman's and you're angry and scary and I don't want to be around you anymore.'

The roses vanished. 'What?'

'Get out.'

'But—'

'You hurt people, you *meant* to hurt them, and you're not even sorry.' Norah clenched her fists. 'You're scaring me and I don't think I want to be your friend anymore.'

The pit in Hero's chest yawned. She opened her mouth.

Norah's arm was straight and strong and emphatic as she pointed to the door. 'Out.'

The pit swallowed her heart.

CHAPTER 11

The jwak sat in its plascrete cradle. It didn't look like the one from the Bayard archives; it was short and fat, just big enough to wrap her hand around, whereas the other had been long and thin.

Hero hunched over the bench, chin resting on crossed forearms, and stared at the tech. Hunger made her stomach rumble even as fear twisted her guts.

She heard Tybalt's shoes clack-clacking over the marble-wood floor before she smelled the pancakes in his hand. The sweet, warm scent made bile rise in the back of her throat.

'You missed dinner.' His deep voice didn't entirely cover the click of the plate at her elbow.

Hero stared harder at the jwak. 'I'm not hungry,' she said, even as her stomach churned.

She knew what the thing was now, knew how it worked, but every time she tried to fix it, tried to stop the power surge from seeking out her brain, the solution felt wrong. There was something she was missing; she could feel it in her bones, even if the knowledge escaped her, hidden in a blue, rose-scented fog. But she'd figure it out, all she had to do was reach into the fog and—

Tybalt's hand swallowed her shoulder, the dark liquorice of his thoughts swamping her brain.

'Don't touch me!' She spun around, throwing his hand off her shoulder and sending the pancakes to the floor.

The plate smashed, slender bits of chinaglas immediately lost amidst the wreckage of old projects, the pancakes satellites of golden-brown oozing mawberries and chocolate.

The sight held her transfixed.

Tybalt didn't say a word; his dark head cast into shadow, the hem of his trouser pants splattered pink and brown. He nodded, just once. 'I'll send the cleaning bot,' he said, voice flat.

His shoes clack-clacked all the way out of the lab and down the hall.

Ice settled in her gut and crawled up her spine while the scent of butter and chocolate filled her nose. She stared at the pancakes until the cleaning bot came, a shiny white disk hovering over the floor, turning back to the bench before it zapped the mess into oblivion.

She loved pancakes.

The thought was strange, settling into her chest, in the space under her heart and above her stomach. Cold. Hard. Heavy.

The jwak glowed, Hero's tears making its edges blur. She sniffed and dashed her hand across her cheeks.

She'd figure this out, the jwak, the blue fog in her brain. She'd figure it out and then she'd fix it, even if she had to blow up another chunk of the city to do so. But first she needed answers, answers she couldn't hack into a network to find because Doctor Zass's lab was offline, even to the Librarian.

A section of the workbench slid into itself and there lay the Librarian's data slide, the little black slither of plasglas and biogel sucking in the light and refusing to let it go.

CHAPTER 12

The lift stopped, doors opening into a foyer, its holowalls shimmering with images beamed directly from under the city, of vibrant blue-green forest ripped apart by the grey-brown of rocky canyons and the bright blue of thundering rivers. At the very top of the image, the massive spires puncturing Cumulous City's underbelly reached towards the planet. It was almost like being there, floating under the city, except for the giant double doors looming in front of her.

Hero swallowed and stepped out of the lift.

The Librarian's data slide was a hot weight in her pocket, burning a hole in her pants with every breath. She folded her palm around the small rectangle of plasglas and biogel and took a deep breath before she stepped forwards.

The Bayard AI flickered to life the moment her foot touched the foyer, the avatar's torso floating in front of the double doors as armless as it was legless. It smiled at her. 'Greetings, Ms Regan. How may I assist you?'

'I want to see Doctor Zass.'

'You do not have an appointment.'

She glared at the avatar. 'Just let me in.'

'I am afraid that I cannot do that, Ms Regan. Doctor Zass's privacy settings are quite strict.'

Hero's hand tightened around the data slide. 'Then page her.'

'Doctor Zass has listed her status as "do not disturb". You may leave a message for her if you like.'

A message wouldn't do. She needed to get *into* Zass's lab, and if she didn't do it now… Hero blew out through her nose. She needed Woolsey's notes, needed to know what this *thing* was inside her head. The mystery of the jwak beckoned to her, and the surge of glee she'd had at the thought of choking Trainer Ella, and it made her stomach churn. She needed to know, and she needed it now.

There were words that would get her in there, that would trump the AI's strict adherence to Zass's privacy settings and whisk her past those double doors. But if she said them… Zass'd have her hooked up to more monitors than she could hack in a week, and her mum… Hero blanched at the thought.

The avatar smiled at her, its expression as bland as it was patient.

Hero took a deep breath. She could do this. 'It's an emergency,' she said.

The avatar's smile became a frown. 'One moment,' it said.

Hero hugged her arms.

'Doctor Zass is on her way. Please wait.'

Nerves danced along Hero's spine. She breathed out and hugged her arms tighter, feeling the edges of the data slide cut into her palm. This was it.

Zass burst through the double doors, blue lab coat flapping around her thighs, the long curly wave of her hair bouncing around her head.

Hero's heart caught in her chest. It was just Zass, she could deal with—

Two more doctors bustled through the door behind her, and Hero would have stepped back, but Zass had already gripped her arm. A bright, tangy streak of curiosity and excitement flooded her mind, almost overwhelming the deeper honey-gold of the doctor's concern.

A memory rode on the mix of emotions – a recent one, still sharp and sparkly – of a slightly fuzzy image and an almost indecipherable jumble of handwritten notes. Excitement made the memory pulse in

Zass's mind, the thrill of facts and research clicking together, making the blue and orange creature in the image – small triangular head, long sleek body, flippered feet and two pairs of fins – pop in the doctor's mind.

The biogel headband was back on Hero's forehead before she had time to process the memory, and then she was being hustled down soothing grey corridors.

Zass's lab was vast and warm, a suite of three rooms divided by semi-opaque walls. Hero was bundled into the smallest; one assistant peeling off into another room while the other hovered at Hero's back.

Zass patted the top of the biobed.

Hero perched on the edge of the bed, her hands gripping the mattress. Zass pressed a thumb to the headband and watched the screen that popped up above her palm, her gaze intent on the lines and numbers that flowed across it. She didn't speak.

Hero's grip tightened. 'Aren't you going to ask me what's wrong?'

She looked past the screen to Hero, her expression bland but her dark blue gaze focused. 'Tybalt called me.'

Hero huffed and looked away. 'Of course he did.'

'He's concerned about you, as any father would be.'

'I have a dad, Tybalt isn't him.'

The bed dipped a micron when Zass sat on it, her hip touching Hero's before the levs compensated for the extra weight.

The gold-brown touch of the doctor's thoughts brushed against Hero's, no longer as hard as they usually were, maybe even just a little sweet. Hero shifted, trying to put some space between where their hips touched. She wasn't averse to peeking at the doctor's thoughts, but it was hard to think of Zass as the enemy when she could feel the woman's concern.

Zass folded her hands in her lap. 'Hero, you're a remarkable girl – intelligent, resourceful – and if you would work with me, we could conquer the world.'

Zass's pause was as good as a finger under Hero's chin, lifting it to meet the doctor's gaze. The focus in those blue eyes was almost enough to make Hero look away.

Instead, she stiffened her spine. 'Why would I want the world?'

'To make it listen to you.' Zass cocked her head, curly brown hair falling over her shoulder. 'And to make it *remember* what you have to say.'

'Why do I need you for that?'

'Because, you're not the only sly person here.' Slowly, deliberately, Zass laid her hand over Hero's.

The memory hit Hero instantly. She saw the doctor at her workstation, an ancient datapad the size of her palm and twice as thick as a micropage glowing on the black surface, the blue and orange creature from Zass's earlier memory projected above. Someone moved in Zass's peripheral vision and she whipped the pad out of sight, hiding it in a little groove under the desktop.

Woolsey's journal.

Hero blinked and Zass smiled, patting Hero's hand before sliding off the bed.

The doctor's eyes really were quite pretty.

'There is a slight, but rather striking difference between the structure of your hybrid gene and Norah's,' Zass said, her eyes back on the double helix spinning over Hero's head. 'Given that your uncle appeared to have the same structure as you in his DNA.' Another double helix appeared beside the first, and with a flick of her fingers Zass overlaid the two. An almost perfect match. 'I've been working on the assumption that it's hereditary, but you seem to have a small mutation.' She pointed to a section on the overlay where the helixes didn't match up.

'And?' Hero prompted.

Zass smiled at her, her gaze leaving the readouts for just a second. 'Haven't you wondered which Jøran genetics Woolsey used to create human hybrids?'

'What do you mean?'

The doctor leaned in. 'Which animal did Woolsey pluck your Jøran DNA from?'

'I never thought about it.'

Zass turned back to her screens, wiping away Paris's DNA and zooming in on the small mutation in Hero's. 'She had a few favourites among the native fauna – the lethyt and the qwan among others – which made finding the genetic donor for Norah's family line – the qwans – rather simple, but you…' Zass shook her head. 'In her journals, Woolsey referenced a sample she obtained in the mountain ranges below Cumulus City, but the species is not in the Farm's genebanks. If I could acquire another sample, we'd have a chance to stabilise your genetics before—'

'Doctor Zass.' Her mother's cool tones stopped the doctor mid-word. Patricia stood in the doorway, her mouth pulled tight and a hard glitter in her eye. She stepped to the side and gestured to the room beyond. 'A word please?'

'Of course.' Zass's smile was stiff. She patted Hero's hand, the image of the hidden datapad clear in her mind before she joined Hero's mum. The door slid shut behind them, the lab's semi-opaque walls turning a solid milky white.

Hero slipped off the bed, the Librarian's data slide in her palm. Three steps and she was at a terminal, a second later she had the input open and the slide was in, the gel lighting up around it as it went to work.

She didn't wait to see what the Librarian's program did. Instead, she headed for Zass's workstation, slipping out of the small room and into the office adjoining it. The workstation dominated the space. Hero ran her hands under its surface, finding the little groove that hid Woolsey's journal. The datapad was an ancient device made of plasglas and Old Terra circuitry, too archaic for her to copy its data with the equipment she had; she'd probably not even make it past the boot screen before Zass and her mum came back. Instead, she shoved it into her pocket and hustled back into the other room.

The Librarian's slide still lit up the terminal. How long would it take? The AI hadn't told her and the vid of her in that room, with that woman… Hero felt her face go cold and her stomach churn at the memory. She'd been too distracted to ask.

She looked over her shoulder. How long would Zass and her mum keep talking? How long before one of the doctor's assistants came in? Would it be long enough? The lab walls were still opaque, the cams still dark, and the only sound was her heartbeat and the hush of air. Breathing deeply, Hero closed her eyes and extended her mind.

The room outside the lab came to life in her head – Zass, her mum and there, just entering from the hallway beyond, Tybalt with Fink hot on his heels. It was the assistant, though, who caught Hero's attention. The man reached for the door, his thoughts on the adjustments he wanted to make to the headband monitoring Hero's condition.

Her eyes flashed to the slide, the terminal still humming around it. Panic clutched at her lungs, just as she clutched at the assistant's mind, ripping the need to check her headband from his thoughts.

Manners. Fink's mawberry-scented slap made her reel.

Her eyes snapped open, and she snarled at the empty room. On the other side of the lab's opaque walls, she felt Fink snarl back.

The minds in the other room scattered like finch-fish, all except her mum's sharp cinnamon scent and Tybalt's liquorice. There was just enough time for Hero to snatch the slide, still glowing, out of the input before the walls flashed, leaving her looking at her mother's stern face.

'What are you doing?' Her mum's voice was crystal clear through the plasglas. Apparently she'd dropped the sound buffer with the opaqueness.

Hero crossed her arms, the data slide hot in her hand. 'Nothing.'

Her mum frowned, while beside her Tybalt's brows scooted towards his hairline. 'Fink doesn't snarl at nothing, Hero. What were you doing?'

She glared at Fink through the plasglas.

A large red-brown mass sitting on his haunches, his head level with Tybalt's shoulder, Fink pinned his ears back and flashed his fangs.

'Eavesdropping, I wanted to know what you were saying.'

Fink huffed. *That wasn't what she'd been doing.*

Going to dob on me? She glared at him.

He huffed again, but in his mind there was a whine, and his ears crumpled. *He'd had to tell Tybalt before. That thing she did, when her mind went blue and smelled like fur-roses, wasn't right, it wasn't her. It scared him.*

It was Hero's turn to huff and turn away, shame making her stomach sour.

It was long past dinner before Zass let her out of the lab, a neural monitor attached to the base of her skull and her mother's stern admonition not to fiddle with it ringing in her ears.

Not for the first time, she felt the back of her neck. The monitor was a tiny bump; if it hadn't glowed, it would have been invisible. Instead, it was a luminous blue pimple in the dark fuzz of her hair. She could already hear the whispers floating around school, feel the stares. A hint of roses teased her nose, and she felt the sensor throb. Red pulsed in the corner of her vision, but when she turned all she saw was the jwak, dull and dark on the workbench.

She dropped her hand and frowned. It didn't matter. She'd done what she had to do.

She sat in the dark, with only the glow of the fur-roses outside her workroom and Woolsey's ancient journal for light. The old datapad lay open, the two halves of its casing side-by-side with a thin tendril of biogel snaking from its datapaks to the bench's input.

A wave of Hero's hand and screens sprang to life above the workbench, with equations, diagrams and an endless stream of handwritten notes. Bright yellow marked sections of the text, expanding into even more notes in the clean, concise letters of a keyboard – they had to be Zass's notes. She flicked through the journal, scrolling through page after page, searching for something, *anything* to point to the clues the Librarian had hinted at, and perhaps, the thing Zass had wanted her to see.

A highlighted passage with 'Hero' in bold letters above it leapt out of the screen, one of Doctor Zass's notes superimposed on top. *Maybe your search will bear better fruit.*

Hero wiped the message aside and squinted at the passage, the sharp, straight lines and loopy bellies of the letters wriggling in front of her eyes. She blinked, zoomed in and tilted her head before pushing the mess aside. Trying to read that was going to make her head hurt, but a few flicks of her fingers and a screen later, and Woolsey herself was reading the words to her.

The digitally generated voice was halting at first, stumbling over sentences, but became bold and smooth as the computer finished compiling.

'Beatrice snuck me into the breach chamber one last time and again I was left to wonder at the colonists who came before. There is such wonder here, such power in the technology they left behind, and yet they were driven back into space by a species with no discernible technology of their own.

'That is why the pact with the swatai had to be struck. They will stay the other two races and I shall use DNA from each of them to create my Jørgens.

'The sample from the swatai shows the greatest potential but Ayumon's early predictive models have disturbed as much as delighted me. The strength of a human hybrid with their DNA will be as unparalleled as it will be unstable, and the need to commune... swatai Jørgens could destroy us as easily as the threatened war.

'Despite it I will keep to the pact, but of the one hundred families selected as unwitting subjects, only my sister's will carry this variation. I must trust Ayumon and the Librarian to keep them safe, and to save us from them should the need arise.'

Woolsey's digital voice fell silent.

Woolsey's sister. 'I'm related to the Crackpot?'

'Indeed, Hero Regan.' The Librarian's head and shoulders appeared above her station. 'She was your great, great aunt on your mother's side of the family. Do you have the data slide I provided?'

'I do,' she said, pulling it from her bracer.

'Thank you, Hero Regan. Please place the slide in your terminal's input. I will access the data from there.'

'No.' Hero took a deep breath. 'Scrub the vid first.'

The Librarian zoomed out until its entire torso sat above the workstation. 'I cannot comply.'

'What?'

'I cannot—'

'But you promised.'

'I made no such assurances, Hero Regan. Indeed, such an assurance would have been foolhardy.'

She gritted her teeth, her hand clenching around the slide, the scent of roses twirling through her brain. 'Why?'

'Once I have reviewed the data, I may have further need of your cooperation.' The Librarian zoomed back in until it was just a head hovering over her station's input tray. 'Please insert the data slide.'

Acid burned through Hero's nostrils and the room took on a blue hue while roses exploded on the back of her tongue, the sensor throbbing in time with her pulse. Anger swamped fear and when she reached forward to place the slide in the gel, it was the former that caused her hand to shake. 'I'll get you for this.'

The gel lit up around the slide.

'You may try, Hero Regan.' The Librarian winked out.

Red flooded the workroom, the jwak a blazing sun on the corner of the bench.

CHAPTER 13

The genes blurred in front of her, chromosomes merging one into the other in a fuzzy mass of colour and light, Doctor Tachi a dark blob on the other side.

She was supposed to be working, straightening out the last of the twists in Bayard's new explorer drones, but her mind was stuck back at the mansion and the holocall in Tybalt's study. She hadn't meant to eavesdrop, but the door had been open and she'd recognised the tall, lean figure of one of Norah's dads, pale green shirt buttoned all the way up to his neck, tie straight and crisp jacket dark. His hair, black like Norah's, had been swept back from his forehead and his expression had been grave.

It was Tybalt's voice though, flat and calm, like when he'd tried to convince her not to test her hover pad by jumping off the mansion's roof, that stilled Hero's feet.

'Legal action seems somewhat… drastic.'

'I'm sorry, Tybalt. We've done it your way for the past year but after what Norah has told us, we don't feel we can any longer.'

'And what, exactly, has she told you?'

Hero scurried away before Norah's dad could open his mouth. She hadn't wanted to hear what Norah had said to her dads. Imagining it, the looks on their faces, the horror and disgust as they learnt about Demona Thy, was bad enough.

Now though, staring through the holoscreens to where Doctor Tachi bent over his workbench, uncertainty swirled in her mind.

It had been forty-nine hours and fourteen minutes since she'd eavesdropped on that call and there had been no sudden scurries of activity, no unexpected visits from Doctor Zass. No pokes, no prods, no Tybalt looking over her shoulder. Had Norah told her parents about Demona? Did she even know that another person was living in her brain?

Except, there wasn't another person sharing her space, or, at least, she didn't think there was. Whatever Demona's presence was, it didn't talk to her, not like Fink did or Norah could. But if it didn't have a voice, then where had the gut-lurching glee she'd felt when Norah had scrambled away from her come from?

The door at the back of Hero's mind throbbed, loomed. She had to know.

She pushed the door open, just a crack, and peered into the space beyond. Her breath, short and sharp, caught in her throat.

It wasn't dark. The tiny space was full to bursting with memories and feelings and knowledge. They curled and twisted, an ever-shifting kaleidoscope of blue – light and dark and so pale it was almost white. A rose-tinted memory tugged at her, the scent curling around her nostrils and pulling her in.

Everything went blue, and then she wasn't herself anymore. She was Demona: taller, older, her knuckles bloody and swollen, aching as much as her face. She spat blood.

A woman stood in front of Demona, short and chubby with grey in her black hair, her hands balled up in front of her face and a steely look in her eye. The woman gestured. 'Again,' she said.

Demona grinned, spitting more blood and worrying at another loose tooth, before striking.

For all her bulk and age, the older woman moved liked grease, ducking, blocking, striking back. She danced around Demona, never flinching, never blinking no matter how close Demona's fists and feet came. Even after an hour, when sweat had long since drenched Demona's T-shirt, the old woman barely even breathed hard, and not for the first time Demona wondered what kind of hybrid freak she was.

Hybrid. The word rang in Hero's head and another memory took hold.

Demona propped a shoulder against the wall and stared hard at the old woman on the biobed, at her softly lined face and the way her hands folded neatly in her lap. She looked normal, even surrounded by doctors with holos of her insides projected above her chest.

Normal. Which is more than could have been said for the other one. Demona's stare slipped to the man with the perfectly parted blond hair. He was talking to one of the lab specimens again – a qwan, a native four-eyed bird – like the dull, scrawny-looking thing could talk back.

As if sensing her, the animal turned one set of eyes – the upper ones, the dark bloody red of fresh meat – on Demona even as the lower pair – a pale, cloudy blue – stayed on the man.

The man followed the qwan's gaze. He smiled, his expression hard, and Demona felt something inside her brain—

No. Hero recoiled, snapping out of Demona's memories fast enough that the scent of roses left gouges in her mind. She winced. Her skull hurt and her stomach cramped and roiled.

Demona had known Paris.

Hero focused, breathed deep and plunged back in. She needed to find her uncle, needed to know what else Demona had known of him, but the woman's memories slipped through her fingers. She saw Demona sitting in front of a cake with a big pink eight on the top, saw her bent over a workbench, a familiar-looking cylinder coming together in her hands. She saw the boy – twice Demona's size – who beat her up on the way to school, felt the joy and the satisfaction when she left him bloody and broken two years later.

And then there was Paris, his skin pale, his cheeks dark hollows, his hair plastered to his face in long dirty strands. The memory slipped away before she could latch onto it, ripped away by the other images, smells, tastes and feelings rushing through her brain. Pain, joy, fear, the sour taste yul-rrots, the dusty scent of a biodome and anger. Anger so hot it burned inside her skin until it erupted, exploding out of her fists and her feet against flesh and bone, turning it to joy.

'Hero.'

Her eyes snapped open.

The world was blue and her body didn't feel right, was too short, too soft.

Light flashed.

Doctor Zass stood in front of her, a glowing ball in her hand, intent on the screen hovering above it. The doctor's mouth moved, but Hero didn't hear the words. The glowing ball, a sensor, shone in her eyes and sent pain ricocheting all the way to the back of her skull. She pushed it away.

There was a pause, a moment of tension carried on the golden-brown of Zass's thoughts, and then the ball was back, piercing her eyes.

Hero winced and pushed it away again.

It was back a split-second later and this time, when she went to shove it away, someone grabbed her wrist.

Fury wound its way up her spine. She growled and tried to tug away.

The hand on her wrist tightened, and another – not Zass's – grabbed her shoulder. There were more words, soft sounds that some part of her knew were meant to be soothing, but only made the world bluer.

The sphere of light disappeared, replaced by Zass's violet gaze. The doctor's mouth kept moving, the sounds coming out of it winding through Hero's ears and gumming up her brain. She wanted them to stop, needed them to stop. There were words to shut them the Terra up, but they wouldn't come, tangled in the mess Zass's sounds were making of her head.

Frustration, hot and jangly, bloomed in Hero's stomach. She smelled roses. She smiled.

Zass frowned at her.

Hero struck. Pain speared all the way from Zass's cheekbone and up Hero's knuckles to her elbow, but she tucked it away to relish later. The grip on her shoulder loosened, and she spun the stool around, hand shaped like a spear and aiming for the other person's throat.

Doctor Tachi stumbled back, eyes wide and mouth open as he tried to suck in air past the shattered cartilage in his voice box.

The image of a stun-stick bloomed in Hero's mind, honey-brown and streaked with a sour note of panic. She was off the stool and twisting on the ball of one foot, using the seat to balance as she brought her knee up high and whipped her other foot towards Zass's head. Her legs were too short and the blow that should have had the doctor spitting out teeth, landed in her ribs, sending her careening into a workstation.

Frustration boiled up from her gut in a thick blue wave that burned the back of her throat and made her bones ache in a way that could only be abated by the curling of her fists.

Zass clutched at the worktop, half on her knees, and said something, but the words burned in Hero's ears and she shook them aside. There was only one way to assuage the emotion eating her insides.

Liquorice, sweet and black, hit her brain a second before the laboratory door slid aside. Tybalt stood in the doorway, one hand on the control panel, the other unbuttoning his jacket. The twin furrows over his nose were deep and black, the lines around his mouth tired. His gaze met Hero's, dropped to Zass, scooted over to Doctor Tachi, who was wheezing as he hunkered with his back to a workbench. She felt Tybalt's mind race, heard the thrum of it, sensed the first salty stirring of fear and then... Nothing. Even the air went still.

'Hero.' Tybalt stepped forward, hands dropping to his sides. 'What have you done?'

Tybalt's voice was slow and calm, just like it had been on the holocall, but his eyes… the thing that was Demona recognised that look, the focus, the way his gaze locked with hers and refused to let go. A thrill rippled up her spine. It was better than Zass's fear, Tachi's pain. It was a challenge.

Hero grinned.

For a moment, Tybalt faltered, his focus stuttering, before his mouth tightened. 'Hero,' he said, his hands held palm out while he took a step forward.

Hero's body tightened, her gaze narrowed. She watched his face, waiting.

He moved closer. 'I need you to calm—'

She struck, but her arm was too short and her fist barely clipped Tybalt's chin, knuckles grazing the stubble. He moved like lightning, but not as fast as Demona's opponent. She ducked and twisted, slipping out from under his arms and struck again.

He dodged, blocked.

She barely had time to see his fist before it connected with her face.

CHAPTER 14

When she woke her head was fuzzy and the back of her throat tasted like menthol. Slowly, lids heavy and her face throbbing, she cracked her eyes open. Just as quickly, she closed them to escape the light piercing her eyeballs.

Hero groaned and tried to lift a hand to cover her eyes. It wouldn't move. She tugged, felt something broad and soft tighten around her wrist and turned her head, cracking open an eye to glance at her hand.

A wide biogel cuff was wrapped around her wrist where her bracer should have been. Hero frowned and tried lifting her hand again. She'd barely raised it a few centimetres from the mattress before yellow bands lit up the biogel and her wrist stopped moving.

Maybe it was all the fuzz clogging up her head, but it took a moment for the significance to sink in.

They'd strapped her to the bed.

Both eyes now open and her heart thumping just a bit harder, Hero checked her other wrist. A similar biogel cuff was wrapped around that too. She tugged and the yellow bands shone through the biogel.

'Fink.' She said his name even as she reached for him with her mind.

Nothing. It wasn't the way the room – the same lab she'd been in before, except now its walls moved with a gentle pattern of soft blues – swallowed her voice that concerned her. It was the silence in her mind, the green gooey feeling at the edges of her brain, where not just Fink but *everyone* – all the minds she should have been able to sense – should have been, that made her panic.

She knew that feeling and remembered the taste of menthol on the back of her tongue. She hated and feared them in equal measure.

Someone had shot her up with the meds that had once, and apparently still did, keep her telepathy in check. There was only one person who would do that.

'Mum,' Hero screamed.

The walls had barely swallowed the sound before a rectangular section glowed white and slid aside.

Her mother stood in the doorway.

Hero glared at her. 'You shot me up.'

Her mum crossed her arms. 'It had to be done. You know I wouldn't have done it otherwise.'

'And the cuffs?' Hero tugged at her wrists.

Her mum remained silent, but her mouth thinned and her gaze was pinched, scrunching the flesh between her brows and at the corners of her eyes before she strode to the bed. She pressed a thumb to the cuffs and the bands of light flashed green before falling from Hero's wrists.

Hero tucked her hands under her arms. 'I want Fink,' she said. 'Why isn't he here?'

Her mum's brow tightened some more and Hero's stomach tightened with it. 'He's fine. Trainer Ella has made him comfortable in the stables.'

The words 'made him comfortable' echoed in Hero's mind. For a second, she forgot how to breathe before she frantically reached out to Fink with her mind, only to get caught in the gooey mess blockading her brain.

She scrambled off the bed, wincing when her feet hit the floor and sent a jolt of pain through her jaw and into her head.

'Honey.' Her mum was at her side, lifting her chin up to meet her gaze before Hero had a chance to do more than blink. 'You need to take it easy. Tybalt—'

Hero jerked her head away, the movement sending another spike of pain through her skull. 'What'd you do to Fink?'

'He's fine.'

'What did you *do*?'

'Hero—'

'Tell me!'

With a sharp breath in through her nose, like she was inflating her spine, her mum drew herself up until she towered over Hero. 'He attacked a trainer, and Trainer Ella did her job.' She held up a hand even as Hero opened her mouth. 'He's fine, Hero. Ella only knocked him out.'

There was something in the way her mum said that Trainer Ella 'did her job', a twist to her lips that made Hero's gut scrunch and turn to ice.

'She called Farm Control.'

Her mum's lip twisted a little more and her eyes darkened. If Hero's brain hadn't been stuffed with meds, she was sure she would have felt the anger in her mum's mind all the way from the other side of the room. 'That too, is part of her job.' Her mum's words were hard and clipped.

Hero shook her head. 'No,' she said and moved around her mum, heading for the door. The Farm didn't give 'pards second chances, not when they attacked a human. If they took him… Her breath caught in her chest. 'I won't let them take him.'

'Honey.' Her mum caught her shoulder. 'You're not going anywhere.'

Hero shrugged her off. 'You can't stop me.'

'I can and I have,' she said. 'I've activated the biometric lock on this room. You can't leave until Doctor Zass or I say so. Fink will be fine – no one's taking him anywhere.' Her mum's brow twitched like it always did when she lied. 'But you need to stay here because *you're* not fine.'

'I'm not crazy.'

'No one's saying you are.'

'Then why are you locking me in a room?'

Patricia's gaze softened and turned sad. 'You hit someone, Hero, don't you remember? Tybalt—' She shook her head and reached touched Hero's cheek. 'You fought him, and he knocked you out.'

A memory of Tybalt's fist rocketing towards her jaw played in Hero's mind. She frowned and put her own hand up to her jaw, wincing at the tenderness there. 'He hit me.'

'And he feels terrible, but I've seen the vid and...' Her mum's mouth hung open for a second, her jaw working like there were words in her throat that wouldn't come out before she shook her head. 'It scared me, Hero. The girl I saw on that vid... that wasn't you.'

Hero looked away, remembering the scent of roses crawling through her brain and the memory of flesh hitting flesh running up her arm. It had scared her too, how much she'd enjoyed it.

'What happened?' her mum asked.

She looked at her mum from under her lashes. 'I...' she began. 'I don't want to talk about it, and...' She took a deep breath and glared. 'I'm not going to talk about it until I see Fink.'

'Hero.' Her mum's mouth flattened. 'I'm sorry, honey, but no. This is not how this is going to work. You're safer up here and *he's* safer with you up here. Trainer Ella is recommending that Fink is taken to the Farm on probation, but if you go down there, chances are good he'll act out again and once he does that... They'll put him down, sweetheart. No second chances for 'pards, remember?'

Her mum clasped her shoulders and bent to look Hero in the eye. 'Just sit still and let us figure out what's happening with you. Once we do that, we can start the process of getting Fink back. Okay?'

Hero crossed her arms.

Her mum stared at her, a thought weighing down her brows, a decision ticking over in her eyes. She sighed and sat on the bed beside Hero. 'There's more going on here than just you and Fink, things I wish I could tell you, but more, there are things I wish you'd told *me*.'

Hero's breath caught in her throat. 'Like what?'

'I think you know.' Her mother's gaze, the same dark brown as her own, held Hero, boring into her brain.

She tightened her arms over her stomach and turned away.

Her mother sighed again, the sound deeper and sadder than Hero had ever heard it, and slipped off the bed before walking out the room, the door sealing behind her.

Hero took stock of the room that was now her prison. There was a way out of here, there *had* to be. No way was she sitting around letting Zass poke and prod at her while Farm Control took Fink away. Her heart beat faster at the thought and a squidgy sense of panic built in her stomach, but she pushed it away and concentrated.

It was hard though when her thoughts kept brushing up against the green barrier holding her in her head. She wiped her palms on her legs, for the first time really noticing the soft blue pants and loose top – the kind Tybalt had worn in hospital – that had replaced the clothes she'd been wearing. The squidgy feeling in her belly contracted and spiked. There wasn't a mirror in the room, not even the walls were shiny enough to catch her reflection; instead, she explored the rest of her body with her hands.

She found the sensors first, three dots on her forehead. She tried to take them off, to slip her fingernails under them, but they were stuck tight. That wasn't the end of them either – there were more, attached to the sides of her head, just above her ears, and two more just above the old one, running from the nape of her neck to her crown. Each one of them a fingernail-sized pimple sticking out from her skull, rough to the touch and no doubt glowing like beacons on her head.

She had to get to Fink, but there was nothing in the room she could use – not her bracer, not a terminal, just the sensors stuck to her head and flat blue walls.

The memory of her last visit to the room played in her mind. Maybe the wall was all she needed.

Hero pressed her hand to the plasglas, smooth and cool under her palm.

'Librarian?'

The wall interface flickered, and the smooth, golden face of the Bayard AI stared back at her. 'I apologise, Ms Regan, you do not have sufficient privileges to access that function. Please consult your sup-super—'

The AI stuttered, static running in a shifting line of multi-coloured boxes through its face. '—supervisor to… Please excuse me, I am currently experiencing a higher than usual lo— load—'

Static poured down the wall, drowning the AI in cubes that shuddered and jumped across its surface. Another face rose out of the mess. White and expressionless, the Librarian hovered over the blue surface before the door beside it slid aside.

'Quickly, Hero Regan. The Bayard AI is adapting to my intrusion. I will not be able to aid you for much longer.'

Hero didn't need further prompting. She raced out the door, bare feet slapping on the floor, and into the small room beyond. There was chair and a workstation, holoscreens aglow, one showing the lab and the others a hodgepodge of graphs. One spiked and beeped in time with her heart.

A small square on the wall behind the station glowed and slid aside, revealing a tidy pile of clothes and her bracer sitting atop. She grabbed the bracer first, almost sighing in relief when the biogel wrapped around her forearm, cool and smooth against her skin, before it activated, sending a fizz from her fingers to the nape of her neck.

She reached for her clothes next, eager to be out of the floppy blue pants and tunic, but before her fingers brushed the fabric, the wall panel snapped closed.

'Leave the clothing, Hero Regan. It will not be adequate.'

'But—'

'Leave it, Hero Regan. There is little time and more appropriate garb will be supplied.'

'I don't even have shoes!'

The Librarian appeared on the wall before her, a purple line shooting from the AI to another glowing doorframe. 'Go,' it said, before disappearing.

Eyes wide and mouth open, Hero stared at the wall for several long seconds before movement caught her vision. The purple line blinked, and the doorway slid open. Beyond it an empty corridor beckoned and thirty-eight levels below that, Fink.

Hero's mouth snapped closed. Shoes sucked anyway.

The plascrete was cold under Hero's feet. The Librarian's purple guideline streaked ahead of her along the off-white walls. It flashed red as they came to an intersection, jumping to the other side of the narrow hallway. Hero followed it, slamming her back against the new wall and barely breathing as a woman in a green lab coat wandered along the other hallway, head buried in the nest of screens projected above her palm-unit.

Heart pounding in her ears, Hero listened while the clack of the woman's shoes faded.

Across the intersection, the purple line flashed once more. Hero dashed after it and into the softly glowing box of a waiting lift.

She slapped the control panel.

The lift doors remained open.

'Librarian?'

Her bracer glowed and shivered against her skin a second before the AI appeared above her wrist. 'I am experiencing difficulty with the Bayard AI. One moment please.'

Hero waited, her gaze jumping around the foyer and the nerves jumping in her stomach growing stronger with every second the doors remained open. She jiggled on the spot, and then froze, her eyes going wide at the sharp clack-clack of shoes from down one of the corridors. 'Librarian, hurry up.'

'One moment please.'

'You said that already, but someone's coming *now*.'

The footsteps grew louder and now Hero could see the woman

from before, green lab coat swinging around her legs, her head still buried in her holoscreens.

'Librarian.'

'One moment pl— Done.'

The lift doors closed and Hero sank against the side of the lift.

'Hero Regan,' the Librarian said. 'Has your medication worn off?'

Taking a deep breath, Hero pushed against the sides of her mind. The green gooey feeling was still there, weaker perhaps, but still walling her inside her own head. 'No,' she said.

'That is unfortunate.'

Her heart froze a little. 'Why?'

'The Bayard AI's immune response is proving to be most aggressive. I have enough control of its systems to deliver you to the stables but nothing more. You will have to manage the rest of the way on your own and your telepathy would have proven most useful.'

'I have my bracer.'

'Indeed and you will need it to free your companion, but once your escape is discovered, I predict that the AI will negate even that advantage. Speed, Hero Regan, is of the essence.'

The gentle hum of the lift stopped and the sign across its doors flicked to *Level 589 – Stables* a second before the doors opened onto a cavernous storage area, dark grey crates stacked almost to the ceiling. The guideline pulsed on the side of the closest box.

'Continue following the purple line, Hero Regan,' the Librarian said before its avatar above her wrist winked out.

Cautiously, Hero moved through the corridors formed by the crates, her gaze on the guideline pulsing in the gloom, straining her ears for the telltale clack of shoes or the clop of hooves. By the time she reached the massive doors at the end, a trickle of sweat meandered down her back. She waited for two beats, the back of her head resting against the wall, before peering around the door.

A wide hallway greeted her, lined on each side with large box stalls occupied by companions shut behind transparent sheets of plasglas. The stables.

A sterdane raised its head, the scales running from its nose and all the way down its back gleaming in the soft overhead lights, and whuffed when she jogged past. There were two more 'danes curled around each other in the next stall, and then a sternard, and then a toa-mare, each after the other. And then there, behind a wall of plasglas, was Fink, curled into a tight ball with his back to the hall.

Hero pressed her hands to the glass. 'Fink,' she said.

He didn't move.

She pressed herself tighter to the glass, rapping on it with her knuckles. 'Fink,' she said again, louder this time.

Still, he didn't stir.

'Hero Regan.' She jumped back when the Librarian appeared in front of her nose. 'Your escape has been noticed. You must open this stall now.'

'Right.' She planted her palm against the plasglas. Immediately the plasglas flashed red and *Unauthorised Access* projected over the back of her hand.

Hero activated her bracer and the code that controlled the lock was tangled around her forearm a second later.

The glass sank into the floor.

On his mound of blankets, Fink didn't move.

'Fink,' she said, her voice small.

His ear twitched.

'Fink,' she said again. 'Get up.'

He grumbled.

'Now,' she yelled.

He snarled and lumbered to his feet.

She slapped his nose. 'I'm rescuing you, you idiot. Trainer Ella sicced Farm Control on you and Mum shot me up with meds again, so we're leaving. Okay? Now stop snarling.'

He grumbled again, but softer, and padded out of the stall after her.

'Hero Regan.' Her bracer glowed, and the Librarian hovered above her wrist. 'This way.'

'This way' led them down the hallway, past more stalls before spilling into the tack room. Two rows of neatly racked saddles – some wide and flat, others tall and skinny with seats made to rise halfway up the rider's back – bracketed each side of the wide corridor. Behind them, names shimmered on the walls.

'Hero Regan.' The Librarian reclaimed her attention. 'The last rack on the left.'

The last rack on the left held a broad, black saddle with a seat deep enough to sink into and a thin line of holo transmitters built into the front. On the wall behind it, her named glowed.

Hero scooted around the saddle rack and pressed her palm against the wall. It made a halo around her hand before a section the size of a door disappeared into the floor. Inside, a neatly folded pile of clothes rested on its own little shelf, while another shelf above held a helmet, below that a set of tall boots sat next to a small mound of bags, the jwak strapped atop the top one.

Hero gaped. 'How did you do this?'

'The tack room is stocked by the Bayard AI. It was simple to request new supplies,' the Librarian said.

'But I left the jwak at home.'

'An explanation will take time you do not have,' the Librarian said. 'Hurry, Hero Regan.'

The blue hospital pyjamas flew off, left in a crumpled pile even as Hero reached for the new clothes. The nanoskin went on first, covering her from toe to chin, a little too loose until she pressed a finger to the seal at the front and the dull grey material suctioned itself to her skin. Breeches came next, then the shirt and vest. The boots with their heavy soles almost slipped themselves on before she swung the thigh-length coat over her shoulders.

Fink took less time to saddle and Hero ducked and wove around his legs, snapping seals into place and securing the bags to the ties behind the seat. The last bag she slipped on her own back before jamming the helmet – the same transparent plasteel as the one she used for racing – on her head.

Next to her Fink stiffened, ears and whiskers pricked forwards.

'What is it?' Hero asked, a hand on his chest, her heart thumping against her ribs.

He rumbled and turned just long enough to nudge her towards his back. She didn't need to read his mind to know what that meant.

Hero leapt into the saddle, slapping vacuum seals into place as the sharp clack-clack of hard-soled shoes echoed in the corridor outside.

'Librarian,' she said, almost before her helmet came to life, screens popping up all around, a map of Bayard front and centre. 'What now? You have a plan to get us out of here, right?'

'Indeed, Hero Regan. You must steal a hover.'

'What? But— I can't drive!'

'Trust me, Hero Regan. All will be well.'

Beneath her, Fink growled, his tail twitching in sharp, impatient jerks.

'Fine then, but don't blame me when we crash.'

Fink gave a short little cough and leapt forward.

They burst out of the tack room, Fink's claws leaving marks on the floor. Ahead of them, Trainer Ella stood frozen in the middle of the corridor, two others standing behind her. Hero had time to see the stun-sticks in their hands and the Farm's distinctive cube logo on their chests before Fink charged.

One of the farmers managed to raise a stun-stick before Fink leapt. Hero ducked, but even so, her helmet brushed the ceiling as they sailed over them.

They raced on, the clack-clack of pursing footsteps lost under the sound of Hero's heart racing and the pounding of Fink's paws. Ahead, the corridor ended in a T shape and Hero had a moment of panic, her pulse in her throat and her eyes scanning the map spread across her visor. She didn't know which way to go and there was no Norah in her ear to tell her what direction to take.

Just as she felt Fink slowing, a line on the map glowed red. 'This way,' the Librarian said.

Hero nudged Fink with her knee and he picked up speed again, leaping and twisting his body in mid-air to bounce off the wall and keep racing down the left corridor.

They burst through double doors into a cavernous space full of hovers and a handful of people. On her map, a spot pulsed red and Hero turned to look at it, her HUD picking out an old, battered hover.

No one noticed them at first, Fink dodging and weaving around the parked hovers until a mechanic slipped out from underneath one, forcing Fink to leap over her.

'Hey,' the woman yelled, her voice carrying over the clank and rattle of tools and equipment.

There were other voices then, shouting 'stop' and 'what are you going here?' Hero's HUD flashed and popped in the corners of her vision, tracking people running to intercept them. She hunkered over Fink's neck and kept her eyes on the hover pulsing red on her screens.

The hover door was already open. She jumped off Fink and climbed inside, heading for the cockpit while Fink squeezed himself into the tiny compartment at the rear.

Hero slipped into the pilot's seat, ignoring the vista of hovers and running bodies on the other side of the canopy, and ran her hands over the flight console.

Nothing happened. The console and the hover remained dark. 'What now?'

The Librarian reappeared in the corner of her vision. 'You must turn the hover on, Hero Regan.' A spot on the console glowed blue.

Hero pressed it. The hover hummed to life, the console lighting up beneath her fingers, the door sliding closed. 'What next?'

'Now, you fly,' the Librarian said, and on the inside of her helmet, other parts of the console lit up.

As soon as Hero touched them, the display on her screens changed, showing the next sequence until her hands were racing over the console. It wasn't until the hover spun and shot forward, pressing her into her seat, that she looked up.

Her eyes went wide and, for a second, her hands stilled on the console. They were flying – *she* was flying, skimming over the tops of hovers, the cavernous hanger speeding away beneath them. Hero gulped. Up ahead the shimmer of an energy barrier played over the bright zipping lights of a busy skylane.

The hover dipped and the sound of grating plasteel brought her attention back to the controls, hands once more flying. They shot out of the hanger before she realised it, straight out into the busy flow of traffic.

Horns blared, lights flashed and the oncoming rush of barges, taxis and maintenance bugs dazzled her eyes. She didn't see the boxy nose of the freight train until it was right in front of them.

They ducked, plummeting, and Hero's hands clutched the seat, before the hover levelled out, threading through the traffic with a mind of its own.

'Librarian.' Hero swallowed, trying to shove the lump that was making her voice high and thready back into her stomach. 'What's happening?'

'Now that you are out of the Bayard AI's territory, I have re-tasked a minor subroutine within the transport AI to pilot the vehicle.'

'Oh.' Her voice squeaked. She cleared her throat. 'Where are we going?'

'To the Grip Core, the centre of the city. From there, you will take an alternative route to your destination.'

'Which is?'

'Patience, Hero Regan.'

CHAPTER 15

The freight elevator was cold and loud. The hiss and clunk of the old tech that shuttled the city's freight from the giant loading docks at its base to its outskirts and all the place in between, deafening.

The freight elevators hadn't been made for people, or companions.

Massive boxes towered over them, rectangular plascrete cubes big enough to house a hover or three and still have room for a maintenance bug in the back. Only their weight and some kind of magnetic charge that buzzed in her ears and made Fink's coat stand on end kept the crates stuck to their palettes. There were no sides, no roof, just the endless darkness of the shaft above, and the patchwork of other palettes, just like the one they stood on, connected in a square the size of a city block.

Hero huddled closer to Fink, folding her body over the front of the saddle and burying her face in the thick fur around his neck. The nanoskin kept her toasty from her fingers to her toes, but was doing nothing for her nose, which felt like a frozen block on her face.

Fink fluffed out his ruff and purred.

'I'm sorry,' she said.

He stopped purring and twisted to look at her from the corner of one eye. She didn't have to touch his mind to read his thoughts, the prick of his ear and the tilt of his whiskers made the question clear.

'For being mean. For not telling you stuff.' She buried her face in his fur. 'It's just… I did something, Fink. Something bad.'

He nuzzled her foot and hummed.

She hugged him tighter. Maybe it was because the meds were still barricading her mind, or maybe because she couldn't stand hiding it from him anymore, whatever it was, the words tumbled out of her mouth. 'I hurt some people when I was kidnapped last year. I thought you were dead, and I was mad, so mad. So I reached into their thoughts and I crushed them.'

Fink stilled.

'The first one, I just wanted her to let me go, but I couldn't make her listen, couldn't make her *do* want I wanted, no matter how hard I pushed. So, I just kept on pushing and pushing and the barrier around her mind, it just kind of went "pop".'

Fink twitched, a tiny jerk like she'd pinched his shoulder.

'Then there was this rush from her mind into mine, and I didn't know what it was so I just pushed it all away, into the back of my brain.'

Hero's breath shuddered out of her nose, her gaze turned inwards, caught in the memory of Demona's back sliding down the wall, her eyes wide, her mouth open in an 'O' of surprise. 'It was an accident, I swear it was. An accident… The first time.'

Fink squeaked and darted sideways, his eyes widening until they were the size of her fist.

A tear slipped down Hero's cheek and she threw herself from the saddle. She was glad of the meds now, glad she couldn't feel what Fink thought of her. It would be worse than Norah, worse than when Fink had been shot, worse than seeing him on the ground with blood pouring out of his chest. Worse than anything.

Hero wrapped her arms around her middle. 'I thought you were *dead*.' The last came out as a strangled yell. 'I was going to get Meren, I was going to make him pay for shooting you, but…' She breathed, the air shuddering down her throat. 'But someone pulled me off him and… and I hurt them instead.'

Fink stared at her, rearing back on his haunches, one forepaw raised and his tail twitching back and forth in sharp little jerks.

There was a strange look on his face, his ears flat and his muzzle wrinkled even as he stared at her with eyes so big she could see the white edges.

She looked away. There was still more to tell and she couldn't bear to look at him while she did. 'The first one,' Hero said as she felt another tear slide down her cheek. 'I can feel her in my thoughts. Not all of her, just her memories and how she felt. It creeps up the back of my brain and smells like mum's fur-roses, and sometimes when it's really bad and I do those things, bad things like attack Mum and Doctor Zass, the world goes blue, like I'm looking out of *her* eyes. It scares me, the things I've felt, the things I've thought.'

Fink just looked at her, his paw still raised, his muzzle still wrinkled.

She hugged herself tighter.

The lift shuddered, stopped and the palette they were on hummed on its maglevs and rose.

'Hero Regan.' The Librarian appeared on her visor. 'Hold on.'

'What?'

'Secure yourself, Hero Regan. The palettes move swiftly.'

The palette hovered and turned in place, joining a string of other palettes doing the same. She looked at Fink – his paw no longer raised and his muzzle no longer crinkled – and then made a mad grab for the nearest crate when the palette shot forward.

Hero fell, arms flailing and hands clawing at the deck. She skidded backwards until she slammed up against a crate and wedged herself in the space between rows. Out the corner of her eye, she saw Fink crouch low, belly flat against the decking and all six legs splayed, his claws scraping the plasteel.

Around them, lights flashed past, streaks of colour too brief to catch hold of. Red, yellow, white, blue, green – just as soon as Hero realised they were moving through a tunnel, they were out again, and she could see up, up, up, into the city above. There was time enough to marvel at the towers and bridges looming over them, the faint lights of hovers and signs pinpricks in the darkness, and then they were gone, replaced by the whomp, whomp, whomp of another tunnel.

Hero shivered and rubbed her arms. Her nose was frozen, and her cheeks ached in the cold rush of air. Fink stayed crouched on the deck, ears flat to his head and his body, from the tip of his nose to the end of his tail, tense. She wondered what he thought, what he felt. Did he hate her? Was he scared or angry or disgusted? Like Norah, would he never want to see her again? What would she do if he did?

Her heart shrivelled in her chest.

There was one way to find out. Tentatively, she pushed against the gooey barrier around her mind. It was thinner than before and it gave, just a little, just enough so that she could reach out and brush the very edges of Fink's mind.

Fink twitched, swivelling to look at her.

Hero shrunk back against the crate and looked away.

It seemed forever before the palette slowed and then stopped. There were clicks and clunks, massive mechanical arms moving overhead, reaching for the crates beside her.

'Hero Regan.' The Librarian was back inside her visor. 'You must exit. Quickly.'

She pushed herself to her feet. 'Okay. Fink—'

'Very quickly.' The Librarian interrupted her. 'The palette will resume moving in eleven seconds. Ten. Nine…'

Hero's eyes widened, and she scrambled out from between the crates, ducking and weaving through the stacks. 'Fink,' she yelled. 'We have to go. Now!'

Fink chortled just before she heard the thump of his paws and felt, more than saw, his large shadow leaping overhead.

'…Six. Five…'

The edge of the palette was just ahead. Her backpack snagged on something and she wrenched it loose, half-stumbling but never losing sight of the clear space ahead.

'…Three. Two…'

Heart pounding in her ears, Hero threw herself the last metre, hitting the cargo dock belly first.

'…One.'

Behind them, the palette shot forwards. Hero watched after it, her eyes wide, but before her heart had time to thump twice, it was gone.

'Well done, Hero Regan. Brace yourself.'

'What?'

'Brace—' the cargo dock shuddered once and plummeted, '—yourself.'

She screamed, just once, wind rushing past her ears as she scrambled for purchase, her stomach going out from underneath her and her feet lifting into the air. Her fingers found the edge of the crate and she held on, knuckles turning white and her jaw clenched. When she had a good grip, she looked around for Fink.

He was right behind her, crouched against the deck just like he had been on the palette, only this time he reached towards her, gripping her calf with his forepaw and tugging, once, twice, the message clear.

Hero let go of the crate and Fink yanked her towards him and into the safety of his embrace.

The cargo dock slowed, coming to rest in a cavernous junction, pausing only a moment before it zoomed off in another direction. There was another junction after that, and another and another, the distance between each growing shorter and shorter until the dock stopped altogether.

For several long moments, neither Hero nor Fink moved.

Hero's breath shuddered out of her lungs. 'Librarian?'

The AI appeared on her visor. 'Yes, Hero Regan?'

'Can we get off now?'

'You can.'

'Okay.' She swallowed. 'How much time do we have?'

'Several minutes.'

'Oh.' Hero swallowed again. 'Good. Fink, let me up.'

Slowly, his muscles tense, Fink rose.

She got to her feet, knees shaky, but her heart no longer pounding so hard she could feel it behind her ears, and stumbled towards what looked like an exit. 'Come on,' she said, one hand tugging on Fink's ruff. 'Let's get off this thing.'

They left the dock behind, another cavernous space opening up before them. Dim yellow lights barely illuminated the corners and the darker shadows of archways cut into walls. A cloud of dust puffed under her boots, creeping up her nose and getting in her eyes.

She sneezed. 'Librarian, where are we?'

'Distribution hub IC879. Currently inoperative. It is the closet unmonitored transport hub to our destination.'

Fink prowled ahead, ears pricked and hackles half-raised, eyes locked on the archway directly across from them. He growled.

A prickle ran up Hero's spine. Tapping the side of her helmet and narrowing her gaze, she peered into the darkness. Her visor flickered, and the darkness was no longer an impenetrable black wall. Instead, picked out in green and black, she saw the unmistakable curved shells and long, pointy feet of roaches.

She froze and then leapt for Fink's back, pulling herself into the saddle and slapping the harness across her legs.

'Librarian, tell me we don't have to go past the roaches.'

'I cannot do that, Hero Regan. The maintenance bots in this sector have not functioned for three years, two months and fifteen days. Monitoring suggests that it is a favoured roach breeding ground.'

'I thought you were taking us some place safe.'

'Safe from those searching for you, yes,' the Librarian said. Inside her helmet, a map replaced its avatar, a yellow line racing away from the blue dot pulsing at its centre. 'Follow this path, do not deviate. It is the safest route to your destination.'

'What about the roaches?'

'You and your companion have proven yourselves capable of dealing with this particular hazard on multiple occasions.'

'And if we deviate from the path?'

'Your passage will be recorded by the city AI. It will then only be a matter of time before the police and Bayard search parties locate you.'

'Great,' she said, her brow furrowed and her mouth hard. 'I don't suppose you packed any goodies that would help us get through?'

'None that will assist in this situation.'

Fink growled, shifting his attention from the archway ahead to another on the side. Hero's attention snapped to the new archway and the antenna waving in the darkness.

She clenched her hands in Fink's ruff. 'Looks like we're doing this the old-fashioned way, you ready?'

He snarled.

'That's what I thought.' She touched her heels to his sides.

He leapt forward.

They pounded towards the first archway. One bound, two. On her visor, the roaches skittered forwards, their antenna moving in short jerks and mandibles clicking in… was that excitement or fear? She gathered herself for Fink to jump over them, but he kept charging forwards, closer and closer until she thought he was going to plough straight through. Then he snarled, a long, vicious sound that curdled the blood in her veins.

The roaches scattered.

Fink kept moving, the snarl still rumbling in his belly.

Shock held Hero still; she'd never heard him make that sound, it had sounded… it had sounded… she didn't know, but it had crawled up the back of her brain and taken roost in her skull. A bloody lump of rage. If the map hadn't flashed a warning on her visor, she would have missed the first turn, but she came back to herself in time to nudge Fink with her heel. He veered left without missing a beat.

She kept her eyes on the map and the darkness ahead, helmet mapping the way in black and green. Beneath her, Fink ran, his neck stretched out and his paws thumping the cold ground. Left. Left. Right and left again they went, following the map.

They saw roaches, lots and lots of roaches. Some no longer than her forearm, others as large as Fink and one – its massive shell glowing a faint, pearlescent blue – the size of a small hover, and all of them skittered out of their way.

Hero clutched her hands in Fink's ruff and concentrated on the map, giving Fink directions with small touches of her heels. The meds were still a barrier around her mind, thin but there, and she wished they weren't, wished she could peek into Fink's mind and find out what he was doing to make the roaches scatter.

They dashed over one last skybridge, lit only by dim yellow strip lights that winked out as soon as they passed, and found themselves in a tiny square. Hardly more than a foyer, a fountain at its centre, dusty and dry, a single door half-hidden in the shadows.

Silently, it swung open. 'Enter, Hero Regan.'

There was an entranceway and another door, which swung open as soundlessly as the first, lights glowing at their approach. Slipping off Fink's back, Hero went through first. It didn't look like anyone had lived here for a long time, the dust tickling her nose, the air stale.

The main room was empty, which was just as well since Fink had to wrap his tail close before the front door would shut.

'Librarian, why'd you bring us here?'

'You did not wish to be located by the authorities.'

'Yes, but why *here*?'

The Librarian's avatar flickered on her visor, and for a moment Hero thought it wasn't going to answer. 'Paris Regan found it convenient.'

Her uncle. Her crazy, *dead* uncle. 'But… why? When?'

Before she could finish the questions, the Librarian winked out, along with the lights.

'Librarian?' Her helmet glowed a cool, steady blue, casting just enough light to see Fink without switching the visor to infrared. 'Librarian?' Hero tried again, this time bringing up the prime-net, or at least, trying to. Not so much as static fizzed across the visor. She frowned; the prime-net never went down, it just… didn't.

Fink coughed, his head cocked and his ears pricked forwards.

'It must be a blue-out,' she said to him. 'A bad one, if the prime-net's down.'

Fink harrumphed.

For a moment, neither of them said anything, then he shook his foreshoulders and twisted to nudge the saddle with his nose before looking meaningfully at her.

She stared at him.

He coughed and shook his foreshoulders again, making the saddle and attached bags bounce.

The bags came off easily, then the saddle, and Fink curled up in the middle of the main room, the end of his tail over his nose.

Hero watched him before retiring to the bedroom and curling up on the bare mattress. Alone.

CHAPTER 16

It was hours before the power came back on. Hours in which she paced the three-room… whatever, the place was. There was a bed in one room, built into a wall of cupboards and shelves, and a tiny bathroom in another so she supposed that it had once been a house if something that was a third the size of her bedroom could actually be called that.

Maybe her uncle had; maybe he'd paced the same path she had, although she doubted he'd had to skirt a six-hundred kilo ruc-pard sprawled in the middle of the… living area? Closet? Butler's pantry perhaps? Whatever, it didn't matter. What did matter was what her uncle had done here, and what things he had left behind that she needed now. There was nothing here except dust, a thick, dense layer of it over everything. She'd run her hands over one wall and found the telltale indentations of panels that she was sure hid something important, like a fridge, but without power she didn't have a way to find out.

Instead, she sat on the bed and watched the end of Fink's tail flick from side to side in little, jerky movements and tried not to wonder what he was thinking. Except the harder she tried not to think about it, the harder it was to actually do. Did Fink hate her? She didn't want him to hate her, but she couldn't help but remember the expression on his face when she'd told him about the other mind she'd crushed, and how she'd *meant* to do it.

Hero shuddered and drew her knees up to her chest.

At some point, the meds wore off. She wasn't sure when; she'd been too wrapped up in her thoughts, so busy worrying what Fink thought of her that she didn't realise when he was *in* her thoughts. The scent of mawberries wound through her brain so slowly, gently stalking her fears and wrapping them in warmth.

'You don't hate me?' she asked his tail, now still, the only part of him she could see through the doorframe.

Fink chuffed.

She uncurled her legs. 'Are you sure?'

He growled in annoyance. There was a huff from the other side of the wall and Fink's tail disappeared from the doorway, only to be replaced by his head and then his shoulders before he stuck his nose in her face. He growled a second time and Hero shrank back a little, but not before his tongue shot out, leaving a warm line of slobber from her jawbone to her forehead.

'Ugh! Fiiiink!' Frantically, she wiped her face with her sleeve before the fish scent could seep into her skin.

He pruckled and flopped to the floor, his head in her lap. *He was sure.* He yawned. *He was hungry.*

'You're always hungry.'

He licked her chin, even as his stomach growled. *They should eat.*

'I looked already. There's nothing to eat. Apparently Uncle Paris lived on air.'

She hadn't looked in the saddlebags.

'You stuck your nose in there already, didn't you?'

His stomach growled again, louder this time. *Hungry*, he thought at her, projecting the churning of his gut along with the word.

Her stomach rumbled in sympathy. 'Ugh, fine.' She grimaced and pushed Fink's head off her lap, climbing over his rump to get to the living room.

The saddlebags were a dark lump in the corner. What had the Librarian stashed in them? Hero plonked her butt on the dusty floor and pulled the first bag into her lap. Clothes, like the ones she was wearing, still in their neat little vacpaks, and a med-kit, bigger than she'd ever seen. What was the Librarian expecting them to do?

A whuff against the back of her neck made her jump. *Hungry,* Fink thought at her.

She snapped the med-kit closed. 'I'm working on it.'

There was a puff of dust behind her, Fink flopping onto his belly. *Work harder.*

Hero growled and reached for another bag. 'Just because you can't undo the seals…' she muttered.

A large, dexterous forepaw reached around Hero and gently popped the vacuum seal holding the bag closed.

Hero gasped. 'They're 'pard-friendly?' She punched him in the shoulder. 'You could have got your own food.'

She owed him, he thought back. *For keeping secrets.*

Hero's shoulder hunched. 'I'm—'

'Hero Regan.' The Librarian appeared on her visor a split-second before the lights flickered on, and Hero almost jumped out of her skin. 'We must hurry.'

Her heart pounded hard a few more times while, behind her, Fink had half-shot to his feet, his fore and midquarters off the ground. She swallowed. 'Why? I thought you said this place was safe.'

'It is no longer.' The Librarian didn't frown but Hero imagined she heard it in its voice.

'Is there a time limit on this?'

'Yes.'

A countdown appeared on her visor. 'Five minutes,' she read aloud.

'It should be sufficient.'

'It's better than five seconds,' she said.

Fink grunted. *He was still hungry.*

'Fink's hungry. Is there any food here?'

A wall panel slid aside, revealing several small shelves of vac-wrapped food. Fink rumbled in pleasure. He had a cube of what looked like cake in his forepaws and was using his teeth to tear it open in the next heartbeat.

Fink was reaching for a second vac-pak, the only evidence of the cake were the crumbs littered at his feet, when Hero threw the saddle on his back. The saddle bags followed, the seals popping into place, and by the time Hero had shrugged the last bag onto her back, there was a barely a minute left on the timer.

She grabbed the last food pack and headed for the door. 'Where to?'

A new map appeared on her visor. 'You will need to move swiftly. The blue-out has led to an increase in activity throughout the sector.'

They were out the door and back in the tiny square with its dusty fountain in moments, Hero swinging into Fink's saddle. For a short time, they wove back the way they'd come before heading down and down again. They were slinking across a dark garden, the trees and shrubs little more than sticks and dead twigs, when she saw the dark blob hanging from the skybridge above.

Hero narrowed her eyes, and the visor zoomed in. At first she couldn't tell what it was, all she saw was black crumpled plasteel and the hole it had punched in the bridge. Figures moved around it, a horde of tiny people in the bright reds and yellows of emergency services. They were pulling something out of the blob, something long and straight.

The visor zoomed in further, and that was when she saw the faces.

Hero pulled back. People, she realised. They were pulling *people* out of the blob, but then, that must make it… The visor refocused and now she made out the stubby wings and the maglevs.

She felt the blood drain from her face. 'That's a hover,' she said.

The Librarian hovered on her visor but didn't say anything.

'It was the blue-out. The blue-out made it crash, didn't it?'

'Indirectly. The blue-out incapacitated the mag-lev system for five-point-seven-three seconds. Currently, there are two hundred and eighty-three confirmed fatalities. Correction, there are now two hundred and eighty-nine. Several more wrecks have been located.'

'But—' All the people who'd been out there looking for her. Her heart squeezed. Had her mum—? Without thinking, Hero comm'd her mum, her heart crawling up her throat with every nanosecond it went unanswered, her stomach churning and twirling.

Tybalt's face appeared on her visor, blood trickling from his brow and the lines around his eyes furrowed with concern. Smoke, thick and black, obscured the figures silhouetted against the red glow behind him. 'Hero? Where are you—'

The comm cut out.

'Is there another blue-out? Why did the comms go down?'

'Because I cut them, Hero Regan.' The Librarian took Tybalt's place on her visor. 'It is imperative that no one know of your location or your mission.'

'But my mum—'

'Patricia Regan has been accounted for, as has your father and Norah Joshi. There is no further need to delay. Please resume the assigned course.'

'But—'

'You must continue, Hero Regan. The mission I have assigned to you is integral to the continued stability of the city. Without your intervention, the blue-outs will only lead to a greater loss of life.'

CHAPTER 17

They moved in silence. The image of the bodies being carried out of the hover was stuck in Hero's mind, the memory overlaid first with Tybalt's face and then her mum's. What if it had been one of them in that hover? What if they'd been killed, and it was all her fault? What if —?

Fink coughed. *Roaches*, he thought to her, *and the glowing purple thing.* A mawberry-tinted image of Phara replaced the bodies in Hero's mind.

Where?

Fink's mind stretched ahead of them and Hero followed, matching her thoughts to his and reaching for the dark purple shadow that was Phara. Next to her, a dark orange-brown smudge marked Timon's mind and around them…

Hero jerked back, the clink and chitter of the roach swarm crawling over her skin. 'They're surrounded.'

The words hadn't left Hero's lips before Fink leapt forwards. She held tight as Fink skidded around a corner and down a corridor lined with tall doors.

'Hero Regan.' The Librarian appeared front and centre on her visor. 'You are going the wrong way.'

They burst out of the corridor and into a bell-shaped arcade.

It was a replay of the street race, except well-lit and, well, worse. Phara was backed against the rounded end of the arcade, rump against a shopfront; Timon was at her side, a stun-stick in his hand.

A host of roaches skittered around them, knee-high to Timon's long legs. Their curved shells gleamed and their pointy serrated mandibles chittered as they weaved and danced in front of Timon and his 'mare.

Fink charged the roaches, bouncing across their backs to place himself between Timon and the swarm while Hero was still taking in the scene. He shook his back and nudged her mind, and Hero vaulted out of the saddle.

Timon sidled up to her. 'Dude, I am glad to see you.'

'You are?' Hero didn't take her eyes off the swarm. She wished she had her drones or a shock-bomb or a slip-field or anything that could help, but all she had was her bracer and helmet, neither of which would do much good against one, let alone a swarm. 'I thought you didn't like me?'

'I don't like your *drones*, although right now, I think I might like them a lot more—'

The swarm pounced. Fink rushed to meet it. Ears lost in his ruff, lips pulled back from his teeth, he growled and snapped and swiped, sending first one and then another roach flying. The insects skidded across the arcade, crashing into their swarm mates, leaving a trail of upturned legs in their wakes, before popping back to their feet and rushing back in.

Movement caught Hero's eye, a shadow behind the main swarm.

The thing that stepped out of the corridor was big, a mountain click-clacking towards them in the darkness. Its antenna emerged first, wispy-thin and then thicker and thicker until they were the size of her two wrists, giant poles with serrated undersides that seemed to go on forever. Then its shell came into the light. Black and knobbly, it caught the light only to let it out again in waves of blue and green and purple. The colours zipped and zagged, moving and morphing, sucking her in, first ripples and then diamonds and swirls and—

Pain, sharp and hot, flared through her wrist and up her forearm. She gasped and looked down. Timon's hand engulfed her wrist, his knuckles white.

'Don't look at its shell,' he whispered next to her ear, his breath brushing her cheek. 'Tell your 'pard. It's how they distract their prey.'

Distract their prey… She frowned, not sure what he meant until something soft and light brushed against her thigh. Hero jerked back, heart pounding hard as the roach at her feet chittered and skittered forwards. She kicked it away, even as Timon pulled her backwards.

'Fink,' she said, as much with her mind as her voice, Timon's hold on her wrist making her stumble. 'Fink!'

The 'pard didn't move, his eyes fixed on the mountain-sized roach, barely even twitching at the roaches swarming around his paws, their antenna poking his neck, their feet pricking at his legs, their shells brushing his belly.

Fink, she yelled again, reaching into his mind, only to slam into glass. Cold and hard, the barrier danced with shifting patterns, except instead of the blue, green and purple of the roach's shell, they sparkled blue and silver and felt different. Earthy and cold, whereas the roaches were sharp and metallic, it left the tang of iron on her tongue, and behind it… Behind it was something *alien,* something that tingled against her mind with long, pointy fingers, something that was keeping her from Fink.

The smooth, brown shell of a roach appeared over Fink's shoulder, its mandibles click-clacking as it climbed on his back.

Her chest clenched, hard and hot. *Fink!* She bashed against the barrier. It didn't even shudder.

Another roach crawled onto Fink's back.

'*Do* something,' Timon said, even as he yanked her backwards, out of the reach of the antenna wagging at their legs.

She didn't tell him she was, that would have taken time, too much time. The scent of roses tugged at her brain. She knew what she had to do.

Hero reached into her gut, wrapping her mind around the hot, acidic fear eating at her stomach and squeezing – tight, tight, tight – before she threw it. Hard.

The barrier shuddered, just once, and the mental wrecking ball she'd thrown at it hurtled back at her. Pain bloomed, a shard of ice between her eyes that drove all the way through her brain and out the back of her head. She slapped her hands to her forehead, as if that would keep her brain in, and thought she might have staggered, that Timon might have caught her, but all she could be sure of was the pain freezing her vocal cords and making her knees weak.

It swallowed her mind, every thought making the shard of ice in her brain splinter, the tiny slivers of bone-numbing cold digging deeper and deeper. But she had to think, she *had* to. Fink, she had to get to Fink.

Somewhere, outside of the flesh-peeling chill that consumed her, Hero heard Timon swear and Phara's high-pitched battle cry.

Purple shadows danced and flashed on the other side of her eyelids, followed by the crunch of hooves on shells and the flsssh-zzt of a stun-stick, but Hero ignored it all. Instead, she gritted her teeth and reached for Fink.

The shard of ice cracked, more slivers driving into her brain. She cried out, her knees hitting the ground – another, smaller pain – and a warm trickle of something coppery leaked from her nose, but her mind brushed the edge of Fink's. The barrier was still there, blue-silver and sparkly. She gathered to throw herself against it once more, pulling against the ice when the barrier *turned*.

It moved like liquid, twisting and pulling. There was a brief moment, a nanosecond when she saw it as it was. Not a roach, but something riding it, seeing through its eyes, listening through its ears. Controlling it. It surrounded her, wrapping her in blue-silver and the scent of earth, before sending cold, tingly fingers into her brain.

Hero froze. It hurt, Old Terra, it hurt more than her mental wrecking ball slamming back into her brain. The fingers dove deeper, freezing and slicing as they went, making memories flash before her eyes as they touched each one in turn – Tybalt in a bath of nanomeds, swaddled in bandages; pancakes splattered across the floor; Norah pointing at the door and telling her to get out. The fingers reached deeper still, crawling into the deepest, darkest place in her brain and nudging open the door. The scent of fur-roses crept up Hero's nose, spicy and sweet, blooming on her tongue and the space behind her eyelids was soaked in blue.

Hero's chest burned, fire spreading out from her heart, boiling in her gut, eating her from the inside out until it burned its way up her throat and out her mouth. Her lips peeled back from her teeth.

The fingers in her brain paused.

She pounced, swallowing the fingers in Demona's rage, feeling it pull back the barrier around the not-roach's thoughts until she could ride them all the way back to the creature's mind.

Recognition. Surprise. The emotions hit her one after the other, coloured in the silver-blue of the not-roach's mind, carried on a jumble of images – strange fragments of memory that felt not just old, but ancient. The creature knew what she was, but hadn't expected to come across another like her...

A memory slipped from its mind to hers, the image of her uncle with a short supple creature standing on flippered feet beside him, its double set of fin-like arms folded neatly at its side. The swatai from Woolsey's journal.

Pain lanced through Hero's thoughts, the not-roach's fingers tightening in her brain. Without thinking, she thrust a mental knife between its eyes.

The creature recoiled, fingers yanked from her brain fast enough to make her gasp.

Sounds came back to her first. The phfst-stak of a stun-stick, the piercing whinny of a toa-mare's battle cry and the thick, wet crack of a roach being torn to pieces.

There was one pinned under Fink's midpaws, his teeth and foreclaws deep in its belly while Phara danced around him, her head up and her eyes wild, scattering roaches with every sweep of her tail and lightning flash of hooves.

Timon stood in front of Hero, jabbing left and right with his stun-stick, its orange glow leaving afterimages in her vision. The few roaches who made it past Phara skittered out of his reach, only to be caught in the next sweep of the 'mare's tail.

Slowly, their feet snick-snicking on the plascrete, the roaches retreated. The biggest ones first, and then the smaller ones, their inky black eyes never leaving the two humans and their companions until even their antenna were swallowed by the darkness. All of them, except the giant roach-that-wasn't. The patterns on its shell moved slowly now, dark blues and purples barely distinguishable from the shadows.

She couldn't see its eyes, but she felt it staring at her, the weight of the alien mind on the other side, cold and sparkling. Considering.

Hero growled at it, the sound rumbling out of her throat and bouncing off the walls.

The not-roach vanished.

The rose scent vanished with it, sucked back into the space at the back of her brain. She was empty, numb, her bones warm goo.

Her knees hit the ground.

'Hero?' Timon crouched in front of her, hands on her shoulders, trying to push her up even as she slumped forwards. 'Man, are you all right?' He shook his head. 'Never mind, we gotta go.' Timon swung one of her arms over his shoulder and hauled them both upright. 'Crap, you're not as light as you look.' There was a wince in his voice when he spoke to Fink. 'Give a guy a hand, will ya? She's your human.'

Fink rumbled. The next thing she knew he was crouched on his belly and Timon was swinging her leg over the 'pard's back, slapping the vacuum seals into place.

Hero slumped over Fink's neck, one side of her face half-buried in his ruff. Thick, warm and just a bit scratchy, it tickled her nose and a few loose hairs caught in her mouth, but she didn't care. He was Fink, his fur smelling of dust and his presence a fluffy pink cushion in her mind.

Old Terra, her brain hurt. The icy fingers might not have been slicing up her mind any longer, but where they had she burned as though her grey-matter was going to turn liquid and drip right out of her ear. She wondered what that would look like: a river spilling over Fink's shoulder or, when Timon lifted her off Fink's back, would he find a lumpy grey pile of flesh under her ear?

Fink snorted, and it was only when he stopped and twisted around to nudge her foot that she realised his presence wasn't just surrounding her mind, it was in it too.

Her brain wasn't going to melt, he thought at her.

'How do you know?'

Because he did. But there was another thought behind that one, a tiny thread of fear that glowed a bright, poisonous green half-hidden by the bright pink of Fink's certainty.

Hero frowned and started to reach for it, and *heard* her brain tear – a wet, heavy shrrrr-it – a split-second before her thoughts turned to fire and acid, trying to eat their way out the other side of her head. She gasped, a strangled inhalation of air, and her vision flooded with stars.

'Hey.' A hand clasped her shoulder, shook it. 'Hey, Hero? Dude, can you hear me? Are you all right?'

Hero didn't say anything, couldn't say anything. Pain and heat were flooding her thoughts and she couldn't remember if her last breath had been in or out.

She thought she heard Fink rumble something.

'Look, dude, Fink. I don't speak 'pard, okay, so you know, whatever you're trying to tell me—'

Silence. Distantly, she felt Fink's mind stretch towards Timon's.

'Oh. Wow, yeah, okay, that was... Dude, the whole silent communication thing is— Err, right. Well, if you just show me— You mean her bracer? Well, dude, why didn't you just say—'

In – her last breath had been in. She squeezed her lungs, felt the air rush out, and blinked when her vision began to clear.

Timon was at her side, Phara glowing purple behind him, rolling his eyes even as he reached for her forearm. 'You know,' he said, and she knew, from the twist of his lips and the distracted look in his eye, that he was talking to Fink. 'I get why you two get along so well. You're both really annoying.'

'At least, he's not a glowy roach-magnet.'

Timon's gaze flew to Hero's, his brown eyes wide and his black brows high on his brow. 'Hey. Are you all right? How d'you feel?' His forehead scrunched up and his eyes crossed, and Hero felt the flutter of Fink's mind reaching for Timon's.

'Okay, okay,' Timon said, lifting her forearm and showing it to Fink. 'I'm calling—'

'Hero Regan.'

'Holy frackin...' Timon leapt backwards, his dark complexion losing some of its colour, his gaze fixed on the head floating above Hero's arm. 'What's the Librarian doin' on your bracer?'

She tried to lift herself up, but everything hurt and she couldn't connect the muscles in her arm to her brain. Fink reached out, thoughts brushing past hers to touch Timon.

The boy's eyes crossed before they snapped straight and he rolled them. 'Yeah, I got this part, man.' Timon waved a hand at Fink, his eyes on the Librarian. 'Look, Hero doesn't look so good, so we need an ambulance or a hospital or something.'

'A moment please, Timon Dane.' The Librarian flickered above her wrist. 'Transport has been arranged. Timon Dane, please follow the instructions on your wrist unit.'

Fink heaved to his feet, Timon swung back up on Phara and they were off, the smooth, gliding rhythm of Fink's gait lulling Hero's eyes closed.

The clip-clop of Phara's hooves and the snick of Fink's claws was soon swallowed by the rush of the wind and the whomp-whomp of another freight elevator. It was dark then, even behind her closed lids, but eventually the darkness grew brighter. Hero cracked her eyes open just enough to glimpse the crosshatch of traffic darting above and the endless thrust of skytowers. They dived through another dark tunnel.

The next time she opened her eyes, it was to see bright open sky and the city disappearing behind them as they headed into the 'burbs.

CHAPTER 18

It was the sound of arguing that woke her, drawing her out of the dream where every time she looked up from the console with its strange carvings, Demona's green hair and eyes reflected on the surface above.

'…needs a doctor!' The words pierced her skull and for a second she thought it was Tybalt, but his voice was too high and the person who answered should have had her mum's cold, tight voice. Instead… the flat, emotionless sound of the Librarian was hard to mistake.

'Timon Dane, rest assured that Hero Regan's good health continues to be a high priority.'

'You keep saying that but she's still here, in an abandoned house on the edge of fartsville and whiter than a polar rucnart in a pile of snow! How is that a high priority?'

Hero twisted away from the sound, burying her face in a warm cushion of fur and wishing her head wouldn't throb so hard.

Something cold and wet nuzzled her cheek, sending a chill, mawberry-coloured wave through her skull. It tingled under her skin, loosening the dream held tight on the edges of her mind and easing the hot throb gripping her brain. Hero sighed and wrapped her arms around Fink's foreleg, letting the tha-tha-thump-thump of his hearts drown the argument and lull her back to sleep.

He rumbled, the sound vibrating through her ear to her jaw. *She should wake up now,* he said.

She frowned, the scrunching of her forehead summoning a wave of pain. *Just a little longer.*

No, Fink said. *Now.*

'Dude.' Timon's voice ricocheted through Hero's brain and she opened her eyes just enough to see him glaring at Fink. 'I thought, like, her safety was your top priority or something.' Silence greeted the statement, with Fink matching Timon stare for stare, before the boy turned back to the Librarian. 'At least let me call someone.' More silence, and through the pain spearing her brain, Hero could imagine Timon's face turning red. 'Dudes, you can't do this. She needs a doctor!'

She forced her eyes open. 'I'm okay.'

Timon jumped, just a little, and he stared at her for a second before his mouth snapped closed and he crouched in front of her. 'There's a trail of dried blood coming out of your nose and a whole patch more of it on Fink's neck,' he said, his voice soft. 'That might not be so bad, except that you collapsed for no apparent reason and have been unconscious for...' He shoved his sleeve up and twisted his wrist to glance at the screen glowing in the hollow of his palm. 'Eighteen hours, fifty-seven minutes and three seconds. So no, you are not okay.'

She blinked and pushed herself upright. 'You've been counting?'

'Yeah,' he said, his brows coming down over his eyes. 'I have, because if you die, I'm telling your parents that it's not my fault, and that I spent eighteen hours, fifty-seven minutes and—' he glanced at his palm-unit again ' —eighteen seconds trying to convince these guys to take you to a doctor.' The last came with a glare, directed first at Fink before he turned his head towards the Librarian.

Hero took a deep breath. 'They can't,' she said.

Timon's head snapped back so fast it was a wonder it didn't detach. Incredulity lit up his eyes and slackened his jaw for a second time.

Hero stretched her mind towards Timon's, ignoring the squishy burning sensation – like lava poured over her brain. She had to know what he was thinking, but before she touched his thoughts, Fink slapped her back.

No, he said.

Timon pushed himself to his feet, hands slapping his knees. 'I don't believe this.' He paced away, boots raising puffs of dust that sparkled in the light sneaking through the windows, before he spun around. 'You were *bleeding* from your *nose* while you were *unconscious*. That usually means there's something wrong with your head, where your *brain* lives, which is, you know, important!'

'We ran away.'

Timon opened his mouth, closed it. 'So?'

'We ran away from a *lab*.'

'Ugh…'

Hero took a deep breath. 'Where they were studying my brain.'

'Umm…'

'Because I'm telepathic.'

'Riiiight…'

'And I did something… bad.'

'Okay.' Timon crossed his arms, one finger tapping his chin. 'Is that "bad" kind of like how your drones were "safe" but still blew up a wall and disrupted power to an entire sector?'

For a second she didn't answer. 'Yes.'

'Dude, you're nuts.'

It was Hero's turn to stare. 'What?'

'There's no such thing as telepathy.'

'Fink's telepathic.'

'Yeah, but he's a Woolsey.'

'So am I!'

'No, you're human, descended from the Terran ape. Although you *could* be descended from Woolsey herself – you're certainly crazy enough to fit the bill.'

'I'm. Not. Crazy.'

Timon spread his hands. 'Dude, you just told me you escaped from a lab where "they" – I'm assuming mad scientists – were studying your brain because you're telepathic and you did something "bad".' He drew the last word out, fingers hooked into air quotes on either side of his head.

Hero's back teeth clamped together and she couldn't help the growl the rose in her throat. 'I. Did,' she said.

'Don't get me wrong, I've seen your work and I'm totally not disputing the bad bit. Just the bit about the lab and the telepathy.'

'But it's true!'

Timon rolled his eyes. 'Yeah, just like that one about the secret alien outpost and the giant sea monsters that suck your brains out.'

'Why won't you believe me?' Hero said, ignoring the ache as she reached for the boy's mind.

'Because—'

Fink growled and snapped, slapping at the mental tendril she'd extended towards Timon. *Enough*, Fink's thought rang in Hero's mind and from the way Timon blinked, it rang in his too.

Timon shook his head. 'Hey,' he said, pointing a finger at Hero. 'She started it.'

Fink pulled his lips back from his teeth, his fangs a stark white against the pale pink of his gums.

'Dude.' Timon stepped back, his hands palm out.

Fink twisted, his big black nose nudging Hero's thigh. *They had to go.*

'Where?' she asked aloud.

'You know,' Timon said. 'If you guys are going to do the whole silent communication thing, the least you can do is include me too.'

Fink ignored him and filled her mind with an image of a sleek white metal bug, with swept-back wings that bent and twisted on the pilot's command and a plasteel dome that reflected the deep blue of the sky.

'A shuttle?' She frowned at him. 'You want us to go ground side?'

'Hero Regan.' The Librarian broke in. Hero had to squint against the shaft of sunlight spearing her head. 'Such an action is not yet wise.'

'Yeah,' Timon said. 'You can count me out of that one too.'

Hero glared at him. 'You weren't invited.'

Timon's dark brows lowered until they touched in the middle, and his brown eyes turned hard. 'You know, you're kind of a b—'

Fink coughed, a low hard sound that made his ribs bounce against Hero's back. He must have said something to Timon because the boy opened his mouth and closed it twice before he crossed his arms.

'Fine.' Timon pointed a finger at Hero but kept his gaze on Fink. 'But that doesn't make her any less of a—'

This time, the sound that came from Fink's throat was more bark than cough.

Timon rolled his eyes. 'Whatever. Come on, Phara, let's go find something to eat.'

Fink's stomach rumbled a second before Hero's. 'Get us something too?' she called after Timon's retreating back.

'No,' he said and closed the door behind him with a solid thunk.

'What'd you say to him?' Hero asked, watching Timon's silhouette through the frosted plasglas.

Fink huffed, his muzzle scrunched and the skin under his eyes tense before he shook his head. *Nothing. It didn't matter.* He nudged her shoulder and popped the image of the sleek white shuttle into her mind, accompanying it with the memory of the roach-that-wasn't – its shell rippling with iridescent patterns – and a sense of urgency that danced and jangled in Hero's gut.

She pushed herself to her knees, sitting back on her heels. 'What's going groundside got to do with the…' She waved a hand around as if she could stir the right word out of the air. 'The… not-roach?'

It just did. An old memory, made hazy and patchy by time, coloured the thought.

Hero tried to grab it, but it evaporated at her touch. She scowled. 'That's not helpful.'

He huffed and heaved himself upright, peeling forequarters, mid and then hindquarters off the cold floor.

'Hero Regan.' The Librarian projected itself outwards from the wall, a white torso hovering a hands-breadth above the floor, pinning her with eyes that shone electric blue. 'I must insist that you complete the next part of your mission.'

'You know, you haven't told me much about what it is I'm actually supposed to be doing.'

'I have told you, it is to save the city.'

'But from what and why me?'

'Because you will do what I say, Hero Regan, while the threat of your past action looms. In addition, your current situation is less than desirable. You are a delinquent teenager who has stolen a hover, caused several collisions and violently assaulted two of her mother's employees. The police have recently opened a file on you.'

A screen opened next to the Librarian's shoulder, and Hero stared at the holo of herself, glaring out at the world from under dark brows, hair a dark shadow over her skull and her mouth twisted into a sneer.

Fink popped his head over her shoulder and huffed. *He didn't like that picture.*

She didn't like it either; the holo made her look... scary.

'There is more,' the Librarian said, and a second screen materialised beside the first.

It was a holo of Fink, a rotating series of images – front, side – bracketed by a snarling close-up and underscored by giant red letters. *Extremely dangerous. Do not approach. Warrant issued.*

Her fingers convulsed in Fink's ruff and her brain just... shrivelled.

Fink poked at his image, his nose disrupting the holo in a shower of static. *What was that?*

Hero didn't answer. Instead, she listened to her heart thump in her ears, sending all the blood from her head straight to her toes. She turned to the Librarian. 'Make it go away.'

'I cannot.'

'Now!' The scream burned in her throat.

Fink stared at her, ears flat, eyes wide, whiskers twitching.

The door slammed open. 'What is it?' Timon stood with his hands braced on the doorframe. 'What happened?'

'Fix it,' Hero said, her eyes locked on the Librarian.

'Fix what?' Timon pushed into the room, coming to stand at Hero's side. She knew the moment he saw the warrant because she felt him stiffen. 'Shi—'

'Hero Regan, I cannot,' the Librarian said. 'I do not have direct access to the Farm's network, without which the warrant cannot be cancelled without authorisation.'

Fink nudged her shoulder. *What was wrong?*

She shook her head, the words stuck in her brain.

'A kill warrant. If Farm Control catches Fink…' Timon left the rest of the thought unsaid. 'That bad thing you did, did he do it too?'

'No.'

'Okay then.' Timon turned to the Librarian. 'Find us a shuttle.'

A map immediately replaced the kill warrant, a line snaking its way from their position through another three 'burbs to a glowing red dot in the midst of the suburbs.

Hero shook her head, reaching for the screen. 'No, I need to get into the Farm's network, erase the order.'

Timon pushed her hands away. 'Later. First, we get Fink somewhere safe. The moment he gets spotted Farm Control will be everywhere.'

'We can hide in the Tunnels, we don't need a shuttle.'

'They'll look for you there, plus, the Tunnels are crawling with roaches.' Timon took a deep breath, an expression on his face like he was about to say something she didn't like. 'We gotta go groundside.'

Hero blinked. 'What?'

Timon grimaced. 'Just for a bit. We stash Fink at one of the abandoned biodomes, where no one will look for him. Then you come back and deal with the warrant. Maybe get it downgraded or suspended or something?' He cocked his head like he was expecting some kind of response, except Hero had stopped listening at the word 'biodome'.

Her eyes locked on the bags attached to the back of Fink's saddle, picturing the food and med-kit stashed inside, even as she flexed her toes in the heavy boots and felt the nanoskin usually worn by groundside personnel.

The Librarian had planned this, maybe not the kill order or the fight with the not-roach, but the rest of it…

She was a Jørgen, a human Woolsey, and the same genes that made her telepathic also made her immune to the Pollen. Just like Fink, she had nothing to fear on the surface.

'Let's go,' she said.

CHAPTER 19

They clung to the freight train, hunkered between containers big enough to swallow a barge and still have room for a hover or two.

Hero crouched with her back against Fink's chest, arms caught around her knees, the *zhhmmm* of the train and roar of the wind filling her ears. Overhead, the giant steelcrete ribs of another tunnel whipped by, adding a steady whomp-whomp-whomp to the noise, while light – brilliant red, white and yellow – left streaks in her eyes.

The scent of roses filled her nose, and tiny slivers of pain pierced her palms where her nails dug into flesh. Trainer Ella stood in her mind's eye, flanked by Farm flunkies, and then again on the training floor, trying to send Fink to the Farm.

Hero clenched her teeth and growled, the sound lost in the rush of the train. *Never,* she thought, and she was going to make Ella Karimi, companion trainer, pay for trying. Her mind flashed to the kill warrant and her fists tightened.

First through, she had to get Fink to the surface, had to make sure he was safe. They'd find an old outpost; there were a few out there, there had to be, she'd seen them on the holos. Tiny things, little more than hermetically sealed boxes explorers had once used as way stations and resupply posts.

They'd have terminals, though, and power – everything she'd need to jack into the planetary net and make Ella Karimi's life miserable.

Fink nudged her knee, the bright tingly touch of his thoughts slipping through hers. *What if they couldn't find them?*

Hero glared at him. *We can and we will.*

But what if—

We will. *The Librarian will tell us where they are.*

And if it didn't?

It will.

But if it didn't? Fink asked again, the thought firmer, just like the look in his big black eye.

Hero pushed the air out of her lungs in a long, angry rush. She peered down the corridor of massive crates, barely making out Timon's silhouette against Phara's purple glow.

The Librarian wanted them on the surface, *needed* them there. 'It'll tell us,' she whispered. And if it didn't…

Fink grunted and she could feel him readying another push at her mind when the train jolted and the whomp-whomp-whomp of the passing ribs slowed. Her bracer glowed, a pale blue sixty appearing above her wrist. It ticked over.

Fifty-nine. Fifty-eight.

She looked up and in the darkness saw a matching glow above Timon's palm.

The train continued to slow until the roar of the passing wind no longer filled her ears and the lights no longer made blazing streaks of colour.

Fifty-one.

Hero scrambled to her feet, vaulting into Fink's saddle even as he heaved himself to his. Out the corner of her eye, she saw Timon doing the same.

Thirty-eight.

Through the thin corridors between crates came the bright glow of a platform. Fink tensed – muscles coiled, ears straining forward – and Phara danced beneath Timon, her neck arched, her tail snapping back and forth.

Timon's gaze caught hers, and with her visor zooming in on his face, she saw him grin.

Thirty.

The train continued to slow. She caught glimpses of the platform and the massive forklifts and hover sledges waiting to shift the cargo. The train slowed further, the roar of the wind had died to a gentle breeze when a sharp clank came from overhead. Yellow beams slid and clanked into place on rails above them, equally giant claws hanging from their ends.

Twenty-two.

Fink shot forwards.

With more clanks and thunks, the crates began to move, lifted from above and hovering a moment before shooting upwards.

Hero hunkered lower, trying not to flinch at the shadows moving over her head.

Fink put on another burst of speed, paws pounding the steelcrete.

Eighteen.

They burst out of the crates.

On the edge of her vision, the purple streak that was Phara raced ahead, already leaping the giant gap between the train and the platform.

Thirteen.

Two strides and Fink was there, forepaws tucked against his chest and neck arched as he jumped.

Hero looked down. Not even clouds met her gaze, just air and the sweet greeny-blue of the planet far, far below.

They landed with a jolt and were off again, weaving around maintenance drones with huge pincers attached to egg-shaped bodies, chasing Phara's tail towards a glowing exit.

Ten.

The alarm almost flattened them.

Fink stumbled, ears flat to his head. Hero wished she could lean forward and cover them with her hands, but it was all she could do to hold onto the saddle. Her helmet had muffled the alarm's screech a split second late, and that one piercing warble was enough to cleave her skull in two.

Her visor flickered and Timon's face appeared, his mouth pulled in a grimace and his shoulders hunched around his ears. In the background, she could see herself and Fink racing up behind him.

'The doors are closing. You gotta hurry up!'

The view on her visor switched, locking on the exit with its glowing yellow ring. Stats rolled across her vision – width: ten metres; distance: two-hundred-fourteen metres; time to target: eight seconds – but it was the shadow of the massive door that hovered overhead that caught her attention.

Five seconds.

The door shuddered.

Timon sailed through, Phara skidding to a halt on the other side.

Hero clutched her hands in Fink's ruff and willed him faster.

He lengthened his stride.

Four.

The steady glow of the ring became a rapid flash.

Three.

The exit loomed, taller and broader than the crates shifting and clanking around them, the door hovering over the entrance like a guillotine.

Two.

She could see the underside of it now, the dark steelcrete grey and shiny.

One.

Pain, Fink's pain, ripped through Hero's mind a heartbeat before he fell.

The saddle's emergency seal released and as she flew through the air, Hero had one perfect moment to see the ragged groove that had caught Fink's paw before she hit the floor.

The pain was hers now, a brilliant red blooming in her shoulder. She rolled, curling herself into a ball and hoping against hope that they'd made it before the door—

A gigantic *whomp*, more vibration than sound, ended her thought.

Darkness.

Silence.

She heard her heart, thumping away against her ribs, and then Fink's panting.

Phara glowed, faint purple light spilling across the floor and the giant lump that was Fink sprawled an inch from her face.

'Holy Terra.' Timon's voice was breathless, his boots making a dull thud when they hit the ground. He crouched beside her. 'Are you all right? I mean, not just with the door almost squishing you and all, but the way Fink flipped...' He shook his head.

Hero rolled to her knees, wincing at the hot throb in her shoulder. Fink's back was to her, and she crawled to his side, hands and mind searching for injuries.

He purred and stuck his nose in her neck, but whined when she reached for his forepaw. She paused a second, catching a shadow of the pain that spiked through his leg at her touch.

'He caught his paw in the groove of the door.'

'Can he walk?'

Fink grunted and tried to stand, but she stopped him with a quick thought. Fink flattened his ears and coughed. *He could walk.*

'Just let me check it.' Her hands were already moving over the rough pads and smooth hide of his toes.

Fink snarled and yanked his paw from of her grip. *He wasn't a kitten,* he thought at her. He gathered his legs and heaved himself to five of his six feet, the injured forepaw curled tight against his chest. *He didn't need her to check it.* Lastly, he sent her an image of the door opening and her leaping on his back before a swarm of maintenance bugs streamed after them.

'I'm not riding you like that.'

He huffed and snapped his tail. *Fine then, ride the glowy roach magnet instead.*

'Fink—'

'He's right,' Timon said. 'Although her name's Phara, not "glowy roach magnet", but we have to go. There's no way the security vids didn't see us and Farm Control's going to be all over this place soon. We need to get to that shuttle before they shut the 'burbs down.'

'But—'

Timon yanked her to her feet. 'No buts. Come on.' Phara was at Timon's side almost before she'd stumbled upright, and he was swinging into the saddle and holding his hand out for Hero a second later.

Hero looked up, way up. She'd never really realised how tall the toa-mare was before, how skinny or how smooth and slippery her hide looked. Hero's heart did a tumble in her chest and she glanced over her shoulder at Fink.

He hunched his shoulders and looked away, forepaw still cradled against his chest.

Slowly, she took Timon's hand.

His fingers wrapped around her wrist. 'Okay, on three. One. Two—' He yanked as Hero leapt. A mad scramble later and she was perched behind Timon, arms wrapped around his waist and her heart beating hard.

It was a long way down.

Phara moved and Hero clung tight. The 'mare's long swaying gait rocked Hero from side to side, making her feel like she was going to slip off the 'mare's back with every step.

Timon urged Phara faster and Hero couldn't help the squeak that slipped past her lips or the convulsive tightening of her arms around Timon's waist.

'Hey, dude, I need to breathe.'

Hero gulped and loosened her grip a fraction. 'Sorry. She's really tall.'

'Haven't you ever ridden a 'mare before?'

She shook her head. 'No. Just Fink.'

Timon twisted around, expression incredulous. 'Seriously?'

She nodded.

He turned back. 'Wow. I just thought, with your mum being who she is, you'd have been on sterdanes and 'mares and all sorts of stuff.'

Phara's bounce wasn't quite that bad, and if she squeezed her thighs just a little more, Hero found she could stay upright. More or less. 'I've had Fink since I was four.'

'Oh, well, that explains it then.'

'It does?'

'Not really. Just thought I'd say that.'

A purple and green feathered streak screeched over their heads.

Fink chortled and Hero's visor locked on the 'adder even as he looped through the air and dived back towards them.

'Harish?'

'Oh crud, you mean the little guy with all the attitude?'

Hero ducked, feeling the gust of Harish's wings as he swooped and banked to land on Fink's head. The little 'adder crooned and wrapped his tail around Fink's jaw.

Hero's visor blinked and then there was Norah staring back at her, the bodies and flashing lights of a street race going off in the background. 'Hero? What are you doing here? You weren't even invited to the race.'

'What race?' Timon interrupted. The screen split and his face appeared beside Norah's. 'And if this is the track then where are the other racers?'

'We're in the lead.'

Timon scoffed and looked back the way they'd come, the tunnel as dark and empty as before. 'Not by much.'

Norah scowled. 'What are you even doing on this channel? I didn't comm you.'

'Doesn't matter,' Timon said, and Hero felt the tap of his fingers on her gauntleted arm, still wrapped around his waist. She sensed it then, the gentle fizz of Timon's palm-unit interfacing with her bracer.

Hero tensed, but didn't yank her arm back; instead, she focused on Norah. 'What race?' she said.

Norah's face twisted, anger, frustration and something else, something uncomfortable pulled at her features until they settled back into a scowl. 'Look, it doesn't matter, okay? Both of you just need to go before you screw things up. I'm sending you a map, it'll get you to—'

'We don't need it,' Hero said and cut the comm.

'So, I take it you guys aren't best buds anymore?' Timon said.

Hero frowned and shook his hand off her bracer. 'Let's just find that shuttle.'

CHAPTER 20

The 'burbs weren't like the city, the buildings were shorter and the spaces between them weren't filled with shops and service corridors. Gardens with high walls, not skytowers bordered them on both sides and above she saw not the restless shift of traffic or the twinkle of holosigns and skybridges, but sky. Deep blue slices of atmosphere darkening with the setting sun.

A big black hover with a boxy nose passed overhead, low enough that the hum of its maglevs vibrated in Hero's ears. She followed it with her gaze, the scent of strapples teasing her brain.

Phara clip-clopped her way down the alley, Timon guiding her with subtle nudges and shifts in weight. Fink skulked behind, injured forepaw tucked against his chest, his thoughts a sullen muddle.

Ahead the alley came to an end, T-boned by a wide avenue where the sun shone brighter and grass replaced the steelcrete. Hero's visor darkened against the glare and her hands tightened on Timon's belt when Phara broke into a bouncy trot.

The 'mare had put two hooves on the grass when pink exploded under her.

She leapt sideways.

Hero grabbed at Timon's waist.

Red-brown filled the corner of her vision, Fink leaping towards them, forelegs reaching out to sweep Hero off the 'mare's back.

Fear exploded in her brain, the deep muddy purple of Phara's mind. The image of Fink distorted in the 'mare's thoughts until he was all fangs, claws and mad, blood-red eyes.

Phara screamed, Timon yelled and before Hero knew what was what, she was on the ground staring at the sky with her lungs stuck together. Air wheezed back into her chest.

Fink stuck his nose in her face and whuffed, while somewhere close, wings whistled through the air and paws pounded the ground, heralding the street race zipping along the avenue at the alley's head.

A familiar yellow belly whizzed through the sky and the faintest touch of lavender teased Hero's mind before it was gone.

Her lungs unstuck, oxygen poured back in and Hero rolled to her knees.

Phara danced, head high and eyes wide, as far away from Fink as the alley allowed, while Timon sat straight in the saddle and spoke to her in low tones. When Phara's dance became a slow shuffle, he turned to Hero. 'Are you all right?'

She winced and rose to her feet, rubbing her already sore shoulder. 'Yeah, but I think my shoulder is going to be more black than blue.'

Fink grunted. *That's what she got for riding prey.*

Hero glared at him.

Fink snarled back.

'Hey, dudes, whatever it is, save it for later. We're almost there and it looks like we're going to have to dodge a street race to make it.' Timon pointed across the avenue. Fifty metres away, past a thick expanse of grass and the bright heads of flowers, was a door set into a wall of frosted plasglas.

A shadow moved overhead and when Hero looked, her visor fixed on the drone hovering above their heads, a cluster of multicoloured bombs held tight to its belly. Her visor pulsed red.

Hero ran, dashing onto the grass even as her visor went haywire, more warnings screaming at the edge of her vision. A bang vibrated the air behind her but she didn't turn back; Fink was already at her side, Timon and Phara jumping ahead.

The mawberry-scented shot of alarm hit Hero's mind a second before Fink knocked her sideways. She fell, rolled and scrambled to her feet before the orange burst of itch gas had time to nip at her heels. Fink wasn't quite so lucky; she heard him yip and felt the fiery rush as the cloud caught his tail, clinging to the bare skin and crawling up his spine.

Ahead, the door loomed large.

Timon was already there, sliding off Phara and reaching for the control panel.

'Hey, watch out!'

Hero spun. A doe-oc barrelled towards her, spindly legs and sharp hooves eating the ground between them. Hero froze.

The companion leapt, delicate legs folding up underneath its chest, neck arching. Its belly was a perfect downy white, the short quills studding its flanks a shiny gold tipped in black. Hero met its rider's gaze as the doe-oc sailed above, saw his mouth move, the word 'crazy' falling from his lips, and then the companion's hooves hit the grass and they were gone.

More shapes rushed towards her.

Hero didn't waste time figuring out who or what they were. Eyes locked on the door, she ran.

Timon had it open, Phara crowding in after him. Paws and hooves pounded the avenue behind her. She slammed into Phara's rump, squishing the 'mare's tail to one side and pushed her through the narrow door. Hero caught a glimpse of the control panel and the small black device stuck to its surface before Fink crammed in behind her.

The door swooshed closed.

Fink butted her back and Hero rested against his side waiting for her heart to slow and taking in the large room, full of sofas and tables. The street race flashed by outside, sterdanes and spiderucks little more than coloured streaks on the other side of the frosted windows.

It looked familiar: its resemblance to the dining hall at school mixing with blue-coloured memories of meals taken with unfamiliar faces and tense conversations whispered in the corner.

'So,' Timon said. 'Where to now?'

Timon's palm unit beeped and when he opened his hand, the Librarian spun above it. 'You must head upwards, Timon Dane.'

'No.' Roses floated on Hero's tongue. 'We need to go down.'

'Hero Regan, I really must insist—'

She shook her head. 'The shuttles are down.'

Lavender teased her nose and Hero took one last look at the street racers still flitting through the avenue. She frowned at the shadow crouched on the other side of the frosted window, right where the door panel with its mysterious black blob would be. A faint pop echoed through the plasglas before the door cracked open.

For the second time that day, an alarm blared in her ears.

'What did you do?' Timon yelled.

'It wasn't me,' Hero yelled back.

'Yeah, that's what they all say.'

'It wasn't!' The gap between door and wall was barely wide enough for her arm when Hero reached through and yanked Norah inside, Harish diving in after her.

Norah's startled gaze met Hero's.

People were coming. Fink projected the sound of hard-soled soles striking the ground into her head.

'Run,' Hero shouted in Norah's ear, pushing the other girl towards the bank of lifts at the rear of the room.

Norah ran, Hero close on her heels and together they squished into a lift, squeezing between Phara's hide and Fink's fur. There was barely a sliver of air between their shoulders and less than that between Hero's chest and Timon's. The doors closed. The lift didn't move.

Timon cleared his throat. 'Ah, you going to tell the lift where we're going or what?'

'Oh, um.' Roses teased Hero's nose, and a memory played itself out in her mind. She pressed a hand to the control panel. 'Basement twelve.'

The lift moved.

Hero locked gazes with Norah. 'The door was already open.'

The other girl frowned. 'What?'

'The door, it was open, I'm guessing by whatever that black device was on the control panel. You didn't need to use an explosive, all you did was set the alarm off.'

'*You* set the alarm off?' Timon said.

Norah ignored him. 'How was I supposed to know that? All I saw was you, sticking your nose in and screwing things up again.'

'Perhaps if you'd told me what you were doing—'

'Why? So you can feel *special*? That's what you accused me of. And so what if you're right? At least I don't hurt people.'

The girls stared at each other, breathing hard, while the alarm blared in their ears.

Timon cleared his throat. 'Can you shut the alarm off?'

Hero looked at him. 'Why? Whoever owns this place already knows we're here.'

'The Klaude,' Norah said.

'What?' Hero turned back to Norah.

'The Klaude,' she said again. 'They own this place and we *really* don't want them to catch us.'

'Then why'd Imogen send you? I sensed her in that big black hover of hers. She's why you're here, isn't she?'

'I wouldn't be here if you hadn't stuck your nose in.' Norah's mouth was a hard line.

Hero snorted. 'It's not like you care.'

The lift stopped.

'Right.' Timon grabbed first Hero and then Norah. 'Finish this later. We've got a shuttle to catch.'

The doors opened, but instead of a shuttle hanger a short thin man with grey in his black hair and familiar blue eyes stood there, a hive of workstations and people at his back. Those eyes widened when they met Hero's.

Recognition flared in Hero's mind. 'You're Imogen's partner.'

Behind her, Norah gasped and yanked Hero backwards. 'Close the door.'

'But he's a detective.'

'No, he's not.'

'Ms Regan,' Dorich's voice rang over the hubbub behind him. 'Wait.'

'Why?' She sent her mind along with the words.

'Because we can help you.' Dorich's thoughts shifted against hers, pale yellow and bland, like water.

'To what?'

'Cancel the kill warrant on your companion to start with.' Dorich stepped forwards, his hands out before him.

Norah's shock exploded against Hero's mind. *There's a kill order on Fink?*

Hope leapt in Hero's chest. 'Why would you do that?'

'Why wouldn't we?'

He's Klaude, Norah spoke in her mind, flooding it with lavender-scented memories of shouting and the terrible, terrible echo of guns.

Dorich took another step forwards, hand stretching towards her – palm up, the nails neat, the pads at the base of his fingers rough with work – while the other inched towards his back. She slipped into his mind and felt the hard plasform of a gun against his palm like it nestled against her own skin.

She slammed the control panel.

The doors closed, the lift hummed and then almost as soon as they shut, they opened again.

The shuttles – two sleek little bugs the colour of clouds – crouched side-by-side, each inside their own circle of yellow light. Hero ran towards the nearest one, aiming for the outline of the hatch in front of the curved wings. It loomed over her, three times as big as any hover.

'How do we get in?' Hero said.

'In?' Norah said. 'Are you kidding me? We need to get *out* before we get caught.'

'That's what we're doing.' Timon stepped up beside Hero and slapped his hand against the hatch, a blue outline pulsing around his fingers. 'You better hope this isn't locked or something.' He looked over his shoulder at the lift, and the numbers on the indicator as it whisked back up. 'Because I don't think you're going to have enough time to hack it.'

'What? You're *stealing* a shuttle?'

The light around Timon's hand pulsed green.

'No,' Hero said as the hatch sighed and popped outwards. She grabbed Norah's hand and pulled her towards the shuttle's glowing interior. '*We're* stealing a shuttle.'

Norah yanked back. 'No.'

'Yes. Do you want to get caught?'

'I don't want to get arrested!'

'Bit late for that.' Timon pushed Norah into the shuttle. 'Besides, not much choice now.'

The lift dinged. Dorich stepped out.

Feet and fur and Phara's purple hide rushed through the opening and Hero was left staring out the closing hatch as Dorich sprinted towards them. Timon rushed to the cockpit, Norah close behind.

The hatch thunked home a bare second before the deck shivered under her feet and the engines roared. Hero was out of the airlock and pushing into the body of the shuttle, gripping Fink's neck when they lurched upwards before slipping past Phara to stand behind the pilot's chair.

Timon sat at the shiny black console, thick straps crisscrossing his chest and waist, hands and head lost amid a forest of holoscreens.

The shuttle lurched again, throwing Hero against a bulkhead. Pain flared in her already injured shoulder, flowing down her arm and making her fingers spasm.

'Do you even know how to fly this thing?' Norah yelled.

'Mostly,' Timon yelled back.

'Mostly?'

Hero gritted her teeth and climbed back to her feet, clinging to the back of Timon's seat.

'Yeah. Mostly. I just gotta remember...' Timon's hand hovered over a screen. 'Ah, there.'

Hero had time enough for one last look out the cockpit, to see Dorich sprinting for the other shuttle and more people streaming out of the lift before the bottom dropped out of her stomach.

The shuttle plummeted, a sickening lurch into darkness with alarms screaming in her ear and Norah screaming in her mind.

Timon cursed, hands flying over the control screens.

The shuttle stopped.

Hero's arse hit the deck, her stomach a moment behind, and tried to decide whether the ringing in her ears was the alarm or the silence left in its wake.

'Right,' Timon said, his voice high and breathless. 'Let's do that again.'

'No!' both Hero and Norah yelled at once.

'I thought you knew how to fly this?' Hero said.

'I do, I just didn't expect the, you know.' He gestured downwards. 'The dropping bit, but I've got it now. See?'

The shuttle hummed. For a moment she didn't think they were moving and then the surrounding darkness started to turn grey, letting her make out the shadows of pipes and conduits before they popped into daylight.

'Easy as cake,' Timon said, his voice steady even though a fine tremor shook his hands. He looked up. 'But we're going to have to move it.'

Hero followed his gaze. The 'burbs spread out above them, a giant sprawling roof of pipes and plates, bisected by the thin silver lines of the nanorail. Lights flashed and popped, artificial stars amongst the shadows.

Overhead the hatch cycled closed, sealing them off from the long dark tunnel that led back to the shuttle bay, while another opened beside it.

A memory of Dorich running for their shuttle's twin flashed in her mind's eye.

She squeezed the back of Timon's chair. 'Go,' she said.

The shuttle dived, nose angling for the white fluff of the clouds, but Hero watched the opening above and the flat white bottom of the other shuttle. It popped out of the tunnel and Hero gripped the chair tighter. Clouds frosted the cockpit's canopy and then swallowed it.

Timon pulled the shuttle's nose upright.

'Why'd you stop?' Norah whispered.

'Because,' Timon whispered back, 'I don't know where I'm going.'

Demona tickled at the back of Hero's mind. 'Here.' She leaned forward, the coordinates spilling from her fingers as soon as they touched the screen she suddenly knew was navigation control. 'Go here.'

CHAPTER 21

The clouds followed them, dense fluffy chaperones hugging the cockpit and turning the dome into a shifting wall of white and grey.

Only the blue lines, twisting away in front of Timon, provided any indication of where they were going, and only Harish's soft snores provided any sound.

Hero sat in the back, Fink's injured forepaw in her lap and one of the Librarian's saddlebags open at her side. She dragged a sanitiser over the cut on the back of Fink's paw, her other hand automatically tightening around his wrist when he flinched.

'Well, if you'd let me do this before, it wouldn't hurt so much now,' Hero said, flicking the soft white cloth, now brown with dried blood and dirt, onto the pack beside her. It was already turning white again, the nanofibres devouring the grime faster than Fink could scoff a cupcake.

He coughed. *They hadn't had the time then.* His gaze followed her as she reached back into the pack, coming out with a thin tube. *Did she have to use the pink stuff?*

Hero ripped the vac-wrap off the tube of nanomeds with her teeth. 'Yes,' she said, spitting the wrap in the direction of the sanitiser and tightening her grip on Fink's paw.

He whined and tried to tug it out of her lap. *But the blue one was right there.*

'We don't have time for the blue one.'

But—

'No buts,' she said and smeared a thick line of bright pink gel over his wound.

Fink whined, his ears clamping tight to his head, his eyes holding hers. For a heartbeat nothing happened and then the gel glowed.

Fink's yelp pierced her ears.

She let go of his paw and he ripped it off her lap, tucking it up against his chest and craning his neck to—

Hero slapped his nose. 'No licking.'

This time, his whine reached all the way into her chest and squeezed.

'What's going on?' Norah appeared in the entrance to the cockpit, Harish peering out from under her hair, his snout open and his tongue lolling out in a huge yawn.

'I used the pink nanomeds.'

Norah winced. 'Isn't that a little drastic? The blue ones would've healed the cut in a day or so.'

'We stole a shuttle,' Hero said.

For several long moments the girls stared at each other. Norah blinked and looked away first. 'I guess we already did drastic.'

'At least we haven't blown anything up this time.' Hero rested her chin on her knee. 'Unless you count that wall safe in the Industrial.'

Norah went still, but Hero felt the lavender-scented tendrils reaching for her mind. 'What are you talking about?'

The nanomeds on Fink's paw died to a pale pink glow, and he settled himself on the other side of the shuttle, his tail flicked over his nose. The memory of his pained whine still tugged at her heart.

'You tried to use my drones to blow open a safe during that practice race, but you put them in the wrong spot and ruptured a power conduit instead. That's what caused the EMP and knocked out the power.'

'You found it?'

'Yeah.' Hero turned her head so her cheek was on her knee. 'You know, I would've helped. We might've actually *opened* the safe.'

Norah frowned, her gaze dropping to her hands. 'Imogen didn't want you to know.'

'Why?'

The other girl shrugged. 'I don't know.'

'Did you ask her?'

'No.'

Silence stretched between them, long and sticky. Hero's brain itched, her skull too tight for her thoughts. She wanted to reach into Norah's mind, to know what the other girl was thinking, feeling, but she didn't. Instead, Hero squeezed her knees tight against her chest and opened her mouth—

'Hey.' Timon stood in the doorway. 'You guys should see this.'

Norah rocketed to her feet. 'See what?'

'Just… come and see.'

Slowly, Hero followed.

The wall of grey and white was gone, replaced by an endless vista of blue-green forest, its canopy flirting with the clouds.

'The surface?' Norah spun on Hero, dark eyes angry. 'You brought us to the surface?'

'Actually.' Timon cleared his throat. 'It was my idea.'

'*Your* idea? Are you nuts? You know the surface will kill you, right?'

Hero stepped up behind Timon. 'He suggested it to save Fink.'

'From what? You?'

Silence filled the cockpit.

'I'd never hurt Fink.'

Norah pushed out of her chair. 'Are you sure?'

Hero's mouth opened and closed, shock holding her tongue and making her stupid, but it didn't matter because Norah was there, mixing with her thoughts, pushing the memory of Fink's yelp and the pink glow of the nanomeds into her mind.

Would a day have made that much difference? Norah hung the thought and the image of the blue nanomeds between them.

Hero looked away first, her eyes catching on Fink, curled in a tight ball with his back to her. Her shoulders fell.

'Yeah,' Norah said, pushing past Hero and taking a seat in the cabin beyond. 'I thought so.'

Hero stood on the threshold, staring at Fink until Timon cleared his throat. 'You should sit, before your neck freezes like that.'

She slumped into the chair vacated by Norah.

'Looks like we're almost there,' Timon said, when the silence had stretched until Hero thought her brain would burst.

'Almost where?'

'You mean you don't know? Dude, you were the one with the directions.'

The Librarian popped up over the flight console. 'Outpost one-three-beta,' the AI said. 'A way station primarily used by explorers mapping terrain and resources under Cumulus City. It's been abandoned for the eighty-two years, seven months, three weeks—'

'Does it have a direct link to the Farm?' Hero interrupted.

'No, Hero Regan, it does not.'

'Wait, wait, wait.' Timon swung his chair around and stared Hero in the eye. 'I'm still catching up on the bit where you knew where we were going without, you know, knowing where we were going.'

'It doesn't matter,' she said and tried to turn back to the Librarian.

Timon gripped her knees. 'I think it does. How'd you know?'

'You don't want to find out,' Norah said from behind them. 'But I don't think it would've mattered if she hadn't known, because it's where the Librarian wants us to go too, isn't it?'

'Correct, Norah Joshi. May I enquire how you surmised that information?'

Norah crossed her arms. 'The Klaude have an outpost of their own somewhere near here.'

'How do you know that?' Hero said.

'I read Imogen's mind, and since even she doesn't know what the Klaude are doing down here, I bet the Librarian doesn't either.'

'No, Norah Joshi, I do not. However, their presence confirms that their location is where I will find the key to the human hybridisation program, as suggested in Augusta Woolsey's journal.'

'What d'you mean "human hybridisation"? Like, human Woolsies?' Timon turned big eyes on Hero. 'That's real?' His voice squeaked on the last word.

'I told you,' she said.

'Shi—'

She turned to the Librarian. 'You said Zass had the only copy of Woolsey's journal. How did you get hold of it?'

'You gave me access, Hero Regan, when you used your workstation to read the journal.'

'You still want to turn everyone into hybrids,' Norah said.

'Indeed, Norah Josh, that is my programming.'

'I'm just going to say, that doesn't sound like fun,' Timon piped in.

'I'm not going to let you do it,' Hero said, ignoring Timon. 'No matter what you do with the vid.'

Timon let out a tense breath, his soft 'thank you' almost lost under Norah's next words.

'Who says it's your choice?'

Hero faced her. 'Who says it isn't?'

'I do.'

'It'll kill millions.'

'Millions will die anyway.'

'So you're going to choose for them?'

'Yes.' Norah was in Hero's face, eyes burning and her breath coming hard. 'Because that's *my* choice and you don't get to tell me what to do.'

'I've never told you what to do.'

'No, you just *do* things and you don't care what other people want, just so long as it's what you want.' Norah held her gaze and her mind.

'I—'

'I don't care.' Norah turned her back and marched into the cabin.

'Oookaay,' Timon said, as the shuttle made a sharp dip. 'So, we're landing now, 'cause, you know, we're here and all.'

The shuttle descended, the blue-green canopy sweeping over the cockpit leaf-by-giant leaf, until it swallowed them. The readout on the shuttle's plasglas dome said the tunnel of greenery was big enough for three shuttles to descend side-by-side, but she didn't believe it.

Giant branches, thicker than her whole body, reached for them with oval leaves so densely packed they turned the space under them into twilight.

The shuttle went down and down and down, sinking into the trees until the space they'd descended through was nothing but a cloud-covered hole the size of her fist. The leaves weren't as dense the lower they went, but the branches grew in size until Fink, or something larger, could have curled up on one.

Light – the bright white of artificial glows – bloomed underneath, and the outpost swallowed them up.

Beyond the circle of the landing lights, the outpost was filled with a grey gloom that sucked the colour out of the air. Hero peered out of the cockpit, her heart beating fast. The shuttle landed with a soft thud and the landing hatch closed above.

She was just an airlock away from being on the surface, and for now Fink was safe.

Relief. Excitement. They mixed in her chest, fizzing until the bubbles escaped into her head, making her dizzy. 'We're here,' she said, voice breathless. 'On the surface.'

'Yeah, I noticed that too,' Timon said beside her.

Hero grinned and shot out of her chair. Norah jerked back when she pushed past, but Hero ignored her, tucking the hurt away and rushing to the airlock.

It cycled open with a hiss of air.

'Dude, forgotten something?' Timon dangled a slim, grey piece of fabric from one finger.

'I don't need an envirosuit.'

'You don't?'

'No. I'm immune to the Pollen. Human Woolsey, remember?'

'Actually,' Norah said, arms crossed over her chest. 'The correct term is Jørgen.'

'Ah, right. Jørgen, got it.' Timon held the suit out to Norah.

She shook her head. 'I don't need it either.'

Timon's eyes just about crossed. 'You're a Woolse— err, Jørgen too?'

'Mm-hmm.'

'Are you telepathic as well?'

'It's a side effect.'

'Seems more like it should be the main effect.'

'Maybe, I guess.' Norah shrugged. 'It depends upon how you use it.'

'And how do *you* use it?'

'Not like she does,' Norah said, and even though she was facing the airlock, Hero felt the finger pointed at her back.

Her spine stiffened, and she slammed her palm against the control pad, the inner doors hissing shut behind her. *It was an accident,* she thought to Norah.

Maybe, the first time, but you did it twice, remember?

She didn't need Norah to push the memory at her, she saw it – the way she'd gripped the man's head and felt the soft, squishy pop when she broke his mind. The other door, the one where she'd stuffed *his* memories, loomed in the back of her head, dark and silent beside the swirling mass of blue that was Demona.

The airlock's outer door opened, the yawning grey of the outpost sucking at her feet just as the shuttle behind her sucked the colour from her lungs.

She jumped out.

CHAPTER 22

The shuttle crouched, its stubby wings almost touching the walls, on the bay atop the living quarters. Dust coated everything from the floor to the stairs – wide and shallow enough that even Phara could clatter her way down – and coated Hero's boots in a fine grey coat that made the dark brown material seem dull. It was worse in the tiny box that served as living quarters, clinging to the bench seats huddling in one corner and glittering in the air. Not even activating the ancient cleaning bot had done more than turn the thick grey coat into a thin grey film.

Now Hero sat on the lower of the two bunk beds that had slid out of the wall; Timon lay above her and Norah hunched over the desk in the corner. The end of Phara's tail snaked though the door that led to the stable and tackroom, Fink was a dark presence lurking in the shuttle bay above. No one spoke.

Hero turned the jwak over in her hands and tried to ignore the way the silence crawled over her skin.

The bunk above her creaked a second before Timon's legs dropped into view, the thick soles of his envirosuit almost hitting her nose. He jumped to the floor.

'We should go,' he said, voice muffled by the helmet.

'Go where? And you know you don't need that, right?' Hero pointed to the helmet. 'The air filters have been running for the last hour.'

'To the city,' he said, making no move to take off his helmet. 'Fink's safe, no one's going to look for him here. Now we go home and your mum can deal with the kill warrant.' He dusted his hands, the gloves making a *whoosh-whoosh* sound.

Norah snorted. 'That's cute, you actually think she's going back.'

'Why wouldn't—'

'The Librarian gave her a mission.' Norah looked past Timon to Hero. 'And you did something, didn't you? Something bad enough to make the Farm issue a warrant when Fink tried to protect you.'

Hero looked away, remembering how Doctor Zass had collapsed against the workstation, and the jwak grew warm in her hands.

Norah nodded while confusion spilled out of Timon's thoughts. 'What'd you do?' His voice was soft.

'I hurt some people.' Hero wrapped her arms around her stomach. 'I hit them. I was in Demona's memories and I just… exploded.'

'Who's Demona?'

'Someone else she hurt,' Norah said.

The sensors on Hero's skull tingled. 'I didn't *mean* to.'

'That's not an excuse!' Norah yelled, her words reverberating around the tiny room.

A loud, short beep broke the tension and a section of the wall above Norah's head lit up. On it, another white-bottomed shuttle descended through the tunnel of green above the outpost.

Hero stretched her thoughts upwards, feeling the sensors throb against her skull, sending a shower of golden sparks through her bones. The jwak tingled in response and power surged up her hand. It hit her brain just as she reached out with her thoughts, rushing past Fink to the shuttle, sending them further and faster than she ever had before. A handful of minds crowded inside the vehicle, pinging and fizzing in her brain, like they were in the next room instead of hundreds of metres above her head. Dorich's thoughts stood out, a pale-yellow void in the kaleidoscope jammed into the shuttle.

'It's the Klaude.' Hero skimmed Dorich's thoughts. 'They know we're here.'

Timon exploded into action, Norah just a second behind. Both of them rushed towards the stairs and the stolen shuttle crouched in the bay above.

There's not enough time. The jwak grew warmer, and it was as easy as breathing to touch her friends' minds. Fink, Timon, Norah, even Harish and Phara, folded seamlessly into her thoughts and they halted in their tracks. *We have to go outside.* The image of the blue-green forest flowed between them, and with one mind they turned and rushed back down the stairs.

Saddles and bags were thrown on with the efficiency of an AI and all the while Hero felt Dorich come closer and closer.

She swung up into Fink's saddle, never letting go of the jwak. Norah climbed up behind her, hands gripping her waist, while Timon leapt onto Phara and Harish activated the door leading from the stable to the outpost's airlock. Overhead, the shuttle bay opened, the sound rumbling through the outpost.

As one, they shot into the forest, the light from the outpost throwing their shadows into the twilight under the trees.

The jwak tingled in Hero's hand, a warm fuzz crawling through her palm and into her bones. She could feel it in her shoulders, her knees and her toes, a million tiny golden bubbles that tried to lift her from the saddle. The little blue sensors attached to her skull fizzed in time to the power pulsing through her bones and she felt like she was thinking in crystal.

She didn't need to look back to see Timon, didn't need Phara's slick muzzle in her peripheral vision or Norah's hands clamped tight around her waist to know where they were. She could feel them, bright sparks caught on the edges of her mind, thinking with her, breathing with her, like extensions of her body.

It was exhilarating and perfect, and wrong.

The first of the trees dashed past – trunks thick and twisted, giant arms spreading wide, leaves catching at her hair.

She slowed Fink with less than a thought, Phara coming to a

standstill beside them. The jwak glowed in her hand, a million tiny bubbles still coursed through her bones, but there was something else there too, a dark spike of lavender she hadn't noticed before.

'Norah?' Hero twisted in the saddle. The other girl stared right through her, eyes glassy, expression smooth except for the shadow of a frown. Hero's gaze skipped to Timon, and he too stared right through her, not even twitching when a bug the size of her thumbnail settled on his nose.

Her hand clenched around the jwak. Something wasn't right. Mentally, she reached for Fink and then recoiled. Chocolate-coloured tendrils, bitterly dark and sparkling with tiny golden bubbles, wrapped around his mind and held tightly to his thoughts. She could feel them, running down his legs, his tail, controlling him, like they were an extension of her.

Blood, warm and wet, splashed onto the back of her hand and she loosened her grip on the jwak to wipe at her nose. Her hand came away red.

A wall of lavender pushed at the back of Hero's mind, sharp and angry, but streaked with sickly green shards of fear. Hero frowned, shoving the jwak into a saddlebag and twisted to face Norah—

Norah's hand smacked her face.

Light burst across her vision, bright little pinpricks that pulsed in time with her smarting cheek.

Norah threw herself off Fink.

Hero blinked, fighting off the grey creeping across her vision.

The other girl stumbled backwards, the blue-green fronds of ferns brushing at her hips, Harish crouched on her shoulder. 'Stay away from me,' she said.

'What?' Hero's gaze flicked to Timon's, but the boy just looked at her, his eyes ever so slightly glazed. She turned back to Norah. 'What'd I do?'

'You know what,' Norah said, and Harish mantled his wings and hissed. 'You were in my *head*.' She jabbed a finger at her skull like a spear.

Hero shook her head and regretted the movement when it made her skull throb. 'No.'

'Yes,' Norah spat back. 'I felt you, crawling through my brain like you owned it, not just telling me what to do but *making* me do it. It wasn't just me either, you did it to Harish too, and Timon, I even felt Fink caught up in… whatever it was you did.'

Hero's heart caught in the back of her throat. *Fink?* She ignored the way the thought made her brain ache.

He rumbled, his ears twisted and his head dipped low. *He'd felt it too.*

'Timon?'

Behind his envirosuit, Timon's eyes were wide. 'Dude, I don't know what that was but don't do it again.'

'I'm sorry.' She turned to Norah. 'Whatever it was, I didn't mean to—'

'But you still hurt people. It's like you don't even care.'

'Hey, man, she apologised already,' Timon said. 'Not being able to control my own body scared the Old Terra out of me, but she just said she didn't do it on purpose and she looks like crud. And you're both, you know… telepaths right?' Timon said.

'Sure, but she's the only one who's *killed* someone.'

Timon blinked. 'What?'

'I didn't *kill* them.' Hero shot back.

Norah smiled, the expression sour and her eyes hard. 'My dads checked. That man you lobotomised *on purpose*? After you sucked his brains out and put him in a coma, he died, so yeah, you're a killer.'

The world froze, the air turned cold and Hero's breath frosted in front of her nose. She'd… Her mind stumbled over the word but threw the image – carried on the hint of roses – at her without trouble. Wide eyes, slack jaw, a cold, still body staring at her with mouth agape and a gaze gone milky with death.

She'd done that.

Her stomach cramped, rolled, heaved—

'*Breathe.*' A memory, blue and rose. Bent over her own shoes – bigger and broader than anything she'd ever worn – a cool hand on the back of her neck and the dark, black eyes of an old woman piercing hers. '*Just breathe, recruit. I don't need your sick all over my training floor.*'

Hero breathed, filling her lungs with the damp scent of soil and the sweet rot of fallen leaves. A breeze caressed her cheek, Fink's paws crushed the undergrowth and overhead a bird rustled its wings.

She looked up.

The qwan crouched on a branch as thick around as she was wide, its long feathered tail curled around the limb. It peered down a long angular nose, nostrils flaring wide, its gaze a piercing blue amongst bright red feathers. The bird cocked its head, short frilled ears twitching, and it shifted, talons leaving marks in the wood. It half-spread its topmost wings – red at the shoulders, tapering into long orange flight feathers – for balance, while its second set – the same deep blue as its eyes – remained tucked against its chest. A delicate silver latticework wrapped around its long neck and dripped down its chest, the whorls and twists embedded with coloured stones.

'A qwan.' Timon's voice was half-exhalation. Hero didn't have to touch his mind to feel his wonder at seeing one of the elusive Jørn natives; she felt it herself, a glowing ball of excitement in her chest.

Fink rumbled, his thoughts dark and tense. He lifted his lip and skittered sideways, putting distance between them and the qwan. *He didn't like this.*

Why? she thought back, her eyes still locked with the native bird's. *It's just a bird.*

No it wasn't.

The qwan flared its nostrils, the insides bright red against its black muzzle, and cocked its head the other way.

Hero reached out to it with her mind, biting her lip against the way her thoughts burned.

The bird's second set of eyes snapped open.

Orange, bright screaming orange was all Hero saw. It reached *in* with long pointy fingers that filled her nose with the scent of earth, wet and cold enough to turn to ice in her skull. Just like the not-roach, a hard glassy bubble formed around the animal's mind, yet instead of being on the outside, Hero was trapped inside. On the other side was Fink. She felt the qwan reach for him as well and threw herself against the glassy barrier, scrabbling for the long cold fingers before they pierced his mind.

A shadow leapt out of forest. Hero felt it smash into the qwan as if the bird's chest was her own, smelled the shadow's hot fishy breath, saw the flash of fangs, the frantic thrashing of limbs. Fear ricocheted through her brain, bright orange and cold. She caught the edge of a thought and the sense of the bird stretching its mind, reaching out to something else and felt that something answer.

Then the qwan, and its orange bubble, were gone.

Hero slumped over Fink's neck.

Beneath her, Fink tensed and Norah backed up until she was pressed against his chest as more shadows stalked out of the trees.

'Whoa.' Timon sounded even more breathless than when he'd spotted the qwan. 'This doesn't feel like it's going to have a happy ending.'

Hero looked up.

Three of the biggest ruc-pards she'd ever seen stood in front and to either side of them. They were bigger than Fink, big enough to make her feel small even sitting on his back. The shortest, a deep rusty red, stood half a head taller than Fink and the largest... The gigantic black 'pard's chest swallowed what little light there was.

Something crunched behind them and Hero twisted in the saddle to see another two 'pards leap from the trees.

They surrounded them, leaves and twigs crunching under their paws, ears twitching, tails carried high and straight above the undergrowth. The 'pards stared at them without moving.

'What do they want?' Timon said.

Hero shook her head, the movement making the blood pound harder behind her eyes. 'I don't know.'

'They want us to go with them, they say...' Norah stepped away from where she'd been pressed against Fink's chest, her head cocked to the side and a frown creasing her brow. 'There are hovers coming, looking for us.' She turned back to the 'pards. 'We're not going with you.'

Out the front, the black 'pard seemed to grow a handful of centimetres, his shoulders rising like mountains behind his ears, and stalked towards Norah.

Norah held her ground for the first step and the second, even when Harish hissed from under the cover of her hair and Phara whinnied in alarm. On the third step, Norah stumbled backwards, coming up short against Fink's chest.

Fink nudged her to the side before growling at the other 'pard.

The black 'pard halted, one paw in the air, and switched his yellow gaze from Norah to Fink.

Fink's growl deepened, his ruff rising.

The black 'pard's answering snarl shook the air. His ruff puffed out to twice the size of Fink's and his chest expanded until the black 'pard blotted out the light.

'I don't think arguing with them is a good idea,' Timon said, even as Hero reached out to Fink with her mind.

He's too big.

Fink twitched, his ears flat against his head and his lips pulled back from his teeth. He shook his back and sent Hero an image of her standing beside Norah. *Off,* he said.

Hero clutched fistfuls of his ruff. *No.*

The black 'pard stalked closer, his head down and tail lashing from side to side.

Phara whinnied, Timon cursed and Norah yanked on Hero's leg even as she scrambled away. 'Stop this,' she said.

Hero reached for the jwak.

A cough and a butter-flavoured mental snap froze her in place.

Another 'pard, older and shorter than the others with white creeping over its blue-grey muzzle and flecked throughout its coat, appeared behind the black one. The others parted around it, sidling out of its way, their heads dipped low.

The black 'pard didn't move fast enough and, quicker than Hero could catch, the older 'pard sank teeth into its rump.

The black 'pard leapt sideways with a strangled snarl, but it lowered its head as the blue-grey 'pard stalked past.

Hero's hand closed around the jwak.

The blue-grey 'pard knocked her sideways, the blow coming not to her body, but to her mind.

The world went black – for one heartbeat, for two – and there was a buzzing in her ears but above it, or maybe beyond it or below it, there was a faint silver hum, the sound of another mind.

Hero hung sideways in the saddle, staring at the ferns at Fink's feet. Her head rang in tune with the buzzing, and her thoughts were slow like her brain had been scooped out and splattered across the ground. The world moved, or rather Fink did, skittering under her, paws dancing over the undergrowth, crushing ferns and crunching twigs. The saddle straps pulled at her thighs and the pommel dug into her stomach, pushing the air out of her lungs. There were snarls and growls and yells. The silver hum grew stronger.

Silence. Fink stood still, save for the quiver working its way up his legs.

Her brain came back in a tired, fuzzy trickle, unsticking in time with the air creeping back into her lungs, and by the time her thoughts had coalesced, she knew two things. One, that the blue-grey 'pard was female and two, that she was strong. Very, very strong.

Slowly Hero pushed herself upright, using both hands to right herself in the saddle. Her head spun and there was a warm, wet trickle wending its way over her lip and dripping from her chin that she didn't have to touch to know was blood.

She rocked back in the saddle, fatigue smacking her between the eyes and dragging at her bones, and had one good look at the blue-grey 'pard – Apani, her name was Apani – before darkness carried her away.

CHAPTER 23

A kitten yawned in her face. The edges of the small 'pard's long pink tongue curling against the roof of its mouth, before it flicked out from between sharp white fangs to lick her nose.

Hero recoiled, trying to scramble away, but there was a warm, fuzzy weight against her back and another draped over her legs. The kittens purred and shifted at her movement, ears twitching and paws flexing, the one over her legs kneading her thigh with needle-sharp claws.

The kitten in front of her, its ash-grey coat marked with hollow circles of inky-black, tucked its head under Hero's chin. It wrapped a paw around her ribs, its delicate little claws sinking through her coat and pricking her skin.

Hero froze, not daring to breathe lest the shifting of her ribs send the claws deeper. There was a sick feeling in the back of her throat to go with the tiredness that burned at her eyes and dragged at her bones, but she levered herself up enough to look around.

Wherever she was, it was gloomy and small, with ragged rock walls and a roof that arched over her head. The smell of 'pards filled the air, dusty and sweet with the distinctive whiff of old fish, and the ground was cold and gritty.

A cave, she was in a cave, and aside from the trio of kittens she was alone.

Where were the others? Her heart hitched in her chest. Where was Fink?

Hero stretched her mind, slipping past the fuzzy grey and blue of the kittens plastered to her sides and pushing against the fog that tried to hold her back. *Fink?*

She waited.

Nothing, not even a tickle at the edge of her mind.

She spread her mind again, pushing harder this time, ignoring the way her vision turned grey and then black. And just… there, an explosion of mawberry – dark and angry – before her thoughts snapped back inside her skull and she hit the floor.

The grey kitten snuggled closer, its nose, wet but not cold, finding her ear.

Slowly, careful of the paw still splayed over her ribs, Hero eased out of the pile, dragging herself backwards until her knees popped out from under the second kitten's weight.

The cave spun when she stood, just enough to make her knees weak and bile rise in the back of her throat. She breathed, drawing the air deep into her lungs before pushing the sick feeling back into her gut and the bone back into her knees.

She had to find Fink, and Norah and Timon. And then she had to get them out of there, wherever 'there' was.

With careful steps, Hero edged around the sleeping kittens, her eyes on the sliver of light wrapping its fingers around the rock. The cave beyond was larger, a long fat rectangle with a high arched ceiling. She slipped around the outcropping that hid the smaller chamber, aiming for the glowing vines trailing along the ceiling from another cavern.

She didn't see the 'pard lying across the opening, until the female's mind touched hers, a gentle orange-pink, rich with patience and amusement.

Hero stumbled backwards but the 'pard only pruckled and herded her forwards with soft swishes of her tail. The 'pard pressed the thought of food – a slaughtered beast that looked a lot like a doe-oc, all spindly legs and long curling horns – into her head, even as she pushed Hero along with a head-butt to the back of her legs.

She almost fell through the wall of vines curtaining the entrance.

More vines trailed glowing lines of blue and green across the stone while luminescent insects were spots of orange and bright yellow amongst the leaves. The vines clung to the too-smooth walls and dripped from the ceiling, a thick curtain of greenery and light that swayed in a breeze she couldn't feel.

The 'pard behind her coughed again and this time the nudge was mental.

Moonlight lit the cave beyond, flooding in from a giant hole in the ceiling, casting the chamber, and the shapes crowded at its centre, into stark relief.

A snarl made the air shudder.

Fink, his ears lost amidst his ruff and his fangs gleaming points, leapt at the black 'pard.

Hero barely had time to squeak before the black 'pard sent him flying, Fink hitting the rock floor and tumbling through the curtain of vines on the other side of the chamber.

'Fink!' Hero ran forward.

A mental shove, as shiny and black as the 'pard it came from, knocked her backwards.

Fink burst back through the curtain, teeth and claws out, muzzle twisted in a snarl and his mind a dark, hard mass of hate.

Shock held her still, and a hard spike of fear bloomed in her chest.

Fink rushed the 'pard.

The 'pard swatted him like a flurry-thyt, pinning Fink to the ground with a midpaw buried in his belly fur and its teeth at his throat. Fink growled and thrashed, forepaws clawing at the 'pard's shoulders, while one mid and both hindpaws scrabbled uselessly at its flanks.

The black 'pard growled, and even with the length of two hovers between them, Hero could make out the bright spots of red blooming on Fink's belly.

Blue soaked her vision, rose coated her tongue, and a scream ripped itself from of her throat. She was on her feet, charging the black 'pard, and before it had time to twitch, she was on its back.

It was thicker around the neck than Fink, its ruff longer and coarse, grating over her forearms and stabbing at her eyes, but Hero didn't care. Arms and legs wrapped around its neck and clamped tight to its shoulders, she thrust at its mind.

And almost bounced right back off.

The 'pard's mind was hard, and it grew scales while Hero watched, thick gleaming plates that clicked into place over its thoughts. Before she knew it those plates grew sticky, sucking at her brain like thick black mud until she was buried in it, mind and body immobilised.

The black 'pard turned his attention from her to Fink. She tried to yell but her mouth remained closed, tried to yank the 'pard's ears or claw his eyes, but her hands were locked in his fur. She felt his mind reach for Fink's, the funny little twist of his thoughts that let him slip past Fink's shields.

The 'pard dove hard into Fink's mind and *pushed*.

Fink went out like a light.

'No!' Before the word was past her lips, she was in the air, the echoes of her yell still fading into the vine wall when she hit the cavern floor. Back first – cold exploding against her spine – head second – stars exploding in her eyes – and Demona whispering in her ear.

The old woman stood over them, boot whistling towards their chest.

Hero rolled to her knees, dragging air into sticky lungs. Spots streaked her vision and blue soaked the edges. The vines trailing from the hole in the cavern's ceiling became the white, shimmering walls of a training floor while the woman ghosted over the black 'pard, stalking her.

Demona burned the inside of her brain, but Hero clamped tighter before the wave of blue swallowed her.

For one perfect moment Hero held Demona in the palm of her mind, knew what she had known, felt what she had felt and saw the same crack in the 'pard's defences.

Darkness slammed into Hero's mind. The black 'pard's thoughts crashed against her shields, surrounding her, and in the crisp, cold scent of a winter night floated his name. Orin.

Orin stalked closer until he towered over Hero, his ruff standing on end and his ears pricked forwards. He blocked out the light and then his mind bore down on hers, hard, yet not hard enough to hurt.

Hero growled and pushed back, searching for the crack she'd seen in the interlocking plates of his mental armour.

Orin's answering growl vibrated in her ears and he bore down harder.

There, a tiny gap where the mental armour didn't quite touch. Hero dove for it.

Lavender, a giant wall of it, met her thrust.

'What are you doing?' Norah knocked Hero on her arse. 'Are you insane? They're helping us.'

Hero stared at Norah, the cavern floor cold against her palms, taking in the glow of the vines and the white light of the moon making a halo around Norah's head, before anger brought her to her feet.

She pushed Norah out of her face. 'He attacked Fink!'

'Because Fink attacked him first.' Norah shoved her back.

Blue suffused her vision again, and Hero welcomed it, just like she welcomed the memories flooding through her arm, curling her bones into a fist.

A hot whuff against the back of her neck had her muscles locking up.

Slowly, Hero turned.

Apani stared back.

The 'pard's eyes were bottomless and as Hero stared into them, she felt that silver hum again, waiting at the edges of her mind. The 'pard's mind opened to hers, silver and sparkling, the faint scent of rain on the wind.

Apani's mind was huge. A great dome that hovered over Hero, until she felt small, insignificant. She'd never felt a mind like

Apani's; it felt like Fink's – in the warm rumble of images and sounds – but different too, like the glassy presence of the qwan.

An image pressed against her mind, of Apani swatting a cub who had just done something very, very bad. She stepped back and back again, retreating across the cavern, Apani keeping pace, until the vine curtain brushed her shoulders.

She jerked to a halt, Apani's snout a centimetre from her own.

The leaves tickled Hero's ear and the matriarch's breath washed her face in heat and fish. It wasn't that she was afraid of Apani, it was just… The 'pard was almost as intimidating as her mother.

The grandmother 'pard snorted in her face, a short, sharp expulsion of air that conveyed satisfaction. Slowly, she sat back on her haunches.

Just as slowly, Hero untangled herself from the vines, never taking her eyes from Apani. She cleared her throat and straightened but still her head barely reached the matriarch's jaw.

The blue-grey 'pard curled her tail around her forepaws.

Behind her, Norah held Timon back and Fink remained passed out on the ground, the black 'pard – Orin – yawning as he stood over him.

Apani rumbled, her thoughts pressing against Hero's. An image of Hero standing in front of Fink's prone form, facing off against a shadowy horde, swam in Hero's mind, the warm honey scent of approval surrounding it. But as soon as she recognised the emotion a new image pushed it out; in it her face was twisted in an ugly snarl and her mind was a chaotic tangle of red and black, lashing out at Norah, at Timon, at Fink, without control.

The cold weight of Apani's disapproval pulled at Hero's shoulders. *But we will take you*, Apani sent to her, *and you will learn.*

Take me where?

Another image: a cavern ten times bigger than the one in which they stood with a lake at its centre, the dark water dappled by the tiny lights of the plants and insects that buzzed, draped and floated over it. *Then we will take you back to the humans.*

'No, we can't go back.'

'You mean, you can't,' Norah said.

'No, I mean—'

'No. *We*,' she gestured to herself and Timon, 'aren't the ones who killed someone and took over their *only* friends' minds. *We* aren't on the run from the police, the Farm and their parents.'

'Norah,' Timon said. 'That's not cool.'

'But it's true, and it's the only reason *you*—' she pointed to Hero ' – don't want to go back to the city, which is just fine with me. At least down here you can't hurt anyone.' Norah spun on her heel and stalked through the curtain of vines, the glowing leaves swaying in her wake.

Hero's vision blurred.

Timon clasped her shoulders, bending down a little to look her in the eye. 'Hey, I don't think you're a killer. I think you've done some pretty scary stuff but—' His hands tightened on her shoulders. 'Not. A killer. Okay?'

The dark orange-brown of Timon's mind radiated from his hands, clear and steady against her brain.

'Okay?' he said again, this time with a small shake.

Hero sniffed and nodded.

'Great. So.' He straightened, hands falling from her shoulders to find the back of his belt. 'While you were out, Norah and I learned some stuff. Wanna hear?'

Apani rumbled, amusement and – was that a reprimand? – carried on the touch of her mind.

Timon blanched, just a bit, his dark complexion turning a little grey. 'Ahh, well, you know, if you wanted to tell it and all…?' He trailed off.

Apani pruckled, a deep throaty sound, like parts of it got stuck in her throat. She nudged Timon with her nose.

'I think she wants you to tell it,' Hero said.

'Right, well.' Timon cleared his throat. 'Turns out, the pack was keeping an eye on that qwan we spotted. I didn't really get why, but there was this impression… like the 'pards were…' He scrunched his face, looking over Hero's shoulder as he searched for the word. Finally, he shrugged. 'Not scared exactly, kind of like the qwan was bad but the thing that came after was worse, and that's why they brought us here, to protect us.'

Hero frowned, remembering the encounter with the bird and the fleeting sense of its mind reaching out to something else.

Apani grunted, her ears twisted, and pressed an image on Hero's mind of a beast that looked a 'pard. It had six legs, and the same sleek, feline-like body, but it was bigger, with a triangular head similar to the qwan and two sets of eyes set on either side of its long, narrow skull.

Hero's heart beat faster, and she turned wide eyes on Apani. She knew what that creature was; part of its DNA had gone into making Fink. 'Rucnarts,' she said, the breath gone out of her voice. 'The qwan was talking to a rucnart.'

'What?' Timon's voice rose with alarm. 'When?'

'When Orin—'

'The big, black 'pard?'

Hero nodded. 'When he jumped the qwan, I felt it reach out.'

'Ugh, isn't that bad?'

They both looked to Apani.

The matriarch was inscrutable, but Hero caught the agitated flick of her tail.

'I think that's a maybe.'

'A maybe.' Timon ran a hand through his dark hair. 'Awesome. So, what do we do now?'

Hero wiped her nose. 'We do what we came to do. We cancel Fink's kill warrant.'

Apani rumbled, and an image bloomed in Hero's mind, of a biodome in the midst of a clearing, its multifaceted sides gleaming in the afternoon sun. She stood in front of it, along with Norah and Timon.

'No, we have to go *here*.' She pushed an image of a door in a mountain, soaked in the blue of Demona's memories, at the 'pard.

He must. A vision of Timon, standing beside Hero in his envirosuit. The suit tore and Timon's face turned yellow, then grey before his eyes started to bleed and his hands to shake. Soon enough he was a twitching, convulsing tangle of limbs, his face contorting while he screamed and screamed and screamed, his body tying itself in ever increasing knots on the cold stone. Abruptly, he stopped, staring up at Hero out of the bloody, lifeless mess of his eyes.

'It doesn't happen like that,' Hero said.

Timon looked at her, and it was clear from the way his dusky brown skin had turned the colour of pale tea that he'd seen Apani's vision.

'It takes longer. Months.' She turned to Apani. 'Doesn't it?'

The matriarch flicked an ear and remained silent.

'You know that's not comforting, right?' Timon said. 'Moments or months, if my suit rips I'm still gonna get Pollen poisoning and I really like my brain the way it is.'

'I—'

Timon held up a hand. 'But I knew that when I suggested we come down here, even if I didn't expect the whole great outdoors bit.' His gesture encompassed the cavern. He took a deep breath. 'So, let's not rip my suit while we do this. Deal?' He held out a gloved hand.

Hero stared at it, at the way the glow from the vines turned it a pale silver-green, and how she could almost make out the shape of Timon's knuckles through the thin fabric.

Apani touched her mind. *It was the cub's choice.*

She lifted her gaze to his, barricaded behind its plasglas shield. 'Are you sure?'

'Would I have my hand sticking out if I wasn't?'

'I don't know.'

Timon rolled his eyes. 'Just take my damned hand.'

Hero hesitated for just a second before she did just that.

His grip was tight. 'Awesome, let's do this, but… ahh, let me be the one to convince Norah.'

CHAPTER 24

The sun rimmed the opening in the cavern's ceiling, a warm golden light that only just touched the top of the vine curtain. Where it did, the leaves grew and turned their faces to the light even as their glow died.

Timon boosted Norah onto Phara's back, while Fink shifted from paw to paw, rocking Hero in the saddle. His thoughts were a dark, huddled mass of grumpiness and his gaze was fixed on Orin.

The black 'pard ignored him, but the red one at his shoulder – younger, with a thinner chest and black markings around his eyes and snout – stared back, the hair half-standing along his back.

The rest of the pack milled around the cavern, the three kittens using the vines to play hide and pounce, while the older 'pards stalked the edges, disappearing and reappearing.

Timon swung up in front of Norah, the glow from the vines still turning his envirosuit a shimmering silver-green, just as Orin gave a sharp cough and shouldered his way through the greenery. The red 'pard followed, but not without a long glower at Fink.

Norah caught Hero's gaze as Phara strode past, her eyes as hard as they were dark. 'I'm doing this for Fink,' she said. 'Not you.'

Hero nodded, looking down to escape Norah, clenching a fist in Fink's ruff.

They moved single-file, Orin leading the way, the red 'pard bringing up the rear, Fink and Phara sandwiched between them. They didn't speak, or at least no one spoke to Hero. She caught snatches of conversation – murmurs more than words – floating back to her from Timon and Norah. At first, she'd tried to decipher them, wondering what they were talking about, if it was her.

Suspicion churned in her gut but didn't have time to fester before it was dislodged by Fink's dark grumble. Some time during the day, his focus had shifted from Orin to the red 'pard. Red's gaze seemed stuck on Fink's tail and Fink's discomfort radiated through the saddle and crept up Hero's spine.

She tried to ignore it, pushing the feeling away by concentrating on the buzz of brightly glowing insects and the trees that pressed in from all sides. Trunks big enough to swallow Paris's tiny apartment twice over were covered in dark, rough bark splattered with pale moss and creeping vines, their flowers bright sparks of colour amidst the vibrant green. Branches big enough to be skybridges arched overhead, weaving and knotting together until, just like the city, she couldn't see the sky. The insects wove through the leaves, a steady stream of orange and yellow and blue, keeping pace with them like a tiny, glowing escort.

Fallen branches formed giant bridges over moss-covered boulders and the vivid green sprays of ferny undergrowth that grew in the valleys between.

Orin wound through the rocks, leading them steadily upwards, just like he had been since they'd left the 'pards' den, his pace brisk. Ahead, Phara stumbled, Timon and Norah clinging to her back. Heat rose from the 'mare in a steady white cloud, her purple hide made darker with sweat while exhaustion had her muzzle almost touching the ground.

Zipping through arcades and dodging drones obviously hadn't prepared the 'mare for a long, steady climb over a mountain.

Not that Fink was faring much better. Hero could feel the deep thrum of his hearts beating in his chest, and the ache and drag of his muscles twisted through the constant grumble of his thoughts. He scrambled over a rock, back legs bunching to push them up a steep section of the trail and she felt the way his lungs burned, heard him wheeze with the need for more air.

She reached for the straps keeping her in the saddle, intending to get off and walk, but Fink twisted and snapped at her hand before she could touch the release.

He wasn't a kitten, she didn't have to coddle him.

I'm not—

Behind them Red pruckled; the liquid, rumbling chuckle more snarl than purr, and Hero caught the echo of the thought he sent Fink, an image of a baby Fink riding on *her* back.

Hero felt the rage burst in Fink's chest, a toxic tangle of frustration and fear, and recognised his need to express it with violence and blood. It called to her, tickled the door behind which Demona slept and filled her chest with the same fire that burned his. But even as her vision turned blue and roses exploded on the back of her tongue, she pulled herself back.

Fink twisted to face Red.

Time slowed.

The knowledge that was Demona's took in the red 'pard's size – the breadth of his chest, the depth of his ruff, the scar on his muzzle and the tiny notch missing from one of his ears – and Hero knew Fink wouldn't win this fight.

Her hand closed over the jwak, the little blue sensors warming against her skull. Even as she slipped past the barriers around the 'pard's mind like they weren't there, she felt something else, a familiar cold and glassy presence hovering above.

Stop, she thought and both Fink and Red froze.

Other minds pinged against hers – Norah's and Orin's – small intrusions as easy to shake off as the exclamations and growls that tried to fill her ears. Hero reached out, past where their small group stood in the shadow of the forest into the thick branches above.

The jwak made her mind tingle, made her brain feel big, her thoughts crisp and powerful, so that the minds in the darkness shone.

Three of them crouched above, circling, while the other two – the cloudy, glassy minds that had first alerted her to their presence – shone brighter than the others. A thought, a flutter that reached for another mind – smaller, barely a dull blip – leapt from one of them.

Hero snapped back inside her skull, her hand slipping off the jwak. She gasped, inhaling blood from the stream coming out of her nose. White suffused her vision for a heartbeat, the sound of her pulse mixing with the voices raised in her ear until the two were a single, endless drone.

The trees came back to her first, the branches, the leaves, the sunlight struggling to dapple the darkness, and imagined the shadows of the five great minds staring down at her.

'They're watching us,' she said.

The drone of voices stopped.

A hand, big and silvery, swallowed hers. 'Who is?'

The muscles in her neck didn't work, and she almost yanked her head from her spine trying to meet Timon's gaze. 'I don't know, but they have us surrounded.'

Behind his mask, Timon's eyes widened. Orin snarled at the trees, Phara skittered close to Fink, and Norah launched Harish into the air a split-second before a glowing net sprung up around them.

A hundred fat little insects, their bodies the size of Hero's thumb, hovered in a perfect pattern of triangles, so closely packed together their wings blurred the air, making the forest beyond hazy.

Outside the net, Harish shrieked and swooped, a fuzzy streak of green wings and yellow scales rising into the air before he tucked his wings and dove.

'Harish, no!' Norah yelled.

The barrier spat and bowed inwards, the tiny lights darkening where the 'adder impacted, before it bounced back.

Harish dropped to the forest floor, his only sound the soft thump his body made when it hit the ferns.

Norah leapt from Phara's back, Timon following, but Hero only had eyes for the shadows descending through the trees.

They moved like liquid, the light catching them only briefly and then only in parts, revealing a shoulder, the tip of a bushy tail, a paw big enough to swallow her chest.

Orin and Red growled, their eyes on the trees. Orin snagged Timon's suited arm, dragging him back towards the centre of the dome, while Red caught Norah's jacket and yanked her backwards.

Norah fell on her arse, trying to shake the 'pard off and reach Harish, still unconscious on the other side of the barrier.

The first pool of liquid darkness dropped out of the trees.

'Holly Terra,' Timon said.

The rucnart padded silently towards them, a behemoth on six long, muscled legs, its tail swishing the undergrowth and two of its four glowing eyes fixed on Hero. It brushed the edge of her mind, hot where the qwan had been cold, salty where it had been earthy.

Fink snarled.

The rucnart turned its focus to Fink.

Another two rucnarts dropped from the trees, as sleek and dark as the first, triangular heads and dappled coats parting the air. One paced over a fallen log that loomed over them while the other perched atop a large, moss-covered boulder.

Hero tried to find the other two, searching the trees. A qwan peered back, its upper eyes closed. A waterfall of coloured stones hung from the delicate collar around its neck and recognition sparked in Hero's mind.

She looked away before the bird opened its other set of eyes, only to slam into the gaze of the second qwan.

Its mind took hers in a heartbeat, the all-too-familiar cold, earthy scent swallowing her thoughts. There was no pain this time, no icy fingers digging into her grey matter; instead the qwan felt distracted, busy, like it was trying to watch a holovid and build an army of drones at the same time. In fact...

Hero reached back along the qwan's thoughts, ignoring the way it made her brain burn. Surprise sharpened the bird's attention, and it dug cold fingers into her skull, before the buzz of a hundred tiny minds fragmenting in a hundred different directions snapped it back. Hero followed, skimming along in the wake of the qwan's concentration.

The insects – the qwan held them in its mind like an AI controlling a cloud of drones. The insect's eyes were the qwan's eyes, their tiny brains an extension of its own.

She pressed closer, trying to slip past the qwan's glassy shields and see what it had done—

Pain brought her crashing back into her own body.

Her head split in two, her vision turned white, then black and only locking her elbows and clinging to the pommel for dear life stopped her from crumbling over Fink's neck. When her vision cleared there were fresh splats of blood on the back of her hand and her head pounded in time with her heart.

Around her 'pards growled – Fink's deep rumble vibrating against her legs; Phara snorted and tossed her head, deep purple eyes ringed in white; and Timon was squished between the 'mare and Orin's flank. Norah still crouched by the edge of the insect dome but she no longer crooned to Harish; instead her gaze was locked with the rucnart staring at her from the other side.

'She's surprised,' Norah said, her eyes never leaving the rucnart's, although her words were for Hero and Timon. 'She didn't think humans had any more telepaths.'

'You're *talking* to it?' Timon said.

Norah nodded, her forehead creased and her eyes focused somewhere distant. 'It's not like talking to Harish, or even Fink. It's more like talking to you, Hero, except there are more pictures and sounds.' Norah bit her lip, frowning harder. 'She's angry – no, that's not the right word. The emotion's different, colder. She wants to know why… It's an image of woman, with dark hair and black skin and she's standing next to Dorich. The Klaude. The rucnart wants to know why the Klaude sent us.'

'But they didn't,' Hero said.

Norah gasped. 'She doesn't believe us.'

The net buzzed, a shudder rippling through the insects before they flowed over Norah, clustering around her face, her shoulders. Their glow changed, going from blue to green then yellow and finally orange, before Norah made a funny sound and collapsed.

The dome shrank, leaving Norah where she lay, the spaces between the insects getting smaller and smaller and the light they emitted brighter and brighter.

Hero fumbled for the jwak, her hand wrapping around the cool metal, squeezing it tight. The pain in her head subsided, her vision cleared, and the jwak lit up the trees with an angry red glow.

She focused on the rucnart standing over Norah, but roses tickled her nose and Demona whispered in her ear. The 'pards could deal with the rucnarts, once the net of insects was down.

Hero looked up and smashed her mind into the qwan's.

The bird's brain shuddered, its glassy shield holding, but the net shattered and a hundred tiny minds paused a second before scattering into the forest.

Snarls ripped through the air and as one the 'pards sidled around each other until they each faced a rucnart.

The one in front of Fink crouched atop its boulder, pinning them with all four eyes. Its dark green, almost black coat blended with the moss it had shredded with long claws, and its ears – long and thin with tufts at the tips – lay flat against its head.

Knowledge and the steady weight of experience flowed from the space in Hero's head where Demona's memories resided. With her vision tinted blue, she took in the rucnart's size, the terrain and the distance between them, before she glanced behind them to the other rucnarts and the wall of glowing insects reassembling itself out of nothing. Hero knew, the same way Demona would have known, that this was a fight they couldn't win.

A large black drone zipped overhead, spitting bolts of vivid yellow light. One struck a qwan in the chest, spreading over its breast and seeking out its head like some kind of straightjacket. The bird shuddered and the wall of insects began to crumble before something small and rock-like plummeted out of the trees.

It hit the drone with a sharp crack, the hull shattering, sending shards of black plasform spewing into the air. As the drone shuddered and smoked, the rock-like object unfurled, revealing long furry legs and a round face. The critter gathered itself and leapt, thin membranes snapping to life between its legs as it glided into the forest, leaving the drone to crash into the undergrowth.

Hero touched the creature's mind a second before it disappeared, recognising the glassy presence of a qwan guiding the animal's actions.

Bark spat and another bolt of yellow light left a scorch mark under the feet of the rucnart on the fallen log. The rucnarts scattered, disappearing into the darkness while the remaining qwan took flight, but they didn't flee. Hero felt their focus shift from her group to their attackers.

More bolts shot out of the forest, and Hero traced them back to a rider winding up the slope. She recognised the sternard instantly – Orth's cloud-white fur, the pearlescent scales covering his chest and belly impossible to miss – and barely needed the zoom on her visor to recognise Trainer Ella, holding a rifle like an extension of her arms.

The part of her that was Demona whispered it was time to leave.

'We have to go,' she yelled.

Timon nodded and then darted towards Norah, still crumpled on the forest floor, a drone hovering over her. Orin leapt in front of him, the 'pard almost knocking Timon to the ground, before the drone hummed and spat a net around Norah.

The drone sat at the centre of the net, the glowing strands that leapt from its body hissing where they met foliage and leaf-litter. Hero didn't need the stats rolling across her visor to know that they'd never get through it; she felt it with rose-scented certainty.

'Leave her.' The words came out of her mouth almost without permission.

Timon spun around. 'You can't be serious.'

'She'll be fine.'

'How do you know?'

She pointed to the riders coming through the trees. 'They're from Bayard.'

Timon looked back to Norah, indecision written across his face. Finally he nodded before swinging up onto Phara.

Orin led the way, and together they raced into the trees, leaving Norah and the sounds of the fight far behind.

CHAPTER 25

At some point, long after sweat lathered Phara's hide and Fink's breath rasped in and out of his throat, they dropped out of their headlong run. But they didn't stop, not even when Timon fell asleep in his saddle, collapsing over Phara's neck and snoring.

It got dark then, and with the dark came the cold, leaving Hero's breath to frost in front of her face and the snot to freeze in her nose. Still, they kept moving, Orin leading the way, winding through giant trees packed so close together their roots formed small, moss-covered canyons. Red snapped at their heels whenever their march slowed to a shuffle.

At first, Hero spread her mind through the forest, riding the jwak's golden tingle, but of the qwans and rucnarts she sensed nothing. Instead she brushed over smaller minds – tiny rodent-like creatures intent on the sound of grubs beneath the leaf litter, and larger, 'pard-like ones stalking dinner from above. They buzzed, purred and slithered past her thoughts, little pricks of light in a rainbow of colours, each touched by the same faint cold, earthy flavour.

The sense of the qwans was sunk deep into the animals' brains, blending with the flavour of their minds, as if they were born with the birds' already controlling their thoughts.

Hero didn't know when they left the dense forest for the rocks and mammoth trunks of the canyon, or how long they clambered over uneven ground, always heading down. All she knew was that the sun, sliding yellow and pink through the gap between the mountain peaks and the sprawling disk of Cumulous City, was warm on her face.

The city itself was a dark lid on the mountains, partially obscured by white clouds. The canyon thrust up to meet it, grey chunks of rock rising above the tips of the trees – shorter than those in the forest, their trunks the width of two hovers instead of four, branches not as thick and leaves not as broad.

Silhouetted by the rising sun, a crag reached out ahead of them, a ragged finger extending over the canyon, atop which an old wind-gnarled tree stood sentinel. Demona rose in the back of Hero's mind, recognition following in her wake.

The world snapped back into focus.

Hero nudged Fink with her heels.

He growled and snapped, thoughts grumpy and tired.

She nudged him again, excitement chasing through her blood. *We're almost there,* she thought at him, urging him to go faster.

With a weary grunt he picked up his feet, breaking into a shambling jog, brushing past Phara and leaving Orin to growl at his heels.

Around a tumble of boulders and a thick wall of bushes – more thorns than leaves – a pitted grey box three times the size of hover-barge was embedded in the cliff face. Fink stumbled to a halt and Hero slid off, holding onto the pommel while her knees became used to standing again.

The airlock looked strange, stuck in the side of the mountain, like someone had dropped a cargo crate in the middle of the canyon and forgotten it. Stones and dirt piled against its sides while dust crusted the lip between wall and door, creating a thick red-brown seal.

Phara clopped up beside her as Timon rubbed the sleep out of his eyes. 'This place has people in it, right?'

Orin coughed and in the tumble of images and sounds from his thoughts, Hero had the impression of many airlocks dotted around the mountain, each bigger than the one directly before them.

'It's a side entrance,' she said, pressing her hand to the control panel.

The control pad turned green, and the airlock *popped* open.

'You'd think it'd be locked.' Timon slid off Phara's back.

'Why? Who's going to risk Pollen poisoning to break in?' Hero stepped over the threshold.

'You mean, besides us?' Timon said, and followed.

Inside, the airlock's clean white walls made it look bigger, big enough not just for Fink and Phara, but Orin and Red as well. But the two 'pards remained outside, their ears flat. Red's ruff was fully raised, right down to the little hairs along his back, as he cowered behind Orin.

'Aren't you coming?'

No. The thought was loud and clear. Orin sat, his back stiff and his tail twitching. *They would wait.*

The outer door cycled closed.

'Looks like there's a lock after all,' Timon said. He stood next to the inner door and peered at the control panel next to it. 'I don't know how we're meant to get past that.'

Without a word, Hero put her hand to the panel and booted up her bracer. A moment later, code danced around her forearm.

'Right,' Timon said. 'I forgot for a second. Criminal mastermind at work.'

A few minutes later the panel turned green, and a hiss filled the air. Hero only had a moment to wonder what the sound was before her lungs seized and her head turned light as the oxygen was sucked from the room. Her vision was turning grey and Timon was gripping her shoulders, his expression concerned, when the oxygen rushed back in.

Hero gasped, hands on her knees. She hadn't expected that, and from the way Fink and Phara were gasping right along with her, neither had they.

'Airlock clear.' An AI spoke from above. 'You may proceed.'

Hero wasted no time, stumbling out of the tiny room before the inner door finished cycling. The chamber beyond was little more than a cube, benches and a handful of envirosuits lining the pale grey walls.

There was a click and Hero turned in time to see Timon remove his helmet and set it on a bench. He shrugged when he saw her looking. 'Have to start sometime,' he said. 'Besides, it'll be harder to explain why we're creeping around if I'm wearing it.'

If they were caught, Hero didn't think they'd get a chance to explain, but she kept her mouth shut.

Beyond the pale-grey, human-made chamber everything was different. The floor flowed into the walls which curved into the ceiling, like a rectangle without its corners, while the surfaces were covered in intricate patterns that caught the light – a soft glow emanating from the curve between wall and floor – turning the hallway into a tapestry of shadows.

The corridor was silent, the strange curving walls eating the clop of Phara's hooves and the snick of Fink's claws. Ahead, another hallway awaited them, walls the same pale sand, thick with carved patterns and shadow, but wider, its arms reaching left and right in a mountain-sized hug. There were no doors but plasglas control panels – the sharp edges at odds with the curved walls – marked the hallway at regular intervals.

'Dude.' Timon's voice boomed in her ear, making her jump. 'I have never seen architecture like this, it almost doesn't look human. Also,' he paused a second, 'I think we need a map.'

Roses tickled her nose and Hero shook her head. 'No,' she said, letting Demona's memories guide her feet. 'I know where we're going.'

'You do? How?' Timon followed. 'It is like a Jørgen thing?'

'I guess so.' Hero kept her eyes on the walls searching for… She bit her lip. The memory floated in her mind's eye but refused to form.

'Can Norah do it as well?'

'I—' The fear and digest that had suffused Norah's face when she found out about Demona stopped Hero's feet. She shook her head.

'Maybe. But she wouldn't.'

Timon was silent for several heartbeats. 'That's what she meant, wasn't it, when she said "depends how you use it", about being a telepath? That's how you killed someone.' There was no accusation in his tone but Hero couldn't look at him, couldn't look at Fink, so she kept her gaze on the walls and resumed walking.

'The location of the outpost, how you know where we're going now.' Timon grabbed Hero's arm and swung her around. 'That urban legend about the sea monsters who suck your brains out. You're like them.'

Hero pulled away. 'I'm not a monster.'

'I didn't—' Frustration twisted Timon's lips and furrowed his brow. 'Why do you always think the worst? I didn't say *you* were a monster, I said you could do the same thing.'

'Whatever.' She turned on her heel.

'No.' Timon spun her back around. 'Not "whatever". Look at me, I'm wearing an envirosuit, I haven't been home for days and my dad's probably *freaking out,* and now I'm following you around some kind of secret alien outpost because, for some really stupid reason, I believe in you. So you don't get to just say "whatever" and walk away.'

'I…' Timon's stare made the back of Hero's neck tingle and her stomach twist. 'Fine. It's just…' She shuffled her feet, her tongue frozen by the confusion clogging up her brain.

Fink coughed. *There were people coming.*

She pulled back, grateful for the distraction, and strained her ears. She heard only silence until Fink lent her his senses and then she caught the faint snick of boots.

'We have to move.' Hero pulled Timon forward, eyes searching the corridor with renewed purpose, until they lit upon a familiar pattern of whorls etched into the wall. 'There.'

She took off, Fink trotting down the hallway behind her, unaware of the tension knotting her back until she heard the thud and clop of Timon and Phara following. They slipped down a new corridor and stopped short at the white slab of wall blocking their way as the bright spots of other minds pinged on the edge of Hero's awareness.

Hero pressed her hand to the square of plasglas attached to the wall. A section of the wall shivered and became translucent – a thin bit of skin stretched between bones – before it collapsed, sucked into the floor like it had never been.

She rushed through, Fink brushing past to scout the room beyond, Timon came next and then Phara, the tip of the 'mare's tail barely clearing the threshold before Hero closed the door.

Too fast to see, the door snapped back into place, once more a solid piece of wall.

'Where are we?' The dark swallowed Timon's voice.

'I'm not sure.' Hero walked into the black, feet guided by rose-scented memories. Lights came on with every step, walls glowing from the bottom up until the room was bathed in soft light and a deep steady hum worked its way into her bones. A workstation, all slim black lines and smooth, shiny surface, sat by itself in the middle of the room, as at odds with the intricately carved walls as the plasglas control panel beside the door. A lead ran from its base, the clear biogel pulsing with a steady stream of light, to disappear under the far wall.

The hum drew her forward. She pressed her hand to the wall, felt the carved ridges even through the thick nano-leather of her glove, and then leapt back when the wall fell away.

The hum became a throb that shook her bones, pulsing with every fourth heartbeat, the vibration hanging in the air and crawling over her skin. For a moment it was all she could take in, the throb blinding her other senses, but gradually they cleared.

The giant tube sat half-buried in stone, what she could see wider and taller than her mother's mansion, either end disappearing into darkness.

'Please tell me you know what that is,' Timon said.

Hero nodded, Demona's knowledge becoming hers and flowing out her lips. 'A magnetic field generator. It's what keeps Cumulus

City aloft. The Librarian said it was broken and that no one knew how to fix it, but...'

She marched back to the workstation. It came alive at her touch, graphs springing up around a diagram of the generator – a ring the size of the mountain – fragmented into sections that pulsed white or orange or red. The orange dominated, the white sections little more than highlights, while the red crept outwards in rough patches, slowly swallowing the ring.

Square icons sat beside each red section. Hero touched one.

A vid opened on another screen. The generator lay exposed, a giant piece of its pale-grey exterior peeled back to reveal metallic muscles contracting around glowing veins, the smooth tubes deformed by dark, ugly lumps. People clustered around one of the lumps, doing something to it until it shrank and was swept away in a flood of power, before they moved on to another.

Timon leaned over Hero's shoulder. 'It looks like they're fixing it.'

'Maybe.' Hero pulled back to look at the diagram where a section of orange turned red. 'Or maybe they're just making it worse.'

She pushed the diagram and its vid aside. There was nothing she could do about it anyway, but that didn't stop the niggle of guilt gnawing at her stomach, or the memory of a hover crumpled in a skybridge from playing before her eyes. She shook the image away.

'The Librarian said the outpost had a direct connection to the Farm. If I can find it and get in, I can cancel Fink's kill warrant.'

'How do you even know you can do that from this station?'

'I don't,' she said and dived into the computer, scanning menus, whipping through screens, on the lookout for the Farm's distinctive cube.

Long minutes ticked past. At first Timon hung over her shoulder, a tall shadow breathing down her neck. She glared at him until he backed up and that's when the pacing began. Back and forth across the lip where room met tunnel.

Hero turned up the opacity on the holoscreen and ignored him. The workstation itself had no connection to the Farm, but she wormed her way into the network that connected to the rest of the complex. She found the connection to the Farm in moments, inserting herself in the complex's data stream and sliding past the Farm's immune system. Fink's kill warrant almost jumped onto her screen and then it was the work of moments to… to… Hero stabbed the cancel button again.

Nothing happened.

Panic crawled up her throat and squeezed her vocal cords. 'It's not working,' she said.

Timon stopped pacing. 'What isn't?'

'The kill warrant. I can't cancel it.' She lit up her bracer and tried to run a diagnostic, but nothing appeared above her wrist except static. 'It's like the entire system is frozen.'

He looked over her shoulder. 'What's that?' Timon pointed to a darker spot amongst the static above her wrist. A robin emerged from the multi-coloured fuzz and fluttered its wings.

'The Librarian.' Hero reached for the symbol. 'But why?'

The AI popped up under her fingers. 'I required access to the Farm's AI, which you have provided.'

'But the Farm's immune system…'

'Is currently combating an infection I acquired from the Bayard archives. Once it has spread, I shall have the control of its systems that I require.' The Librarian inclined its bald white head in her direction. 'I thank you, Hero Regan, for your cooperation. Now, I need you to run.' The AI vanished.

Timon was already tugging on her arm. 'That doesn't sound good. Come on, let's find Norah and—'

Behind them the door snapped open.

Trainer Ella stood there with a gun in her hand, the barrel assembling itself as she aimed it at Fink.

CHAPTER 26

Light caught the edge of the gun barrel and Hero's heart stopped. 'No,' she said. Time slowed. She thrust at the woman's mind.

And collided with lavender.

Norah? Where are you? Hero pushed against the wall, but it didn't budge. *She's got a gun!* A frantic image of Fink standing in front of them.

I'm right here. The other girl stepped out from behind Ella. *You left me behind.* A memory of the forest exploded in Hero's head, the ferns tickling her cheek, the buzz of the net spread above her and Ella kneeling at her side.

I knew they wouldn't hurt you. We were coming for you. Hero turned her thoughts to smoke and tried to slide past Norah, but the lavender wall was everywhere.

I don't believe you. You could have rescued me, if you wanted to. But you didn't.

She's going to shoot Fink.

No. She felt Norah shake her head. *She won't, she told me she wouldn't.*

And you believe her?

More than I believe you.

A resounding crack filled the room. Hero turned, shielding her head from the bits of plasform flying through the air, to see the workstation shattered. The indentation of Phara's hooves made a giant crater in its side, the jagged edges oozing biogel.

Ella's gaze was on Phara, the gun wavering just a fraction, and then there was Timon – a tall, dark streak – charging the trainer from the side. The woman spun around, the gun whined. Timon jerked to a halt, stumbled back a step. Fell.

Fink leapt at Ella and Norah's mind leapt at Fink. The lavender wall fractured, shock and fear but also a desperate need to protect leaking through.

Demona tickled the back of Hero's brain and this time, instead of pushing, she wrapped herself around Norah's mind and pulled. Time stopped.

It was like body-slamming Fink: a jerk and bounce and then nothing. No sound, no room, no Timon lying on the floor, just her and Norah standing in an endless field of grey.

'What'd you do?' Light cracked behind Norah. 'Where are we?'

The answer rose from Hero's bones. 'In my head.'

Fear, an ugly puke-yellow fog, emanated from the ground at Norah's feet, clinging to her legs, while lightning cracked again, closer than before, the edges dipped in lavender. 'Is this what you did to Demona?'

'No.' Hero bit her lip and stepped forward. 'Look, I—' And slammed into a wall of lavender-coloured air.

'I can see her.' Norah's voice shook, her dusky skin turned to ash as the miasma at her feet reached for her knees. 'It's like she's standing behind you but *in* you too, and your thoughts… They're not just chocolate anymore, they've got streaks of blue in them, like you're absorbing her.'

'It was an accident.'

'But she's still *dead*.'

'She's not dead.'

'She might as well be.' The miasma at Norah's feet turned red as her voice rose. 'And you're walking around doing whatever the Terra damned thing you like and if your friends don't like it, you'll just take over their minds!' Lightning crashed.

'It's not like that.'

'Isn't it? What were you planning to do to Trainer Ella then?' A shadow of Ella appeared at Norah's side and then was gone. 'Pull her into your brain and have a chat?'

'I—' Hero's insides turned cold, Ella's apparition returning, this time holding a gun to Fink's head. Roses crawled up her nose and her voice was as cold and hard as the ice in her gut. 'She has a gun.'

She reached out, used her eyes just long enough to let the outside in. Everything was frozen in place beyond the borders of her mind: Fink leaping, his lips pulled back, and Trainer Ella's finger tightening on the trigger.

Fury worked its way up her spine, carried on a tide of blue, and she embraced it. Hero gathered her mind. 'She *still* has a gun.'

Lavender cracked and thundered. Norah replaced the wall of air, eyes shining with light. 'I won't let you hurt her,' she said and shoved lightning-filled hands through Hero's chest.

Hero flew, Norah's lightning numbing her brain, eating her insides, burning across her skin, and then she fell. The grey field cracked under the impact, delicate spider webs running away from her hands and knees. Blood trickled from her nose, dropped from her lip, splattered on the fractured ground.

Blue rose up to meet it, turned the floor the colour of a cloudy sky, seeped through the cracks and pooled around her hands.

Norah's shoes, heavy black boots that encased her calves, encroached on Hero's vision followed by the other girl's hands, still crackling with purple light.

Chocolate-coloured streaks, too dark to be called lightning, exploded around Hero's fists a split-second before she slammed them into the ground.

The boom shook her ears, and it was Norah's turn to fly. She crashed through the dull grey floor, great shards of it spewing upwards in her wake, the fragments raining down on Hero, slicking her skin, spearing her arms.

Blood flowed, but Hero didn't stop. She swallowed Norah, wrapped the girl's hands in manacles of brown and caged her in a sea of blue.

Lavender lightning flashed, turned to acid and ripped at Norah's bonds. They recoiled, snapping back into Hero's chest, leaving a long line of red to seep through her shirt.

Pain played on the edges of Hero's mind, a cold tearing, but the roses crawling up her nose gathered it, sucked it into her marrow. The coil of chocolate writhing around her fists darkened, burned over her arms, her neck, her chest, until it was curled up beside the roses.

When Hero breathed, it was chocolate shadows and blue fire that puffed from her mouth.

Norah pounded on the walls of her cage, fists wreathed in lightning. Every strike made the sides shudder and sent steelglas spikes through Hero's head. The roses swallowed them up, and the chocolate sparks burned darker.

A thought brought Hero nose-to-nose and palm-to-palm with Norah, the rippling blue wall all that stood between them. For a moment they stared at each other, breathing heavy, the air clouding with the chocolate and fire on Hero's breath.

Norah slammed her hands against the cage. 'I won't let you hurt anyone else.'

Hero snarled, feeling blood trickle over her lip, tasting it on her teeth. 'She has a gun,' was all she said before dark lines of chocolate shot from her hands. They wrapped around the cell and squeezed. It crumpled, the sides collapsing, the roof, the floor, until it was just a thin bit of vac-wrap bound in boiling coils.

'Hero.' Norah's voice was a breathy squeak and there was fear in her eyes. It slithered against Hero's mind, closer and closer as the barrier protecting Norah's mind became thinner and thinner.

Pain, not from the shards or the scratches tearing up her brain, but carried on the scent of lavender, bled though.

Hero froze. Norah stared back, wide eyes and shallow breaths, fear in her gaze but something else as well – a dark, angry certainty that said, 'I told you so.'

Hero threw herself backwards, the chocolate bands turning to smoke, the blue vac-wrap vanishing like it had never been.

What had she done? What had she been about to do? 'I'm sorry.'

Lightning smashed her in the face.

The real world was cold and her knees hurt.

Blood dripped onto the floor between her hands, the bright red spots the only colour she could see, the rest of the world gone grey and fuzzy around the edges.

Her head pounded, but she dragged it upwards. Timon was still sprawled on the floor, blood spreading across his shoulder in a wave of red. She crawled towards him, ignoring Fink crouched over a limp body in the corner of her vision, until a sound drew her gaze to the door.

Norah leaned against the wall. Hero wasn't sure if it was the pain sucking the colour from her vision, but the other girl looked as pale as she felt. Her gaze was locked on Fink, on Trainer Ella's corpse beneath his paws. She stumbled backwards.

'I always just thought it was Hero who hurt people, but now...' Norah swallowed and backed up another step before she turned and fled down the corridor.

Timon moved, groaning and then gasping as he rolled to his side.

Hero scurried to his side, pushing him back to the floor, trying not to think too hard about the way his envirosuit squished under her hands.

He frowned and reached up to wipe the blood from her lip. 'You're bleeding again.'

She dragged a fist over her mouth. 'So are you.'

'I am?'

'Yeah.'

'Is it bad?'

'There's a lot of it.'

'Huh.' He tried to rise again, winced and lay back down. 'I guess that's why it hurts then.'

Phara nickered and leaned over Hero to nuzzle Timon's hair.

'I don't know what to do,' Hero said.

'That's okay, I don't think you're meant to. I think you're just meant to go.'

'What?'

'There'll be people coming, to see what happened, they'll fix me up and that kill warrant's still out on Fink, but even if it wasn't...' His gaze flicked to Fink peering down at him, the 'pard's head cocked and blood staining his muzzle. 'The woman who shot me is dead, isn't she?'

Fink looked back over his shoulder and growled.

Timon nodded, closed his eyes and gulped. When he spoke his voice was high and breathy. 'Yeah. That's what I thought. So,' he cleared his throat, 'you need to go.'

'But—'

'Dude, you came all this way to save him, don't screw it up now. Besides, it's not like I can go with you, what with the bleeding and all.'

'But—'

'No buts.' Footsteps pounded in the distance. 'Go.'

Hero staggered to her feet. 'No,' she said, fighting the lights that danced in front of her eyes and drained what little colour was left from her vision. She clutched at Fink, her knees trembling, and fumbled with the seals holding the saddlebags in place. 'We've got nanomeds, and I can take over the mind of whoever comes looking.' Her fingers slipped, the digits suddenly thick and clumsy.

A hand on the back of her leg made Hero jump.

Timon was on his knees, his face grey, pain pinching the corners of his eyes and frustration twisting his lips. He looked at Fink. 'Dude,' he said.

Fink's ears twitched, and he twisted to eye Hero before lying down.

Hero swayed as Fink's back became level with her knees. 'What are you doing?'

He didn't say anything, just slipped inside her mind. She recognised the way he twisted his thoughts, remembered how Orin had sent Fink to sleep.

There was a moment for alarm, a second to try to slam mental shields in place, to feel Timon's hand on her back, toppling her into the saddle, and then…

CHAPTER 27

A gloved hand tapped her cheek. 'Come on Hero, wake up.'

She cracked her lids open and Zass's face floated before her, the doctor's round eyes and pointed chin shielded by a thin sheet of plasglas.

'Is she awake?' Tybalt's deep voice rose from behind the doctor.

'Yes.' Zass threw the word over her shoulder but her eyes never left Hero. They were clear and unafraid, like Hero had never kicked the doctor in the chest. Slowly, hand moving an inch at a time, Zass reached for the button that would release the seals holding Hero in her saddle. Fink huffed and shifted his feet, tension holding his muscles tight. 'We're going to have to move quickly,' she said, hand inching closer to the release. 'Just as soon as I—'

A snarl ripped the air and a big black muzzle knocked Zass aside.

Orin planted himself between Hero and the doctor. *She wasn't going with the humans. She had to learn.* An image of the underground lake floated from Orin's mind to Hero's.

Hero frowned and with arms as wobbly as noodles, pushed herself upright. She looked around, taking in the clearing – the trees thin and sparse, the ground between them a riot of giant ferns – and the shuttle crouched off to the side, its swept-back wings folded against a sleek round body. In the midst of it, Red and Orin faced off against Tybalt and Zass.

'What's going on?' Hero asked. 'Where's Timon?'

Tybalt shifted, his gaze never leaving Red, standing between him and Hero. 'You're the only one we found, Hero. Tell the 'pards to stand down.'

Orin grunted and bristled his ruff. Hero didn't need to translate – the 'no' was clear.

Behind his faceplate, Tybalt's brows made a dark line over shadowed eyes. He marched forward, only to have Red block his way. His mouth turned grim and his hand inched towards his gun.

'Don't,' she said.

Tybalt's hand froze, and although his words were for Hero, his eyes never left Red. 'It's time for you to come home.'

Hero shook her head. 'Not while there's a kill warrant on Fink.'

'We can't do anything about that.'

'But Mum could, she knows people.'

'Hero.' Zass had crept around Orin just enough to lay a hand on Hero's knee. 'I'm sorry, but your mother...' She didn't need to say the rest; Zass's memory shot down her arm and exploded in Hero's mind, crisp and honey-bright.

Sirens blared in her ears, the sharp cry of emergency equipment cutting through plasteel speared through her brain. The bright strobes of police and ambulance lights turned the mangled wrecks of hovers that had crashed during the blue-out into a stark play of shadows. And there, a smaller, darker lump amongst the chaos was Tybalt, face bloody as he bent over a body—

The memory cut off, the scent and gentle fizz of mawberries a wall between her and Zass, but it was too late.

That last glimpse of her mother's charred face would haunt her nightmares. Giant black spider webs, craters oozing red at their core, spread across her mum's cheek and over her chin before they crept into her hairline and wrapped around her head. Half her mother's perfect blonde hair smouldered while the rest... Hero struggled to comprehend the blob of skin melted against her mum's skull as an ear.

'No.' Hero pushed Zass's hand from her knee. 'No. You didn't remember it right. Mum can't be... She can't be dead, not because she was out looking for me.'

Zass's face turned white behind her faceplate. 'I'm sorry, I didn't mean for you to find out like that.'

'She's not dead,' Tybalt said.

Hero's attention snapped to him. 'She's not?'

'No.' Tybalt stepped closer, Red shadowing his every move. 'But you need to come home, Hero. You need to be there for her.'

She needed to be there. The words echoed in Hero's skull, bringing with them images of baths full of nanomeds and hard chairs in corridors that sang with the snick-squeak of nurses' shoes. Except as soon as they returned to the city, the snick-squeak would turn to the sharp clack of Farm Control coming for Fink.

Fink couldn't go home, couldn't 'be there', not with a kill warrant on his head, and Hero wasn't going home without him. But she knew, with absolute certainty, that Tybalt wouldn't let her stay.

She reached for the jwak.

'I'm sorry,' she said, welcoming the little golden tingles as she meshed her thoughts with the jwak.

'For what?' Tybalt stepped forward, his hand once more inching towards his gun, his gaze sliding to Red.

Hero tried to smile, but her mouth wobbled at the corners and tears clouded her eyes even as she slipped into Tybalt's mind, just as she felt Fink slip into Zass's. 'We're not going with you.'

'Of course you are.' Zass reached for the harness release. 'It's our job to keep you safe, Hero.'

She shook her head and saw the twitch run through Zass's shoulders a split second before the doctor hit the vac seal and the saddle harness came loose. Zass barely had time to reach for Hero's waist before her eyes rolled up and her knees collapsed. Tybalt followed a half-second later.

Hero wiped the wetness from her cheeks. 'No,' she said. 'It's mine.'

The pack moved. Adults and juveniles trotting through caverns and forest, ears alert, strides sure, kittens riding on their backs as often as they scampered over rocks and through undergrowth. They didn't stop for hours, or maybe days – she wasn't sure. All she was sure of was that Fink kept moving, and she stayed slumped over his shoulder, the harness the only thing keeping her in the saddle.

She might have slept, she might not have. Her body was tired, arms and eyes heavy and her neck too limp to hold her head, but her mind ran, the pack a cocoon of fur and claws, their mental shields a gentle hum at the back of her mind. She pressed outwards, brushing against creatures she'd never felt before. Some were sharp points of light that hummed and scurried and squawked, others were tiny prickles clumped together in huge fuzzy masses that buzzed against the edges of her brain.

Over it all hung Demona, shading the inside of Hero's eyes in blue while the woman's memories mixed with hers. They were different from before, still layered in rose but softer, easier, no longer assaulting Hero's mind and sweeping her away. Instead they came when she called, slotting in amongst her own memories like they'd always been there, distinct but the same.

Behind Demona, the other door in her brain cracked open and new memories peeked out, pale green and salty. They gave her names for the things she saw – *ound* for the trio of slim, feathered creatures pulling a basket of eggs and *adefr* for the blue-veined tree they disappeared under.

The pale green memories had no words for the endless tunnels the pack tiptoed through, and only wonder for the delicate ribs of stone and vines, the deliberate march of insects and the flights of birds trimming and tidying with single-minded intensity.

The packs' paws crunched over carefully arranged pebbles and their tails flicked in short little jerks, tension running under their skins. They skirted around the edges of giant caverns, the older 'pards holding tight to kittens who wanted to scamper through carefully tended flowers and scale the trees at their centre.

Hero felt the lake before she saw it, an icy breeze carrying the sweet dusty scent of water as it shivered over her cheek and raised goose bumps on her skin. It wafted down the tunnel, rustling the vines in its wake while orange insects the size of her thumb buzzed towards it and blue ones buzzed away. The breeze grew stronger, colder as the tunnel widened and then widened some more, while around her the 'pards grew tense, their ears twitching and ruffs rising with every short, choppy step closer.

The tunnel ended in a shower of brightly coloured vines. The cavern beyond stretched high, giant ribs of rock reaching upwards to form a vaulted roof. Thick vines and the golden-yellow honeycomb of something that looked like plasglas – *tartz*, the pale-green memories told her, a resin made by the orange insects buzzing around – filled the spaces in between the rocky ribs. Sunlight filtered through it all, filling the air with swathes of light that grew dim before it reached the lake. It caught in the trees that reached over the water, their branches lacing together, leaves the size of her head spread wide.

A million tiny flowers trailed over the bank and into the water, a pale glow rising from starburst-shaped petals in reds and purples and greens, that reminded her of her mum's roses.

The pack crept to the lake's edge, hides twitching an agitated dance in time with their noses, eyes and ears focused on the water – a deep, dark blue rippling over pale sand that faded into the depths.

Apani stopped at the water's edge and the pack stopped with her, arrayed in a fan at her back. She glanced over her shoulder and Hero felt the thought go out to the pack, bypassing her and Fink.

The pack moved, a subtle shifting of bodies pressing inwards, of noses reaching and nudging, of tails and ears flicking and twitching as they herded Fink into their midst and towards the lake.

Knuckles feeling like balloons and fingers like sausages, Hero clenched tired hands in Fink's ruff. *What's happening?* she asked him.

He didn't know. He nudged Orin's flank.

Orin touched his nose to Fink's. Memories passed between them,

Hero felt the flow of images and emotions on edge of her mind, the stream moving too fast for her to catch anything but the impression of age and the imprint of many minds.

Fink froze, ears flat against his skull and the whites of his eyes stark against his tawny fur. He shook his head and tried to step back, away from the water, but the pack was there, pushing him forwards.

Fink?

He whined, the sound high and strangled, his paws digging into the bank as the pack pushed him forward – one step, two steps – until he was almost sitting on his haunches as the water lapped at his knees.

Fink's panic flooded her mind, a dark, grungy pink that curled around her brain and arrowed straight for her chest. Her heart skipped a beat and a cascade of old, hazy memories swept away her ability to breathe. She had the impression of water and fear, of many, many minds handling the same thoughts and she knew that the memories weren't Fink's. They were older than him, older even than the pack. Teaching memories.

'Stop it!' Hero looked towards Apani. 'What are you doing?'

The matriarch didn't answer, and the pack kept pushing.

The water crept over her toes, icy and sharp, stealing the breath from her lungs, clearing just enough space in her mind that she knew she had to get away, but the 'pards pushed Fink in deeper – huge, furry bodies herding them with nips and snarls. Water swallowed her ankles, her shins, reached for her knees.

Fink snarled back, trying to spin on his haunches and dance out of reach, but the whole pack was there, their ears laid back and teeth bared. Behind them, Apani stood on the bank, her old grey-flecked muzzle held high, her eyes hard. *In,* she said, the command carried on the image of the lake, the force of it breaking over Hero's mind.

Beneath her Hero felt the same command wash over Fink, felt it seep past his shields and heard the whine building in his throat even as he backed up one slow step and after another.

'No.' Hero pushed herself upright, arms shaking, and reached for the jwak, the sensors on her skull growing warm even as she felt her mind expand and the colour leeched from her vision.

Yes, said another voice. Bigger and deeper, it echoed in Hero's head like a million voices rolled into one.

Movement caught at the edge of her gaze. She spun in the saddle, head spinning, eyes turning to starlight and nausea twisting her gut. A man stood on the lake, a lone spot of colour amongst the overwhelming grey, his perfectly parted hair gleaming gold in the light, his blue eyes twinkling. He smiled at her, lips parting over perfect teeth and arms crossed over a blue racing uniform – all that was missing was the pea-dragon and her mother, standing at his side.

Her heart skipped a beat. 'Uncle Paris?'

You surprised us, little fish. We did not think there was another.

'We? Another? But... You're alive?'

Almost. He looked down and Hero followed his gaze to the cold, blue water and the tiny ripples that caught the light and carried it away.

DO YOU WANT MORE HERO?

I love keeping in touch with my readers, it's the second-best thing about being a writer (writing being the first best). Every fortnight (or thereabouts), I send out a newsletter with details about upcoming offers, new releases and extra special projects.

If you sign up for the mailing you'll receive exclusive behind-the-scenes extras, such as:

- free short stories
- deleted and alternate scenes from The Hero Rebellion
- previews of my upcoming books
- pancakes
- quizes
- and much, much more!

Sign up here
www.belindacrawford.com/newsletter

ACKNOWLEDGMENTS

There are a lot of people who made this book possible, not just those who check my spelling and design covers, but also the people who have inspired me and given me emotional and financial support. Chief among them is my aunt, Dinah.

Over the years, a number of people have told me I should write a book, but it was Dinah who succeeded in planting the bug in my ear. Unfortunately, she passed away before Riven was completed, but I'm grateful that she saw my first book, Hero, become a reality.

Other people I'd like to thank are: fellow authors and friends, Tracy M. Joyce and Vicki Renner, who have provided advice, support and ears when I needed a sounding board or someone listen to me rant; my beta readers, Oscar, Brendan and Jen, who read Riven as it was in progress and offered invaluable feedback.

Finally, and as always, thanks go to Mum and Chuck, for providing me with the time and space in which to write this second instalment in The Hero Rebellion.

ABOUT THE AUTHOR

Physics makes Belinda's brain hurt, while quadratics cause her eyes to cross and any mention of probability equations will have her running for the door. Nonetheless, she loves watching documentaries about the natural world, biology, space, history and technology.

She's also a sucker for a fast horse, a faster computer and superhero movies. When she's not doing the horse, computer or superhero thing, Belinda writes science fiction (emphasis on the fiction), where she loves to write about butt-kicking girls who blow stuff up.

You can keep in touch with Belinda, or just pick her brains about sci-fi via her website, Facebook or by sending her an email (she loves email).

www.belindacrawford.com
belinda@belindacrawford.com

Have news delivered straight to your inbox
via her mailing list. Sign up at:
www.belindacrawford.com/newsletter